RIP YOUR
HEART
OUT

A Ripple Effect Cozy Mystery
Book Four

Jeanne Glidewell

Shauna –
Enjoy! :)

Book design by eBook Prep
www.ebookprep.com

Cover and Book design by eBook Prep
www.ebookprep.com

April 2018
ISBN: 978-1-947833-40-1

ePublishing Works!
www.epublishingworks.com

ACKNOWLEDGEMENTS

I'd like to thank my "quality control department"—Sarah Goodman, Shirley Worley, and Janet Wright—for donating their time and expertise to proofread my manuscript. A special thanks to Janet, my nightly walking companion, for her ever helpful input into my stories and the use of her late great-aunt's name, Mabel Trumbo. My dear friend even gracefully accepted the fact I killed Aunt Mabel off in my story. Our evening strolls are usually more talking than walking, but our discussions are invaluable to me when I'm in the midst of an evolving mystery.

My gratitude also goes out to my two wonderful editors—Alice Duncan, of Roswell, New Mexico; and Judy Beatty, of Madison, Alabama. And, as always, my deepest appreciation goes to my publishers, whom I'd be helpless, and probably hopeless, without. They are Nina Paules of eBookPrep, and Brian Paules of its sister company, ePublishingWorks.

Last, but not least, I'd like to thank my wonderful and long-suffering husband, Bob. He patiently tries to help me when I ask him things like, "Do you know how much arsenic it'd take to kill a man about your size?" Or, "What's a good way to kill a person without leaving any evidence?"

Bob doesn't admit to being concerned, but I swear he's learned to sleep with one eye open. I made him promise to never die in a questionable manner. As you know, the spouse is always the number one suspect, and if homicide detectives were to ever confiscate my computer and discover all of the suspicious-sounding topics I've researched over the past few years, I'd likely never see the light of day again.

DEDICATION

I was fortunate to have the best grandparents a girl could ask for, with all four of them living in close proximity to me throughout my school years. The first grandparent I lost was my maternal grandmother, Adelaide Hallberg, with whom I was residing at the time, in Longview, Florida. She died of a heart attack at the young age of seventy-three on Halloween night in 1978. I'd like to dedicate this book to Grandma Hallberg, along with all others affected by cardiovascular disease. This includes my friend and neighbor, Melody Zumbrunn, and her sons, Gage and Max, who lost their husband and father, Brad, in December of 2016. He passed away suddenly and unexpectedly at fifty-two years old with a previously undiagnosed heart valve defect. Brad was just one of many incredible individuals gone way too soon due to cardiovascular disease.

I'd also like to dedicate this health-related book to my transplant surgeon, Dr. Daniel Murillo, and the entire staff of the Research Medical Transplant Institute in Kansas City, Missouri. I owe it to them that I'm still alive, writing cozy mystery books. Along with them, my second chance of life was afforded me by my (pancreas and kidney) organ donor, my donor's family, the support of my family and friends, the phenomenal love and care my husband has *always* provided, and the awesome power of prayer. My heartfelt gratitude goes out to all of the above and to everyone who has ever said a prayer on my behalf. The prayers worked!

CHARACTER LIST

Rapella Ripple: Rapella is a sixty-eight-year-old woman with an inquisitive trait that's just powerful enough to be dangerous. Never one to accept things for the way they appear, she's determined to uncover the truth behind the death of a woman she's never even met.

Clyde "Rip" Ripple: Recuperating from open-heart surgery, Rapella's soon-to-be sixty-nine-year-old husband, Rip, is unable to be as involved in the case as he has been in the past, but he always has his wife's back.

Mabel Trumbo: Following double bypass surgery, Mabel passes away unexpectedly. Her death is presumed to be caused by post-operative complications. But soon after the Ripples move into her home, they see signs that not all is as it appears.

Sydney Combs: Sydney is Rip's cardiac surgeon's private nurse. She is kind, caring, and a bit of a drill sergeant when it comes to the patients under her care. She offers the use of the new "Heart Shack" to the Ripples after Aunt Mabel bequeaths her old Victorian home to the heart center to be used as temporary housing for the families of cardiac patients.

Adelaide Combs: Adelaide is a hairdresser in Yakima, Washington. Mabel Trumbo's niece is all about what she stands to gain from her aunt's death.

Tasman Combs: This disrespectful dude is Mabel's pot-smoking nephew who, like his sister, Adelaide, alienates Rapella at their first meeting. Tasman's just as interested in claiming his inheritance as that snobby sibling of his appears to be.

Ridley Wickets: Mr. Wickets has been Mabel's caretaker for nine years. But considering the condition Rapella finds the home in, he hadn't been earning his keep for a long while.

Itsy Warman: The widow next door impresses Rapella as eccentric, unpredictable, and occasionally annoying. But she's also fun to be around and makes Rapella think of her as the sister she never had. When the two are together, anything could happen.

Chase Cumberland: This deceptive hunk of eye-candy is just another piece of the puzzle that Rapella tries to put together to discover the truth behind her late host's death.

FROM THE DESK OF
JEANNE GLIDEWELL

Dear Reader,

As I mentioned in my dedication, my family has been touched by cardiovascular disease. I'm certain many, if not most, of your families have also been affected by this number-one leading cause of death in both men and women. I hope you find the information regarding cardiac health I've included in this story interesting and useful, rather than tedious and boring. It's important we all take our heart health seriously, and take steps to ward off heart issues that are often preventable, and *too* often fatal.

As always, I apologize in advance for any words I have made up and any grammar I have mangled. My editors are remarkable, but not magicians. And that's probably a fortuitous thing for me. If they were magicians, one of them would probably have already turned me into a pile of dust, or something equally as incapable of writing.

With sincere gratitude, I thank you for giving me the opportunity to entertain you with *Rip Your Heart Out*, the fourth installment in my Ripple Effect Series. To all of the fans of my Lexie Starr cozy mystery series (who I'm proud—and still in disbelief—to say hit the *USA Today* and *New York Times* best-sellers lists in early 2016) who have written and implored me to release another book in that series, my next release will be Lexie Starr, book seven. Many have expressed a desire to see Wendy Starr and Andy Van Patten get married. So, as they say, ask and you shall receive. I anticipate releasing *Marriage and Mayhem* in the fall of 2018.

I'd love to hear from you via my website - http://www.jeanneglidewell.com. I always respond. Now sit back, relax and enjoy the ride.

Jeanne

CHAPTER 1

The view from White Pass Summit was breathtaking: a panorama of mountains, waterfalls, glaciers, gorges, tunnels and trestles. At the summit, nearly three thousand feet higher in elevation than the Skagway Harbor where our cruise ship was moored, we could see the headwaters of the Yukon River. My husband, Clyde "Rip" Ripple, and I were celebrating our fiftieth wedding anniversary in Skagway, Alaska, aboard the White Pass and Yukon Route Railway.

Skagway was one of five Alaskan ports of call on our seven-day cruise of Alaska's Inside Passage. We'd toured the town of Ketchikan on foot the previous day: visiting the Beaver Clan House, the Libby Salmon Cannery, the traditional totem poles of Saxman Village, and, of course, Dolly's House.

Dolly's House was formerly a brothel, but is now a museum on Creek Street, which was the red light district of Ketchikan in the early 1900s. We have a chubby grey and white tabby named Dolly, who is gracious enough to let us reside in her domain as long as we tend to her every need. With that premise in mind, I'd wanted a photo of the two of us standing in front of the Dolly's House sign to use on our Christmas cards in December. I'd asked Rip, "Do you think 'her majesty' will realize the house was not named after her, but rather a long-ago brothel owner named Dolly Arthur?"

"Probably not, Rapella," Rip replied. "After all, she *is* just a cat. She only cares about two things: her next meal and a comfy place to nap."

"Are you describing Dolly or yourself?" I asked playfully. "I realize Dolly's just a cat. But the Dolly House *was* a 'house of ill repute'. And where do you think the term 'cat house' came from?"

Rip smiled at my bantering, but the smile didn't quite ring true. It seemed forced to me. It was as if he was trying to convince me he was enjoying the excursion as much as I was. But I knew better. My sixty-eight-year-old husband, and the love of my life, could not easily fool someone who'd been by his side for over half a century.

"I'm going out on that open-air area behind this passenger car so I can get a better photo of Dead Horse Gulch." The rear "porch" had a metal railing with spindles enclosing it, and I could run from side to side as we passed by different landmarks without the risk of making an early, unplanned departure from the train. Convinced Rip was not feeling up to snuff, I decided to test the theory. "Want to join me?"

"You go ahead," Rip said. "I'm perfectly content to stay right here for now."

"Do you feel all right, honey?"

"Of course. Just a little tired. We've been on the go so much that I'm kind of enjoying being off my feet for a spell. Besides, I'm conserving my energy to do some serious grazing at the midnight chocolate buffet this evening." Rip's face bore an ornery grin.

"There's nothing like a self-induced bellyache to finish off our anniversary celebration, is there?"

"Nope! My goal is to not stop eating milk chocolate until one bite *before* I've reached belly-aching status." Despite the twelve pounds he'd lost, while I'd gained three, on our self-imposed low-carb diet the last six weeks, Rip still suffered from "Dunlap Disease". As everyone knows, that's when your belly has done lapped over your belt. He patted his paunch and smiled. "I can't maintain this sexy spare tire without working at it."

I knew he was trying to alleviate my anxiety with his attempt at levity, but it was doing nothing to calm my concerns. Before I missed the opportunity for a magnificent photo, I patted his shoulder and said, "You rest. I'll be back in a couple of minutes."

"Don't hurry on my account," I heard as I hustled down the aisle toward the door leading to the outside viewing area. After the three-hour excursion along the narrow-gauge railroad route, once used by Klondike Gold Rush prospectors for transportation to the gold fields in Dawson City, we were scheduled to do a little gold panning ourselves and enjoy a salmon bake in the Liarsville Trail Camp before returning to the cruise ship. If not for the fact we were on a shore excursion with twenty other passengers from our ship, I'd have opted to take Rip straight back to our cabin. He had appeared pale and lethargic all day. I hoped he'd get a chance to nap before our celebratory supper in one of the ship's specialty restaurants that evening.

After Rip had retired from a lifelong career in law enforcement, we'd sold our home and bought a thirty-foot travel trailer we affectionately call the "Chartreuse Caboose". Now we travel around the country in our home on wheels as full-time RVers. The previous week we drove from Buffalo, Wyoming, to Seattle, Washington, where we'd signed up for a site in an RV park near the Cascade Mountain Range. From our site we could see the tip of Mt. Rainier in the distance. We planned to park there a full month so we could tour the area after we'd returned from the Alaskan cruise.

On our way to the Port of Seattle, where we'd boarded the cruise ship earlier that week, we'd dropped Dolly off at a pet-boarding facility that had great online reviews. I'd tried to convince our eight-year-old housecat she'd have a wonderful time there while we were on our trip, but I'm pretty sure I saw her raise her furry little paw to flip us off as we handed her carrying cage over to the nice lady at the check-in desk. I noticed Rip's eyes had gotten misty as we drove away from the Paw Spa Ranch and Resort. For a retired sheriff of Aransas County, Texas, the man was very soft-hearted.

It'd been a hectic week, and it wasn't just Rip who was feeling the effect of a much busier schedule than usual. While he napped on our cabin's king-sized bed, I planned to sit out on our balcony and relax with a cup of hot tea from the single-cup hot beverage dispenser in our over-sized cabin, while reading the last few chapters of a novel I was deeply immersed in. I might even place a call to our personal porter and request a refill of our complimentary fruit basket. Just because I could!

I could get used to all the pampering and individual service that came with booking a suite on a cruise ship. I'd already developed a sense of superiority in just four days aboard the floating resort, and wasn't sure how well I'd be able to adapt at being a mere "commoner" when the cruise was over.

Who, I wondered, is going to place my linen napkin on my lap for me before every meal? Who's going to deliver an apple fritter when I have a hankering for a pastry? Who's going to attend to my every want or whim? And most importantly, who's going to make sure I have a chocolate mint on my pillow every night and a white cotton elephant or monkey crafted from one bath towel and two washcloths at the foot of my bed?

We had decided to splurge on a penthouse suite to celebrate such a milestone occasion. As promised, we'd been treated like visiting royalty from the moment we stepped on board the recently renovated ship.

I'd noticed that with each day following our embarkation, Rip had seemed more lethargic, and less interested in the beautiful and fascinating sights we were visiting. However, I figured the following day would be a restful one for both of us. We'd be cruising Glacier Bay all day, enjoying the stunning scenery: bone-chilling clear water, glaciers, floating icebergs, breaching whales, and snow-capped mountains.

As we boarded the bus that would transport us to the Liarsville Trail Camp, I prayed Rip would be back to his normal, lively self by the time we sat down for our anniversary supper at the popular onboard steakhouse. He'd warned me in advance when he said, "I'm planning to completely devour one of their thirty-two ounce porterhouses—or die trying."

Had I known at that time how ironic and prophetic his declaration would turn out to be, I'd have demanded the locomotive engineer kick it up a notch so I could get Rip back to civilization and airlifted to a cardiac care center as soon as humanly possible.

And, had I been able to foresee that I'd soon be immersed up to my elbows in the mysterious death of a woman named Mabel Trumbo, I likely would've cancelled the trip altogether. A party in our hometown of Rockport, Texas, with our family and friends present, would've been a fun option to celebrate our golden wedding anniversary. But we all know that hindsight is twenty-twenty, and it was too late to change our minds.

So, in retrospect, I'm glad I was unaware of the trials and tribulations that were about to befall us. Sometimes ignorance truly is bliss!

CHAPTER 2

"**W**hat do you mean by 'I'll pass on dinner'?" I asked Rip as he sprawled out on the rattan couch on our large balcony on the aft of the ship.

"Just that, dear. Our porter brought in a fresh basket of fruit and a few pastries. I'll make do with that if it's all right with you."

It actually sounded better to me than the broiled lobster I'd been planning to order at the specialty restaurant that evening. After a healthy serving of salmon at the Liarsville Camp in Skagway, I wasn't particularly hungry. But it *was* our fiftieth anniversary, and a banana and cherry tart sounded like a pitiful way to celebrate it. However, if Rip didn't feel up to the thirty-two-ounce porterhouse he'd been talking about for the last several weeks, I didn't want to force him to stuff himself on my behalf.

For one thing, Rip's primary physician, Dr. Kristy Herron, would have my head on a platter if Rip were to spill the beans at his next appointment. We returned home to south Texas every year for our annual checkups. For years I've tried to get him to see his doctor more frequently, but it was like trying to convince a ten-year-old to eat a heaping bowl of garlic-crusted Brussels sprouts because they were beneficial to his health.

At his recent appointment, Dr. Herron had warned Rip of the consequences if he didn't immediately change his diet and lifestyle. "No more junk food like pork rinds and ice cream, no more vegetating on the couch for hours on end, and absolutely no more avoiding my office like the plague. Or, at least not if you want to be around for your next birthday," she'd told him. To which my bull-headed husband had laughed, and replied, "If I were to adopt those lifestyle changes, I'm not sure I'd want to be around to see my next birthday."

Rip's birthday was two months away. Considering how he was behaving that evening, I wouldn't have bet a plug nickel he'd be around to attend his own party. By the way he was gasping for air, I doubted he could blow out more than three of the sixty-nine candles on his cake anyway. He appeared pale and clammy, and had the energy of a slug that'd just been showered with salt.

Rip stating he'd prefer a pear to a juicy steak were words I'd never thought I'd hear come out of my husband's mouth. I'd have been less surprised to hear him say he'd prefer to spend the evening in the cabin; painting his toenails while we watched *The Notebook* on TV, after a day of being pampered at the onboard spa.

"Are you okay, honey? You don't look well. In fact, you look pale and sweaty."

"I've been resting outside for a while. If you'd been out here, instead of inside reading a book, you'd probably be perspiring too."

"We're in Alaska, dear. Look out there to the right." I pointed to a large iceberg we'd just skirted past. "I'm wearing a jacket and you have a heavy blanket covering you because, according to the ship's channel on TV, it's fifty-two degrees out here. I hardly think there'd be perspiration pouring out of my goose bumps if I'd been out here on the balcony with you."

"I'm fine. You worry too much, darling. Just a little worn down. Then again, perhaps it was the salmon I had for lunch. It might have had a touch of salmonella in it, or just didn't agree with me."

"Nice try, Rip. We split a piece and I'm not ill. Besides, you've appeared under the weather for the last several days. Are you nauseated? It's rare for you to be 'off your feed', as my pappy used to say."

"I'm a wee bit queasy. That's all. Could be a touch of seasickness from the constant movement of the ship. That's why I enlisted in the air force rather than the navy during the Vietnam War. Remember?"

"Yeah, that's a possibility I hadn't considered," I said with a nod. Even though I knew it was merely wishful thinking, I convinced myself that Rip was right. Motion sickness probably *was* the cause for his discomfort, and once his feet were back on solid, non-undulating ground, my gray-faced husband would be back to his old self. Although I could sense no movement at all, as if I were in a hotel room rather than a cabin on a cruise ship, I knew some people were very sensitive to motion. And, as he'd just mentioned, I did recall Rip basing his decision to join the air force on the high probability of puking throughout his entire tour of duty if he chose to become a "swabbie". As it turned out, being a military police officer in the United States Air Force was what had inspired his lifelong career in law enforcement.

"I'm going to the gift shop to buy some Dramamine, in case your self-diagnosis is correct. If it's not, we're going to visit the ship's doctor tomorrow. We'll be at sea all day so the timing is perfect."

"But—"

"No 'buts' about it, Rip. In the meantime, we can toast our anniversary tonight with a couple of glasses of 7-Up, which I have in the fridge." The carbonated soft drink had always been my go-to beverage when anyone in the family had a bellyache, served with three or four saltines on the side. "And I'll go down to the buffet and grab a few crackers, too."

"All right, dear. If it'll make you feel less anxious, I'll share a 7-Up with you."

"Um, thanks, dear, but no 7-Up for me. *I* actually feel quite good, and would feel even better after a shot or two of tequila. So, I believe I'll have Armando bring me a cocktail. In fact, I'll order two of them to make the trip to our suite worth his while." Armando was our personal porter, a soft-spoken, polite young gentleman from the Philippines. I could call him and request a poached egg and a fresh, thinly sliced kiwi at six in the morning, and he'd deliver it with the utmost courtesy and a pleasant, but probably forced, smile on his face as if I were the Venerable Mother Ignacia he was serving. I wouldn't do such a thing, mind you. The kind, hard-working man put in a long enough day without me requesting that he cater to some silly whim of mine.

I must have had a hard-to-decipher look on my face, because Rip assessed my expression for a few seconds and read it all wrong. I was only concerned about his health, but with his next remarks, he made it clear he thought I was upset about missing out on our special supper. "I'm sorry, honey. I'll make it up to you tomorrow night. Okay?"

"I don't give a flying fig about the anniversary dinner, Rip. It's you I'm worried about. It breaks my heart to see you feeling badly."

"Honey, I appreciate your concern. I really do. Bring me an apple, along with the crackers, and between them they should settle my stomach. You know what they say. 'An apple a day keeps the ship's doctor away.' And other than a little tummy upset, I'm fine. After our belated feast tomorrow, I plan on dancing the heels off of those shiny new shoes of yours in the Lido Lounge, so you better get some rest, as well. Trust me, your old man's healthy as a horse."

His words did nothing to ease my anxiety. For one thing, I'd witnessed a seemingly healthy horse keel over in mid-stride at the Sam Houston Race Track a few years ago, rendered dead as a doornail by a faulty ticker. While I felt bad for the filly and its owners, I'm still ticked off about the twenty-dollar wager I'd lost on her. The fact Lucky Lady was leading the race by three strides when both my luck, and hers, ran out on the final turn did nothing to quell my disappointment, either.

Another cause for concern was that I knew from past experience Rip would tell me he was fine and to quit nagging him, even if he was dangling from a meat hook with a cleaver embedded deeply in his skull and an arm and six toes severed. I don't know if it's just a "man thing", or being a lifelong law enforcer, but he appeared to think the words "ill" and "injured" were equivalent to "weak". And the last adjective my husband wanted to be branded with was "weak".

I didn't worry as much when he was moaning and groaning as if his next breath could be his last. If he was acting like a big baby, I knew he had some little short-lived bug and was milking it for all it was worth. Rip enjoyed being coddled and fussed over as much as the next man. However, when Rip withdrew from his normal activities and went out of his way to convince the world he was "just fine", I knew it wasn't just some little virus that would resolve itself in twenty-four hours.

"Would you like me to have Armando bring you a Crown and Coke?" I asked.

"Yeah, sure. A shot of whiskey always fixes anything that ails a person."

I wasn't so certain, but was encouraged about his desire for a drink. Since shortly after we'd retired and hit the road as full-time RVers, we'd always made time for an afternoon cocktail. We'd relax over our drinks and discuss the issues of the day, whether it'd be the latest terrorist attack monopolizing the news or the size of a hairball Dolly had just hacked up.

A couple of hours later, Rip was sleeping fitfully on his side of the king-sized bed. The bed was so comfortable, it had a tendency to knock us both out as if we'd each downed a half bottle of Nyquil before hitting the sack. The slight rocking of the ship lulled us to sleep like newborns.

My sense of relief evaporated like early-morning dew on a muskmelon when I went out to the balcony to make sure everything was stored properly. I found an apple, with one small chunk missing, four of the six crackers I'd gotten for

Rip, and a full glass of Crown and Coke that was watered down from the melted ice. I realized then Rip was sicker than he was letting on and had only requested the items to alleviate my worries.

A full gallon of Nyquil would not have cured my insomnia that night as I lay staring at the ceiling and wondering if Dr. Herron's comments had been more of a prediction than a warning.

CHAPTER 3

The following day was, without a doubt, the worst of my nearly sixty-nine years of life. What was supposed to be a relaxing day—cruising Glacier Bay and enjoying the beautiful scenery on either side of the ship—turned out to be one of fear, anxiety, and dread.

The horrible day in question started off with a scrumptious buffet in an exclusive restaurant aboard the ship that was only open for breakfast to suite passengers. It was a heady feeling to be treated as if we were VIPs. The variety of food at the buffet was unbelievable. There were eggs and potatoes available in every way a chef could conceivably prepare them, and meat of every variety. The fruit bar was incredible, as fresh as if its contents had been picked just minutes prior to our arrival. Kiwi, papaya, mango, and pineapple aplenty. There were a few fruit options, like prickly pear and acai, which looked absolutely dreadful to me. And there were even a couple of scary-looking selections, such as "dragon fruit" that I wouldn't have touched with a ten-foot pole, lest I be spending the remainder of the cruise on the proverbial throne.

I'd been pleased at how much better Rip appeared to be feeling after he'd awakened. Although still a bit pallid, he seemed more like himself than he had in several days. Just seeing Rip anxious to partake in a hearty meal had seemed a reassuring sign to me. I felt less assured, however, when he didn't end up eating enough to keep a bedbug alive. It was as if consuming a single scrambled egg and piece of toast had left him dragging his own wagon.

When I expressed concern, Rip said, "We're not spring chickens anymore, darling. You've had me on the go for days. It's apt to take me a day or two to regain my strength and energy. Don't you worry your pretty little head, now, you hear?"

"Okay, honey. I'm just not accustomed to seeing you so lethargic, and I never thought I'd see the day you turned your nose up at bacon."

Rip laughed. "Well, don't tell Dr. Herron about it. As far as she's concerned, I've set the bar extremely low, and I want to keep it that way. I don't want the doctor to think I've taken her concerns to heart and turned over a healthy new leaf."

I was so relieved to see his sense of humor had returned that I didn't want to argue, so I didn't remind him that Dr. Herron had warned him he was a ticking time bomb if he didn't make some lifestyle changes. Instead, I did as he implored me to do and chalked his lethargy up to five straight days of nearly nonstop activity.

After breakfast, we proceeded to the gift shop. We planned to spend much of the day on our private balcony, but I had not expected Alaska's late spring to be quite as frigid as it was. My wool sweater wasn't cutting it. I needed to buy a thick sweatshirt to wear over it, preferably with a hood to prevent the sharp wind from chilling me to the bone.

"While we're here, I'd like to buy you a souvenir of Alaska," Rip said.

"I am. I'm buying this Alaska hoodie. I love the teal color, and it'll keep me warm while we cruise the bay today."

"That's fine. But I'd also like for you to pick out something more meaningful."

"Why?" After a disapproving glance from Rip, I added, "Like what?"

"Something special to remind you of Alaska and our fiftieth-anniversary cruise."

"I'll never forget this trip, sweetheart. I don't need some little trinket like a shot glass or magnet to remind me." It wasn't only the fact I'm financially conservative that made me hesitant to spend money on a souvenir. The limited space in a 240-square-foot travel trailer was also a factor. If I crammed one more trinket inside it, we'd have to find a home for Dolly because there'd be no room left for her to park both pairs of her chubby cheeks. "Besides, we'll have pictures, too. You know how every time we turn around one of the ship's photographers are snapping a photo of us."

"Yes. And I'm also aware that you've yet to purchase a single one of those photos." Rip smiled as he spoke. He'd earlier agreed with me that fifteen bucks was too much to pay for an eight-by-ten-inch photo. After all, we could take our own pictures for nary a cent. And, if we didn't like them, we could simply delete them and snap more. I'd been doing exactly that throughout the entire trip.

"Well, of course not, but we agreed that—"

"Besides, a shot glass or magnet was not what I had in mind. Let me show you something I saw in a glass case back there." Rip pointed to the far corner of the store.

I followed him until he stopped at a case full of jewelry. I glanced at a diamond and ruby broach and gasped at the price. "Oh my! We can't afford this stuff."

"I want you to have a nice gem to wear in honor of our fifty years of happiness together."

"And, I love you for that thoughtful sentiment, dear." I meant what I said, but my heart skipped a beat at the price his thoughtful sentiment carried with it. In case I'd misread the price, I checked it again. I hadn't. "It's so expensive. We could make a decent down payment on a new travel trailer for that amount. And everyone would probably assume the gems were fakes anyway. So why not buy something with fake gems to begin with?"

"Considering how tight you are, you're no doubt correct. Everyone probably will assume the gems are phony. But you and I will know they're not. And that's important to me because my love for you is anything but phony, darling."

"I know your love for me is true, as mine is for you. But I thought you were considering the idea of trading the Chartreuse Caboose in on a larger trailer? We'll want to put a good down payment on it, won't we?"

"I *am* considering a new RV. Maybe a fifth wheel this time, with two or three slide-outs for the extra space to spread out in. But relax, sweetheart. We have more than enough money in savings to buy a new one outright and still leave plenty of padding in our emergency fund."

"That's a relief. But, I still think we—"

"See this ring?"

I looked down at the ring he was pointing at. It was so stunning it took my breath away. It had a gold band and an oval jade stone anchored in the middle of it. On a shore excursion tour earlier in the week, we had visited a shop near a small jade mine. We'd been given an interesting demonstration on how many of the indigenous gems, including amethyst, fluorite, and garnet, were transformed into beautiful jewelry in their facility. Our tour guide had told us jade was the official state gemstone and prolific in certain areas of Alaska. And, as one would expect, gold was the official state mineral.

"It's a gorgeous ring," I admitted. "But it's outrageously expensive."

"Not nearly as much as a lot of these other pieces, like that broach you were looking at. Besides, I don't care what it costs. How often does a man get to celebrate his fiftieth year of marriage to the most beautiful woman in the world? If you like it, I want you to have it."

"Oh, Rip, honey. You are so sweet. No wonder you swept me off my feet all those years ago. I do love this ring. But what can I get for you in return?"

"Just yourself, my dear. *You* are a gem. My gem. And

that's all I've ever needed, or ever will need, to make me the happiest guy in the world—not to mention the luckiest."

Rip was being uncharacteristically romantic and emotional, bordering on cheesy, and I was deeply touched by his sincerity. It was almost as if he wanted to make sure I had something meaningful to remember him by should something happen to him. The mere thought made the hairs on my arms stand straight up like a zillion little flag poles. I wasn't looking forward to the "until death do us part" clause in our marriage vows. Although that sensation made me uneasy, I agreed to let Rip purchase the ring because I could see how much it meant to *him* to give me something that meant a lot to *me*. And I truly did love my dear husband—and the gold and jade ring, as well.

"Are you certain you feel up to going to La Buena Vida tonight, Rip?" La Buena Vida was one of the onboard specialty restaurants that featured steak and seafood. We'd cancelled our dinner reservations there the previous night, but were able to reschedule them for the following evening.

"I promised you an anniversary supper, and I'm not going to renege on that vow any more than I've reneged on any other marriage vow. Besides, I'm starving. I'll need the energy for dancing in the Lido Lounge afterward."

"But—"

"Don't fret, honey. I'm fine now. If I drop dead of anything, it's going to be malnutrition."

"But—"

"But nothing. I've made reservations for six o'clock, so you best be getting ready. I'm going with or without you."

Despite Rip's smile and the warm embrace that followed, I still had reservations—about *his* dinner reservations. But I didn't want to disappoint him, despite the niggling premonition that the day was not going to end as happily as it had begun.

I took a quick shower and struggled into a pair of panty hose, which reminded me of why you rarely see women wearing them these days. Next, I stepped into my new black dress. It had a black and gold brocade bodice, a straight silk skirt, and a gold belt. I slipped on the black heels Rip had promised to dance off of me and, lastly, I fastened a necklace around my neck, and proudly donned my new gold and jade ring. I couldn't recall the last time I'd dressed so sharply. Rip must have approved of my attire because he whistled at me when I entered the main cabin.

At the time I'd purchased the outfit for our anniversary cruise, it had crossed my mind the dress would double as stylish attire for any funerals we might have to attend in the future. Now, as I looked at myself in the mirror, I prayed that opportunity would not present itself any time soon.

CHAPTER 4

◆

"**Y**our husband is having a heart attack." Seven little words that rocked my world. Those seven words made me feel as if my heart had been ripped out of my chest, stomped on by a pair of mad circus elephants, run over a time or two by a cement truck, and then shoved back into its original cavity in a tattered, bloody mess. Shaken to the core, I collapsed onto a nearby chair before my unsteady legs failed me.

The last time I remembered feeling that petrified was when I was seventeen and my pappy caught me making out with Rip in the woodshed. At that long-ago moment, I feared Rip was about to meet his maker at my father's hands. Now I feared it was *the* Father, Rip's maker himself, that was about to steal my husband from me.

Scrutinizing my reaction, the ship's physician, Dr. Dyer, patted my shoulder in an attempt to console his patient's hysterical spouse. "I think there's a fair chance he'll survive it, Mrs. Ripple. But he needs more critical medical attention than my staff and I can provide on the ship. Take a deep breath, ma'am. It's probably not as serious as it might appear."

"Urg, but I, uh, is he going to, oh my, um, but—" I tried to respond to the doctor's lame efforts to comfort me, but couldn't seem to form a complete, coherent sentence. Finally, I took Dr. Dyer's advice and sucked in several deep breaths before he needed to drag out another gurney. I felt my heartbeat, which had been thumping like a jackhammer inside of me, ever so slowly begin to ebb. "What are we going to do?"

"Not sure yet. I need to go have a word with Captain Radwick."

"Don't leave! Please don't leave Rip's side!" I grabbed hold of the doctor's left forearm. It would've taken a "jaws of life" contraption to withdraw his arm from my grasp at that moment.

Doctor Dyer used his right hand to try and free himself from my grip, but I was still squeezing his arm like a c-clamp. "Don't worry, Mrs. Ripple. My trained staff is well-prepared to handle the situation without my presence until I return."

His reassuring statement did nothing to bolster my confidence. I studied the staff to which he was referring: two young women who were busily fiddling with their cell phones and giggling about something one of them had read on her phone's screen. Rip could have jumped up, yanked the heart monitor leads from his chest, done a merry little jig on the bed, and sprinted out of the ship's hospital without notice, for all the attention the nurses were paying him. But I nodded at the doctor and released his arm, knowing that if I were to do otherwise, I'd only delay the help Rip so desperately needed.

Earlier in the evening, we'd gone to La Buena Vida for our belated anniversary dinner. I had ordered the grilled salmon on a bed of kale and spinach, lightly spritzed with a raspberry vinaigrette. Rip had debated for a few seconds before doing the same. As the waiter had walked away, I gave Rip a questioning look. He had shrugged his shoulders before responding. "I decided I should pay more heed to Dr. Herron's advice and start eating healthier. I don't want her to think I'm not making an effort to improve my diet."

Bull crap! I'd thought. Rip had never given a rat's behind what Dr. Herron thought about his unhealthy eating habits. When it came to eating, "salad" was not in his vocabulary. Nor was "lightly spritzed" or "vinaigrette". I had to wonder even then if my husband's sudden decision to start eating better wasn't akin to closing the barn door after the horse had already bolted.

Suddenly, before I could delve into what was really behind my meat-and-potato husband's suspicious menu choice, Rip sat his Crown and Coke down forcefully, clutched his chest, and groaned like a cow laboring to deliver a two-headed calf.

With no thought for other diners, I had screamed as if a dozen pirates had just stormed the restaurant with their long Samurai swords slashing the air.

"Help! Help us!" I'd hollered. "My husband needs a doctor. Now!"

Several waiters had rushed to our side, along with a fellow passenger claiming to be a physician. Calvin, the physician we later learned was a dermatologist, appeared almost as terrified as I felt, and did little to calm me or the patient. I bent down to assist my husband while waiting for someone to arrive who could actually render assistance. I spent the time praying silently. Looking back, I assume Calvin spent that time scanning his writhing fellow passenger in search of suspicious moles. Despite the fact the dermatologist was sorely lacking in cardiac training and experience, I did appreciate his offer to help, and told him so.

Meanwhile, a member of the restaurant's staff summoned the ship's doctor, who was at Rip's side in what seemed like no more than six-and-a-half days. It was probably more like five minutes, but those five minutes passed by agonizingly slow.

In the beehive of activity that followed, Rip was stabilized, loaded onto a gurney, and whisked away to the small hospital on the cruise ship. The other diners had all stopped eating and were rubber-necking to get a glance of the unfortunate passenger who had fallen seriously ill as he sat at his corner table. I'm almost certain I heard a diner tell his waiter, "I don't want whatever that poor sucker ordered."

I wanted to yell at the gawkers. Tell them all to mind their own business. I felt as if Rip and I were on display for their onboard entertainment that evening. But then I realized I would've been rubber-necking myself, had the stricken diner been anyone else in the steakhouse other than Rip.

Once Rip was lying flat on a bed in the small onboard hospital, I waited in trepidation to find out what would happen next. When I heard Rip whisper my name, I glanced at him. Pardon the expression, but he literally looked like death warmed over: ashen skin, eyes shrunken into his head, and appearing as if he'd aged twenty years in as many minutes. I swallowed hard and said, "Do you need something? What can I do for you, honey?"

"You can relax. I'm going to be all right. I promise."

"But, how can you promise me that—"

"Have I ever let you down before?" Rip's voice was barely a whisper.

Before I could reply, with his right hand pressed against his chest, Rip's eyes closed. He became so still that he appeared to have stopped breathing. I gasped and clutched my own chest.

"Oh, my God! Is he—"

Not certain herself, one of the young nurses checked his vital signs on the monitor, and said, "No, ma'am, I'm sure he's just exhausted. Heart attacks have a way of taking it out of a person, you see. They can be a real buzz-kill."

Not appreciating her turn of phrase, I breathed a sigh of relief and watched closely to detect Rip's chest move up and down and his nostrils flare slightly as he inhaled.

"I have good news and bad news," Doctor Dyer said after he re-entered the curtained-off partition surrounding Rip's bed. He briefly scrutinized the information on the heart monitor. Without asking me which one I wanted to hear first—the bad news or good, he continued. "I've decided the best plan of action at this time is to do nothing."

"What?" I was aghast, justifiably baffled by his remark. "Was your plan to do nothing the good news or the bad?"

"That was the bad news. I'd considered having him airlifted to the closest trauma center, but finding a reputable cardiac hospital near our location in the middle of Glacier Bay would have been challenging, to say the least. Not to mention, the captain informed me that landing a chopper on the helipad during the current weather conditions would be next to impossible. Loading your husband into a basket from a hovering helicopter would be even more risky than waiting until we reach port in the morning. We'll arrive in Victoria, British Columbia—"

I hated to interrupt, but I was at my wits' end. I couldn't quite visualize any silver lining to the cloud the doctor had just painted with his bleak remarks. "Please, tell me the good news!"

"Your husband's vital signs have improved greatly. I think he's out of the woods. For the moment, anyway. I'm not a cardiologist, mind you. But, judging by the EKG we just ran, I don't think his heart has sustained any permanent damage. I think this cardiac event was more of a warning sign of clogged arteries than a potentially lethal case of cardiac arrest. Mr. Ripple should be fine resting in here under close observation until morning."

"Okay." Not comfortable with the doctor's "should be fine", I glanced at the dark-haired nurse who was smoothing out a ragged edge on the nail of her right index finger with a metal file. I felt uneasy about Rip's fate if left under the "close observation" of Dr. Dyer's young nurses. I'd feel better if he were left under my own close observation. I'd watch him as if I were a soaring red-tailed hawk waiting for a mouse to quiver on the ground below. If the heart monitor even hiccupped, I'd summon the doctor immediately. Although I'm sure the nurses were a lot more capable than my shaken mind was giving them credit for, at the time I wasn't convinced they'd bother summoning the doctor unless the heart monitor had flat-lined. "Would it be all right if I stay in here with him overnight, Dr. Dyer?"

"Absolutely! In fact, I'd recommend it. Naturally, we'll monitor him continuously until we reach port. If he takes a turn for the worse, we'll have an ambulance summoned to the port to transfer him to the best hospital in Victoria. Once they believe Mr. Ripple is stabilized and it's safe to do so, they'll transfer your husband to a cardiac center in Seattle. But, if he maintains the vital signs he's showing now, we'll wait until we're stateside, in the Port of Seattle the following day, to transfer him. That would be much better for both convenience and financial reasons." With that, the doctor conversed briefly with the nurses and then parted the drapes to exit the cramped cubicle.

I felt a sense of relief at the doctor's assessment of Rip's current condition. I prayed my husband's vital signs would remain stable, at least until we reached Seattle. I knew Canada practiced socialized medicine and wasn't sure how, or if, our Medicare policy and insurance supplement would be of any use in the neighboring country. I could see visions of our dreams of an upgraded RV, if not our entire nest egg, being destroyed like a mobile home park during a tornado. I glanced down at my anniversary ring and briefly wondered if Rip had purchased it under an "all sales are final" constraint. But I couldn't have returned it anyway. It'd meant so much to Rip to buy it for me.

I moved my chair next to Rip's bed and picked his hand up off the sheet to hold it while he slept. Within minutes, I'd dozed off into fitful slumber. But not before I'd said a heartfelt prayer, asking God to spare the love of my life and make him well again. "Lord, take me if you need an extra angel. I can't promise I'll be quality angel material, but I need Rip more than he needs me."

I knew my husband would not have agreed with me. But once again, as in the majority of disputes we'd had over the last half-century, he'd be dead wrong. Pardon the pun.

CHAPTER 5

"Vroom." I jumped in alarm as something white and willowy flew over my head at break-neck speed. I glanced around the dim, dusty room I found myself in, but saw nothing disconcerting. I then dropped to my knees following a loud scream that reminded me of the sound Penelope used to emit. Penelope was a pet peacock my family had owned when I was young, and her loud screeches could cause even the healthiest person's heart to skip a beat. The next thing I knew, the lights went out and I was alone in pitch darkness. I suddenly felt something feathery running up and down my arms and began to see flashes of light exploding all around me. I knew, without a doubt, I was in a building being invaded by angry spirits. From out of nowhere, I heard a low, resonating voice whisper, "You'd better leave while you still can."

I knew the threat was directed at me, and leaving is exactly what I wanted to do, but I couldn't locate an exit. Squinting in the darkness, I scanned the room but saw no doors or windows from which to escape. It occurred to me that I might be in the process of losing my ever-loving mind—one flipping marble at a time. At sixty-eight, I was too young for the men in white jackets to come take me away and put me in a home for the mentally unstable. Not for my own protection, of course, but for the rest of society's safety. Because, after all, there's no telling what a deranged lunatic who heard and saw things that didn't exist might do! More importantly, my husband needed me right now more than he ever had. Bat-crap crazy, or not, I was determined I wasn't going to let him down. But first I needed to find a way out of the room full of horrors.

Just then, I felt a slight breeze and spotted faint light coming from a narrow window in the far corner of the room. I made a mad dash for it. As I reached the open window, it slammed shut and the face of an older woman stared through the glass at me with an accusatory expression. I felt myself losing consciousness and reached out my arms to break my fall. Just before I hit the floor, I jerked awake. I sat up in bed instantly and glanced around to get my bearings. I breathed a sigh of relief when I recognized the bedroom in our travel trailer and saw Dolly curled up on Rip's pillow beside me.

I realized it was only a nightmare I'd experienced, but I couldn't shake the feeling that the terrifying dream had been a premonition of things to come.

CHAPTER 6

◆◆◆

"Not on your life, Buster Brown!"

"Oh, come on, Rapella! What's one cheeseburger and a few fries gonna hurt?" The pleading look on Rip's face nearly made me give in to his request that I make a run to the nearest fast food joint and stealthily sneak a combo meal back into his hospital room. But I stood my ground. I wasn't going to love him to death—literally! And I wasn't going to tell him about the nightmare either or he'd be worried about my mental state. I needed him to focus on his own well-being instead of mine for a while.

"It was things like cheeseburger and fries that landed you in this cardiac care unit to begin with," I said. "You'll just have to make do with whatever's on the tray they bring in for you, which should be arriving any time now."

"Oh, joy!" His grumbling turned into a cough. He clutched a red heart-shaped pillow to his chest to lessen the pain as he attempted to clear the phlegm from his throat. His cardiac surgeon's personal nurse had brought him the pillow while he was still in ICU following his triple-bypass surgery.

As if on cue, a skinny, haggard-faced woman, who looked like she should be a patient in the ICU enclosure next to my husband's rather than carting trays of food from one hospital room to the next, scurried into the room. She sat the tray down in front of Rip and lifted the lid off of his plate in a tentative fashion, as if she wasn't totally sure whatever was under the lid wasn't hazardous material. Her uncertain expression was unchanged even after she'd observed the contents. She studied Rip's face for a moment before saying, "Sorry."

As the stick-thin woman left the room, I looked over to see why she'd apologized. On the tray was a carton of milk, a wiggly square of green gelatin, a dinner roll, some sad-looking green beans and a glob of mystery meat. I'd have bet on chicken, but couldn't be certain it wasn't pork, or not even meat at all. If it was something like tofu, it was best for everyone concerned if Rip wasn't made aware of the glob's true identity.

The only thing I was certain about was that I couldn't have choked that sorry selection of hospital food down if my life depended on it.

But my husband's life very well *could* depend on his willingness to adapt to better eating habits, even if the food selections weren't what he would've chosen if given his druthers. This particular cardiac center was renowned for its outstanding cardiac care, not its mouth-watering cuisine, so I tried to put a positive spin on his lunch. "Hey, look! You're not on a liquid diet like yesterday. The roll looks quite tasty." *Too bad they didn't give you any butter to spread on it,* I wanted to add, but kept my own roll-hole tightly closed.

Rip gave me a look I tried not to read too much into. I'm sure it was meant to make me feel like the worst wife in the world for not agreeing to pick him up a decent meal at a nearby fast-food restaurant. I blanched as he picked his knife up and banged it down on the roll several times. THUD! THUD! THUD!

"Got a chain saw handy I can cut into it with?" Rip asked.

"Well, um…"

"You want it? Wanna see if it's as tasty as you think it looks?" Without waiting for a response, he flung it toward the trash container. I'll admit that a dinner roll really should not sound like a brick hitting the side of a dumpster when hurled into a metal trash can. But I couldn't cave in every time he complained. His health depended on my perseverance. I'd have to maintain a tough love attitude until Rip was back on his feet.

"What were you expecting for lunch, Rip? Mashed potatoes, gravy, and a thick juicy T-bone? And perhaps a hefty slice of cheesecake for dessert, just in case there's still an artery inside your body that's not on the verge of being clogged shut with plaque?"

In response to my question, Rip shoved the table away from his bed. "This crap's not fit for a dog."

"Fine! Go on a hunger strike if you'd like, but I doubt it'll improve your menu options any time soon. I'm not going to sabotage Dr. Murillo's good work by smuggling in junk food for you to kill yourself with. If that's your goal, why don't you just ask to be put on a morphine drip until you keel over like a hollowed-out oak tree in a windstorm? Why not just save me and everyone caring for you here the time and trouble of trying to give you a second shot at a longer lifespan?"

I'd about had it with the pity party Rip was throwing for himself. Except for genetics, perhaps, he had only himself to blame for his current predicament. Doctor Herron had warned him repeatedly of the potential ramifications of his devil-may-care lifestyle. The cardiologist, who'd performed his bypass operation, had done the same but more emphatically. And yet, even after the open-heart surgery, Rip was refusing to take either one of their professional recommendations seriously.

I decided to change the subject to steer his attention away from the unappetizing lunch. In hindsight, I probably should have segued into a more appealing subject. "We need to get you set up for the therapy Dr. Murillo recommended."

"I'm not convinced it's necessary." Rip shook his head in denial. "I've heard several people say that cardio rehab is vastly overrated."

Are any of these people still among the living? I wanted to ask. I didn't, because I didn't want to get Rip riled up when he should be relaxing and resting quietly. I was pretty sure one of the "several people" Rip was referring to was a fellow police officer he used to work with who pooh-poohed the idea of rehab following his doughnut-induced quadruple bypass. He'd died six months later of a massive stroke. The others were probably the imaginary friends he always counted on to back him up when he needed support for one of his more preposterous opinions.

The man was seriously stomping on my last nerve. I momentarily visualized myself wrapping my hands around Rip's neck and trying my damnedest to choke the life out of him. I was *that* annoyed by his attitude that evening.

More than being merely irritated about the situation, I was scared. How would I ever make Rip follow his doctors' orders once we left the hospital? I wouldn't, I suddenly realized. As hard as I tried, I'd likely never make him see the light.

Like many teenagers who attempt risky things, Rip thought he was invincible. He was a lifelong cop, for goodness sake. And now, after all those years of dodging bullets—literally, on a couple of occasions—he was going to be taken out by those chocolate long johns he'd routinely gobbled down while keeping our streets safe. I was determined not to let that happen.

As Rip scanned through the channels on the room's television, I sent up a silent prayer. I asked God to help me find an answer to my problem before He, the Lord himself, got so annoyed with my husband that He called him home prematurely just to put an end to Rip's incessant whining and self-destructive behavior. Maybe *He* could make Rip see the light. I just prayed it wasn't the one at the end of the tunnel leading my bull-headed husband straight to the pearly gates.

* * *

At five-thirty that evening, I felt as if my prayers had been answered. The answer arrived in a pretty little package—around five-feet-four, one hundred and twenty pounds, auburn-colored hair, and horn-rimmed glasses—all wrapped up in a set of baby blue scrubs with white bunnies across the front. She had a name tag hanging from a lanyard around her neck that had SYDNEY COMBS, CARDIO NURSE printed on it.

Oh, boy. A new unsuspecting, undeserving butt for Rip to chew on for a while, I thought. Rip had been grouchy and ill-tempered all day, and his mood had not improved as the hours droned on. He'd snapped rudely at the man who'd wheeled him from ICU to his new room on the third floor, and then almost reduced a young hospital volunteer, or "candy striper", to tears when she'd come into the room to put a pitcher of fresh water on his table. He'd hollered, "What the hell do you mean I can't have coffee?"

After he'd grumbled to the scrawny woman who brought his evening meal, I turned to Rip. "Okay, Clyde Ripple! I've officially had enough of your repulsive, unappreciative attitude for one day! I'm going home to feed Dolly, and I'm not coming back until tomorrow afternoon. For several days I've been scared senseless that you would die on me. Now I'm starting to entertain the thought of killing you myself."

Rip looked at me in surprise. He knew when I used his given name, I was so ticked off that I was seeing red. I suppose saying I was seriously thinking about killing him might have been a clue, too. Before he could reply, Nurse Combs walked into the room with a stethoscope around her neck.

"I won't stay long, Mr. Ripple. Just going to write the night nurse's name on your chalkboard, and then I'll leave you in peace to finish your supper." As she spoke, she picked up a piece of chalk and wrote "Travis" on the board at the foot of Rip's bed. I gritted my teeth, waiting for her patient to respond. I trusted he'd be unpleasant with the nurse, as he'd been with everyone else he'd interacted with the entire day, and I wasn't disappointed.

"How do they expect all of us heart patients to eat this god-awful garbage?" Rip asked.

Without batting an eye, Nurse Combs politely replied in a soft, but stern, voice. "They don't expect *all* of you heart patients to eat it. Just the ones who want to live to see the outside of this hospital again."

"But…" Rip's mouth hung open. His complaint clearly did not get the response he'd hoped for.

"Do you enjoy living, sir? If so, you best get used to the fact you're going to have to make some lifestyle changes. You're going to have to take medications, as prescribed, go to your cardio rehab appointments, exercise as scheduled, and eat this low-fat, low-sugar, low-sodium 'god-awful garbage', that's been ordered for you for the specific purpose of helping you restore your health. If you have other plans, please let me know. I'll put a DNR sign on your door and—"

"DNR?" Rip asked. The look of bewilderment on his face made me want to give Nurse Combs a high-five. "What's that?"

"It stands for Do Not Resuscitate!"

"Oh."

Without raising her voice or altering her pleasant, matter-of-fact tone, Sydney Combs continued by nearly echoing my earlier comments to Rip. "I will inform the nurses, kitchen help, physicians, and all other hospital staff to stay out of this room because you've opted not to make the effort to heal properly in order to survive the cardiac event you recently experienced. That will allow you to die peacefully without all the intrusions caring for you entails. More importantly, it will allow all of the cardiac center staff members who have patients who *do* want to live and who *do* appreciate our hard work and efforts, to use their time more wisely."

Rip was rendered speechless. He glanced at me for support. Instead of offering any, I smiled smugly. *Where are those imaginary friends when you need them?* I wanted to ask, but bit my tongue and remained silent. *I'm fairly certain your story about that dead cop, who's six-feet-under now because he didn't believe rehab was necessary, is not going to impress this nurse much.*

After waiting an adequate length of time for her patient to reply, Nurse Combs asked, "Would you like me to take this tray of god-awful garbage back to the kitchen now?"

Still at a loss for words, Rip shook his head. His apprehension was blatantly apparent. Finally, he picked up his fork and knife and began to cut into what the kitchen aide had referred to as grilled fish. We'd have to take her word for it, although I've never seen a squiggly, square fish before. It appeared to be way past its prime, whatever "it" was.

I did feel sorry for the poor guy, who I knew was craving something more palatable to consume. But I wanted him to get better and never have another heart scare like this one that had nearly killed him. I needed him to be around as long as I was. So I was relieved to hear Rip mutter, "I'll eat as much of it as I can choke down."

"See that you do." The nurse's voice was terser than it'd been earlier. Rip was looking down at his supper in horror, as she added, "And don't upset one of my young candy stripers again. Coffee is a stimulant and off limits to all of our recent open-heart surgery patients. You hear me, Mr. Ripple? There's a pitcher of water on your table. If you're thirsty, I suggest you drink it."

"Yes, ma'am."

Nurse Combs walked over to Rip's bed and put her hand on top of the bandage on his leg where they'd harvested part of a saphenous vein to use as a means to bypass the clogged area of his blocked arteries. As you can probably tell, I'd learned more about the cardiovascular system and what's involved in bypassing clogged arteries than I'd ever imagined I would—or ever hoped to. Rip winced at the nurse's touch as she poked and prodded the wound area. "Tender?"

"Yes."

"That's to be expected. It's a little warm due to the inflammation, but that's normal too. It's a natural part of healing."

"At least it isn't throbbing like it was yesterday," Rip said. He then picked up his spoon and began to pick at the food on his plate. He was rearranging it more than eating it, which wasn't fooling me, or the nurse. After watching Rip for a few seconds, Nurse Combs confirmed his entree actually was fish.

"That tuna's not a toy, Rip. Eat it. Don't play with it. I'll be back to check your vitals in a couple of minutes, after I figure out where I left my COW."

Rip almost choked on his gelatin, as I asked, "You misplaced a cow?"

"Yes, I can't remember where I last used it. Oh, sorry. Sometimes I forget most patients and their families aren't familiar with the slang we use in the medical field. COW stands for 'computer on wheels'. We have to tow them around to record our patients' vital signs and other important information. For lack of a better word, we call them COWs. However, we just heard a rumor the use of that term may soon be prohibited."

"Why's that?" I asked. "It's rather clever, if you ask me."

"Apparently not everyone agrees with you. A grossly obese patient heard a couple of nurses using that term outside her room one day and thought they were making fun of her. Supposedly, she's filed a lawsuit against that hospital. Word is we're going to have to start referring to them as a WOW, or workstation on wheels." Sydney smiled and placed her right hand under the automatic anti-bacterial soap dispenser to the left of the door. "Now finish your supper, Rip. When I return for your vitals, I'll help you get registered for the rehab facility which, incidentally, is conveniently located one block from this hospital."

"Swell." I detected sarcasm in Rip's tone and wondered if Nurse Combs had picked up on it, as well.

She made it clear she had with her next question. She

bent her head and stared straight into Rip's eyes over the top of her eyeglasses. "You *are* planning to participate in the rehab program, aren't you?"

"Yes, ma'am." Rip sounded as if he was responding to a drill sergeant who'd been on him like ugly on an opossum since the day he'd enlisted.

The cute and crafty nurse winked at me and walked out the door. But not before she smiled at her grumbling patient and said, "*Bon appétit.*"

I absolutely adored Nurse Combs.

CHAPTER 7

As promised, when Nurse Combs returned to take his vital signs at nine o'clock that evening, she brought Rip paperwork to sign regarding his registration for the hospital's cardio rehabilitation program. She discussed the program and scheduling, explained what he'd be required to do, and how frequently he'd have to do it. Rip had wisely waited until Sydney left the room to grumble. "Rehab sounds worse than boot camp!"

"Relax, honey. We will get through it," I said.

"*We?*" Rip's sarcastic retort was not appreciated. I'd been trying to offer moral support but had instead encouraged a new round of complaining. "I don't see you on this bed with a zipper down your—"

"Oh, my! Look at the time! I best be heading back to the campground. Visiting hours are nearly over." I had glanced at the clock at the foot of Rip's bed and cut him off. I'd listened to all of the moaning and groaning I could stand for one day. I collected my purse and walked out of his room before he could utter another word.

I felt a twinge of guilt later on while I enjoyed a toasted cheese sandwich and cup of minestrone soup for supper, knowing this combo was one of Rip's favorite meals. I washed my dishes, fed Dolly, paid a couple of bills, and laid down for some much-needed rest at eleven-fifteen.

As I was drifting off to sleep, the phone rang. As always, being awakened by a phone call during the night scared the devil out of me. I sat straight up in bed like I'd been yanked upward by a block and tackle pulley.

Who'd call at this time of night unless they had bad news to report? I'd always think as I reached for the phone on my nightstand. When someone you love is in the hospital, an unexpected nighttime phone call is even more alarming.

"Hello," I answered breathlessly.

"Relax, honey," Rip said. He'd recognized the fear in my voice. "It's just me."

"Are you okay?"

"Yes, of course. I just wanted to tell you goodnight and that I loved you."

"I'm kind of sweet on you too, handsome. I'm sorry I had to leave so abruptly this evening. I'd just remembered I hadn't fed the cat."

"No problem, dear. I would've left too if I were you. Speaking of 'her majesty', how's Dolly doing? Does she miss me?"

"Absolutely! She asks about you all the time."

"Really?" Rip asked with a chuckle. It was nice to hear him in good spirits for the first time in days.

"Trust me. She's feeling totally mistreated without you here," I teased. With me, Dolly was a typical feline: aloof, independent, and unaffectionate. But when Rip was around, she turned into a "cling-on" that stuck to him like a postage stamp. Rip called her his Star Trek kitty. She'd be curled up on his lap, on the windowpane behind his head, or stretched out on his chest while he was lounging on the sofa. She always had at least one paw touching some part of his body. Rip claimed it was her way of demonstrating love. I thought she was demonstrating possessiveness.

Hearing a flash of the old Rip I knew and loved was refreshing. I was caught off-guard when next he issued a heart-felt apology.

"I'm sorry about the cranky mood I've been in lately. It's not your fault I had to have my leg nearly sliced in two and my ribcage split open like an English walnut. Yet you've been more than patient with me. I don't know what I'd do without you, honey." I could hear the emotion in Rip's voice and I felt the sincerity in his words. If I wasn't so dog-tired, I'd have thrown some clothes on and drove back to the hospital to hug him and kiss him goodnight, something I'd neglected to do before leaving the hospital earlier that evening.

"I couldn't survive without you, either, Rip. So please, for my sake, pay heed to what the medical professionals advise you to do."

"Okay. It's the least I can do." Rip was acting so compliant, I had to wonder if Nurse Combs had been back in his room, putting the fear of God into him, following my hasty departure from the hospital a couple of hours earlier. He made it apparent she had with his next words. "I don't want them to wash their hands of me for being negligent about my own health."

"No, you don't. What else did Nurse Combs say to you?"

"How did you know she—"

"Woman's intuition." I had to laugh that he couldn't see how I instinctively knew she'd been reading him the riot act. "So, what'd she say?"

"Rehab three days per week, for an hour each session the first week, and increasing with time. Regular checkups and lab work, too, of course, and a healthy eating regimen. Basically, she said I'd have all of the enjoyment sucked out of my life until I reached the point I was praying for another heart attack – a fatal one, to be more exact."

"Oh, good grief. It won't be all that bad. Can you at least *try* to look at the bright side of things for once? You have a lot to be thankful for, you know."

"How's that?" Rip asked. There was a good measure of bitterness in his tone. His bubbly mood was sinking faster than an untied anchor. He'd never been the glass half-empty type before his health had taken this turn for the worse. There was no reason for me to tolerate that type of attitude now, either.

"You're alive, for starters. You very easily could've been on the wrong side of the grass right now."

"Well, I guess you have a point there," Rip consented. "And, there's another bright spot I hadn't thought of until just now. Cindy also told me, because of the anti-blood clotting medication they've put me on, I'm supposed to limit my intake of foods that are high in Vitamin K, like spinach, Brussels sprouts and kale. She said that vitamin K thickens the blood and can cause dangerous clotting."

"The nurse's name is Sydney, not Cindy. And how is having to limit your intake of foods high in Vitamin K a bright spot?"

"Now I won't have to keep coming up with excuses to avoid salad bars." Rip spoke with obvious amusement in his voice. I was happy to see his mood brightening again and his sense of humor returning, and told him so.

"I suppose the only bad thing is," he continued, "the commute three times a week is going to put a lot of miles on the truck, and get tiresome."

"Yes, but it's a small price to pay to get you back on your feet. We'll figure out something. Perhaps we can find a closer campground to stay in." I wasn't going to sweat the small stuff at this point. Rip's full recovery was all I was concerned with. "Good night for now, honey. I love you, and I'll see you tomorrow."

"Love you more. Give Dolly a hug for me."

"And get my nose scratched up in return? No, thanks. But I will give her your love. And an extra treat, to her from daddy."

I could hear Rip laughing as he disconnected the call. Our fifty-year old daughter, Regina, thought our habit of treating our beloved cat like we'd conceived her ourselves was laughable.

Despite the nightmare I'd had the previous night, it didn't take me long to fall into a deep slumber, most likely with a smile still planted on my face.

Just before I dozed off, a funny thought crossed my mind. Instead of calling the home-on-wheels we towed around the country the Chartreuse Caboose, we could simply call it our HOW.

While I was getting around the next morning preparing for the long commute to the hospital, I thought about the upcoming drive back and forth to Rip's rehab appointments. I put my Googling skills to work, only to discover there was no good alternative RV park to relocate to. Seattle is not exactly riddled with designated RV parking areas, I discovered.

Once again, the answer to our quandary came in the form of Nurse Sydney Combs. When she stopped to visit Rip on her morning rounds, I chatted with her about the rehab facility and asked her if she knew of any nearby RV parks I might have missed on the Internet. She didn't, but she had an idea that might be ideal for us.

"I don't know if this would interest you or not, but I have a dilemma myself that could result in a win-win situation for both of us."

"What's that?" I asked.

"I'm running behind at the moment, but I'll stop by after my morning rounds to discuss it with you two. All right?"

"Of course!" My attention had been instantly piqued, and I was anxious to hear more. Patience had never been one of my virtues, but I didn't want to appear over-anxious in case it wasn't something we felt would work for us. "Whenever it's convenient for you is fine, dear."

I'd fill the time watching two families competing on *Family Feud* while Rip tried to keep from gagging as he suffered through his breakfast. And, really, don't you agree with him that something as revolting as powdered eggs should be outlawed?

CHAPTER 8

"My great-aunt, Mabel Trumbo, had open-heart surgery here, too. Doctor Murillo performed a double bypass on her about a month ago. Unfortunately, she passed about ten days later from complications," Nurse Combs stated matter-of-factly. "That was two weeks ago tomorrow. She was seventy-five when she died."

"Oh, no!" I exclaimed. "Seventy-five is very young. Especially now that I'm closing in on that age myself. I'm so sorry for your loss, Nurse Combs."

What part of this win-win situation didn't I understand? I wondered. Her aunt, who was only six years older than Rip, had one less artery bypassed than he had, yet hadn't survived. What did that say about Rip's chances for a complete recovery? I could physically feel my anxiety level ratchet up a notch or two.

"Aunt Mabel took my siblings and me in after our mother died. I was fifteen at the time. We just refer to her as Aunt Mabel because adding the 'great' before 'aunt' every time gets tedious. So, anyway, my aunt was in worse condition than Rip when she went into surgery. She'd suffered a nearly fatal heart attack about ten years earlier, and it was the staff here at the center that saved her life. But there was permanent damage done to part of the heart muscle, a condition called myocardial infarction."

"Do you know if Rip's heart sustained any permanent damage?"

"I don't think so. If it did, it was minimal. Aunt Mabel was lackadaisical in regards to her recovery process, not taking any of the cardiac center staff's instructions or precautions seriously. She refused cardio rehab, for starters. To make matters worse, she was beginning to show significant signs of having Alzheimer's, so making sure she remembered to take the right medications at the right time was challenging."

I glanced at Rip, who couldn't remember his own grandkids' names half the time. However, he had me to remind him about his meds, so I wasn't too worried about that aspect of his recovery process. I noticed his face pale and his eyes widen following her remarks. Sydney had indeed made an impression on him that I never could have. She seemed to have single-handedly turned Rip into a staunch believer of following the doctor's recommendations. Where Rip most likely thought I was over-reacting when I warned him of the consequences of noncompliance, he clearly thought the words of his surgeon's personal nurse were gospel. She was speaking from knowledge obtained from her vast experience in the field of cardiac health, and more importantly, post-bypass survival.

"I don't know why, but I feel as if I'm partially to blame for her death," Sydney said. "As an experienced cardiac care nurse, I was the logical choice to take care of her following her operation, both here in the cardio ward and at her home after she was released."

"Why do you feel partially responsible for her death?" I asked.

"I did the best I could to take care of her after she went home from the hospital. I did her shopping for her, paid her bills, took care of her pets, and checked to see if the medications she was supposed to have taken were indeed absent from her pill box. And I tried to get her to get up and move around the house as much as possible. It would probably have been easier to get that antique grandfather's clock in her dining room to run than it was to get Aunt Mabel just to walk." Sydney followed her quip with a remorseful smile that told me how deeply Sydney had loved her aunt, quirks and all. Her eyes glistened with tears that threatened to spill over.

"Once again, I'm so sorry for your loss, honey. It sounds to me like you were quite generous with the time and effort you expended on your aunt's well-being. No one could have expected any more from you. You're only human, for goodness sake! You should certainly not feel guilty about anything, my dear," I said to Sydney in an effort to console her. She ran a sleeve across her face to blot the tears on her cheeks, and the swipe appeared to wipe away her sorrowful expression, as well.

"But *we're* not going to be negligent and non-compliant, are we, Rip?" She asked her patient, as if she hadn't heard a word I'd just said. *I did say all of that out loud, didn't I?* I asked myself. It was as though she had tuned me out completely. As she spoke to Rip, she stared directly into his eyes. "Nor are we going to convince ourselves that we're invincible, are we?"

"No, Miss Cindy. We aren't."

"It's Sydney," I reminded him.

"That's okay, Rapella. He hasn't gotten my name correct yet. But Cindy's closer than Candy, as he called me earlier this morning."

"I'm sorry, Miss Sydney. I must have gotten you confused with the young candy striper who stops by on occasion to see if I need anything. I'm still waiting for that cup of coffee I requested yesterday."

Sydney nodded. "You'll keep waiting, too. You want me to go back over why you aren't allowed coffee in the cardiac ward?"

"Not really."

"And the young lady's name is Jasmine."

"Oh." Rip had the decency to look ashamed, even though I'd guess Sydney knew the expression was a farce as well as I did.

"So, back to what I was telling you about Aunt Mabel. In her will, she left her house to the cardiac center to use as a boarding house for families who have a loved one recovering here in the hospital. Of course, she hadn't expected the transfer of ownership to occur so soon. She was looking ahead a decade or so, but fate intervened, as it so often does. The center will take over legal ownership of the large house in the next week or so. They delayed it so we could get any personal items we wanted out of her home."

"Yes, of course. How thoughtful of your aunt," I replied. "She obviously didn't hold the center, or Dr. Murillo, personally responsible for her death then, did she?"

Sydney looked at me oddly. Her tone sounded a bit snappish as she responded. "Well, actually, she was dead before she could consider holding *anyone* responsible. She died suddenly and unexpectedly. However, I believe she was the sole individual responsible for her death, as I said before."

It occurred to me then my question had been a stupid one. It was like asking someone who'd just plummeted to his death from three thousand feet if he had plans to sue the parachute manufacturer.

I understood the nurse's defensive reaction. After all, she was the nurse who'd been responsible for taking care of Dr. Murillo's patient following her open-heart surgery. To imply the cardiac center was at fault for the woman's unexpected demise post-surgery would be like pointing a finger directly at Sydney Combs. "Of course, she was the cause of her own death."

"Well, not totally her fault, but her noncompliance didn't help matters any. Although I cared for my aunt following her surgery, due to my responsibilities here at the center, I couldn't be there to monitor her 24/7 after she was sent home. So I couldn't control what she did or didn't do when I wasn't able to be with her. But even while I was working, I made sure there was a part-time day nurse attending to her needs. I called regularly to check in on her, as well. I'd remind her to take her medications, tell her it was time to apply antibiotic ointment and change the bandaging on her leg, and encourage her to get up and take a few laps around the house to help build up her strength, endurance, and circulation. Unfortunately, I couldn't be certain she'd do *any* of those things after I disconnected the call."

"That must have been frustrating for you," I said.

"You better believe it was frustrating! But elderly people in their seventies can be quite set in their ways, and stubborn as old mules. Oh, excuse me. I hope you didn't take that personally." She and I both turned to gaze at Rip, who looked away quickly.

"Oh, well, I know I didn't. We're only in our sixties, you see," I replied. It was a statement that expired in just over a year for Rip, and not much longer for me. Still, I took offense when someone inferred we were elderly, and/or, already in our seventies. My next remark was said while still staring directly at my husband, who was directing his attention out the window. "But trust me, Sydney, I understand exactly what you're saying. This one here takes 'set in his ways' to a whole new level."

Sydney laughed. "So I've noticed."

"Go on with your story. I believe you were about to explain what it was exactly that caused your Aunt Mabel's untimely death." I was hopeful my gentle prodding would coax the nurse into a detailed clarification that'd clear up my confusion about the heart patient's post-surgery demise.

Unfortunately, it didn't! Instead of elaborating on why she thought her aunt's death was to some extent the lady's own fault, she reverted to the topic of the woman's donation to the cardiac center. "Aunt Mabel has a large Victorian home just two blocks north of the hospital, making it an ideal location for families of patients here. The huge house has seven bedrooms. One of them may have been occupied by a former caretaker. According to my aunt, he'd been taking care of the place for a number of years. I don't know his name, but I'm certain if he did actually live there, or even exist, for that matter, he moved on after Aunt Mabel passed."

"Your aunt's home sounds very nice," I said politely.

"It was a stately mansion at one time, but it's deteriorated some in the past few decades. The master suite, which Aunt Mabel always used for herself, has its own bathroom and sitting area with two recliners and a large television."

"That sounds cozy," I replied. I had no clue where Sydney was going with this, but assumed she was going to offer us a room to stay in while Rip was going to daily cardio rehab sessions. I was partially right.

"Indeed, it is. Very cozy. Although I'm not sure I can honestly say that about the rest of the home. The problem for me is that I was left in charge of Goofus and Gallant and am responsible for them for as long as they're alive."

"Goofus and Gallant? As in the *Highlights* cartoon?" I asked.

"*Highlights* cartoon?" Rip inquisitively chimed in.

"Yes," I replied. "If you'd spent as many hours in the waiting rooms of pediatricians as I did while Regina was growing up, you'd be familiar with *Highlights Magazine for Children*. In this particular cartoon that appears in every edition, Goofus is a young boy who is rude, discourteous and downright mean, and Gallant is just the opposite. Gallant, who is polite, kind, and thoughtful, shows how young children should behave and react in different situations. It's a cartoon with a positive message."

"Exactly," Sydney said. "I remember Aunt Mabel reading articles in that magazine to my sister, little brother, and me as we were growing up. In this case, though, Gallant is a full-grown St. Bernard, who could devour my two yorkies in one bite. Goofus is a cockatoo with an impressive, and rather irritating, vocabulary. I could be staying there if I chose to, but with two dogs of my own that don't get along at all with Gallant, it's kind of necessary that I continue to reside in my own home. I'm afraid if I moved into my aunt's place, my dogs would injure Gallant."

"Huh? I thought you just said Gallant could eat both your yorkies in one bite. Why would you worry about Gallant's well-being?"

"Gallant would have to catch the hyper little things first. And in the meantime, they'd be doing a number on his ankles. He's too gentle to hurt a flea, even if those fleas were biting the heck out of his legs. So you can understand why I'm reluctant to move into Aunt Mabel's house, can't you?"

"Yes, of course." I understood why she'd hesitate to move herself and her pets into her aunt's home. However, I didn't understand what all this had to do with us. But I was willing to hear the nice lady out.

Sydney went on to explain her idea. "Rip told me you two were staying at the Sunset RV Park near Tacoma, which I know to be quite a commute from here. With Rip having to attend thrice-a-week rehab sessions for something like eight weeks, it's going to be an inconvenience for you guys. During that time, if you two would be interested in residing in Aunt Mabel's old home, which we now call the 'Heart Shack', you can occupy the master suite free of charge while you're there. And, of course, you'd be welcome to stay longer if needed."

"The Heart Shack?" Rip asked, taking the words right out of my mouth. I thought it was a cute name, but an odd choice.

"Yeah. We all offered suggestions and then voted on the entries."

"Was the clever name your idea?" I asked.

"No. It was submitted by an anesthesiologist named José. I think it's kind of a silly name for a hospital housing facility." Sydney was obviously disgusted with the winning entry, but I thought it best I didn't ask her if she'd entered the contest with a suggestion of her own. If she had, the fact her entry lost out to José's could be a sore spot. I smiled politely as she continued.

"The only stipulation is that you'd have to take care of Goofus and Gallant while you're staying there. Please consider the fact you'd have a free place to stay and a short commute to the rehab facility—within walking distance, in fact. It'd be a relief for me, as well. I have very little time to devote to Aunt Mabel's two pets. So, what do you think?"

What I actually thought was that she was trying too hard to sell us on the idea. It was as if she were an encyclopedia salesman at my doorstep in this day and age when any information you had a hankering to explore was but a Google search away. I looked at Rip, who shrugged and asked, "What about the Chartreuse Caboose?"

"The what?" Sydney asked.

"That's what we call our home, a thirty-foot travel trailer," I explained. "We painted it that color and added sunflowers to spice it up a little."

"Sounds like that'd do the trick!" Sydney said with an amused chuckle. "You could always park it in the driveway, and even plug its electric cord into an outlet in the garage if you'd like to keep the refrigerator in your trailer going. I know there's still power to the garage because there's an old chest freezer running in it."

"That'd be great," I said. "That way we wouldn't have to pay site rental for the travel trailer."

"Awesome! It sounds like we have a deal, then," Sydney said enthusiastically. She was clearly in a hurry to close the deal. I almost expected her to whip out a contract to have us sign on the dotted line before "buyer's remorse" set in. Her next question did nothing to dispel the notion. "How quickly can you move in?"

"Not until Rip is released," I replied. I felt a nagging sense of reluctance, but my tight-fisted nature took over as I accepted her offer. "I'd be happy to take care of Goofus and Gallant in the meantime. I can stop there on the way here each morning, and once again as I head back to the RV park. According to Dr. Murillo, Rip should be released in the next few days."

"Oh, that'd be wonderful!" Sydney said. Obviously optimistic we'd accept her offer, she'd brought along a set of keys to the house. She pulled a key ring out of a pocket in her scrubs and handed it to me. "The three old-fashioned keys open up the doors into the house. As you can see, I have them labeled for you."

"Ah," I said with a hint of nostalgia in my voice. "I haven't seen a skeleton key in ages. Those were the only kind of keys we used back in my growing-up days. And this smaller key?"

"I have no idea what that one goes to. Still, I hesitate to throw it away quite yet," Sydney replied.

"Heavens, no! If Aunt Mabel kept it on this key ring, it must open up a lock somewhere on the property. So, dear, how do I find her house?"

"Take a right out of the heart center's parking lot and then another quick right. Drive two blocks west and it's the big red house on the right at 666 South Hart Street. You can't miss it. Trust me!"

"A red house on South Hart Street sounds very appropriate," I said.

"A bunch of us who work here in the cardiac ward just painted the house red two weeks ago and put up a 'Heart Shack' sign in the front yard. The street being named South Hart was just an ironic coincidence."

A red house sounded rather gaudy to me, but I guess someone who'd painted their own home-on-wheels chartreuse should not throw stones. "Terrific! I'll run by there when I head out in an hour or so."

After I made sure Rip was able to hold down his horrid-looking lunch, I left the hospital with the Heart Shack key ring jingling in my left hand. As I walked out of his room, Rip said, "I'll see you later, honey, providing I haven't been stoned to death by Nurse Cindy in the meantime."

I didn't bother to correct him on his nurse's name. I was so thrilled by the turn of events I wouldn't have minded if he called her Nurse Nightingale. I'd decided to overlook the ill-at-ease feeling Sydney had aroused in me with her over-exuberance at convincing us to accept her offer. I marked her reaction up as relief at having one less item on her already full plate.

I'm financially conservative by nature and was all over the idea of free rent for two months. I wanted to do cartwheels across the parking lot, but it wasn't an opportune time for a broken hip. I simply skipped to the truck, instead.

I had no idea what to expect at the late Mabel Trumbo's house on South Hart Street, but it certainly wasn't what I discovered when I arrived there about two minutes later.

CHAPTER 9

It was a typical Seattle day: cool, overcast and with intermittent showers. Even in the gloomy conditions, the Heart Shack was not difficult to spot. The Victorian mansion stood out like a sore red thumb and a coat of fresh paint had done nothing to make the house look fresh or welcoming. In fact, it had the opposite effect. It looked more like a hideous haunted house than a temporary housing facility for family members of cardiac patients.

Several shutters dangled by a single screw, listing to one side or the other. One had tilted completely over and stuck out at a ninety-degree angle from the window casing. The yard was full of crabgrass, dandelions, and Johnson grass, and the noxious weeds were in desperate need of mowing down or drenching with *Roundup*. To make matters worse, overgrown foliage, shrubs, and bushes engulfed the house like a shroud. Sydney had mentioned a caretaker but had appeared dubious about his existence, for some reason. If he did exist, I wondered what he'd taken care of because lawn and building maintenance didn't seem to be on his list of responsibilities.

There was a detached three-car garage that resembled an old carriage house. At one time it would've been an impressive structure. But with the ravages of time, it was now little more than a ramshackle hut. One would not dare park a vehicle inside the building for fear the roof would collapse on it. I was glad to see there was a level bare spot alongside the garage where we could park the Chartreuse Caboose while we lived inside the old home. For a moment, I wondered if we wouldn't be safer and more comfortable residing in the travel trailer and only entering the Heart Shack when necessary to care for Mabel's pets.

I parked our truck on the street. Walking up the sidewalk to the covered front porch, I heard a wailing sound that seemed to be coming from inside the house. I would have felt more comfortable had there been any lights on inside, or even outside, the woebegone structure. I stopped and debated returning to the truck and driving back to the hospital to ask Sydney who might be inside the home besides Goofus and Gallant. In the end, however, my curiosity was stronger than my self-preservation instinct.

Climbing the front stairs involved side-stepping numerous broken and missing boards. The same held true for the porch. Considering the groaning I heard as I walked across the porch, I wondered if it'd be prudent for Rip, who weighed a good fifty or sixty pounds more than me, to find another entrance into the crumbling monstrosity.

Turning the skeleton key, simply labeled "front", in the lock took nearly all the strength I possessed. I didn't know how in the world the owner, in her weak and ailing condition, could have even unlocked her own front door. *Remember to bring a can of WD-40 with you tomorrow*, I told myself. As the key finally rotated enough to turn the tumblers inside the lock, I heard the wailing again, louder this time. Startled, I resisted the urge to flee.

The sound seemed to come from above me. I looked up to see a hole in the lean-to style roof over the porch and realized the wailing sound was caused by wind whistling through the gap. I breathed a sigh of relief and opened the door. The creaking that ensued was incredible. *Bring two cans of WD-40. This entire house may need to be doused with it*, I thought.

Tentatively, I stepped into the spacious foyer. Looking around, I saw a number of old, oval frames hanging from the walls. The photographs inside the frames were of stern-looking people who appeared to be my age but were probably only in their twenties and thirties. The photos were evidently taken before the smile was invented.

All of the antique frames were in dire need of a dusting, as was everything else in the entryway: a wooden church pew, a full suit of armor, a marble table with a vase of dead, dried-up flowers, and a large wool rug that had a paisley design woven into it.

As I took a step onto the rug, a clearly-discernible cloud of dust arose from the fabric. I wheezed at the thought of the zillions of dust mites that had to be swarming throughout the room.

I looked around the foyer and saw several sizable dust bunnies, each of which had hopped into a different corner of the room to hide. Using my index finger, I could have written my name in the thick layer of dust on the top of the marble table. *A can or two of furniture polish along with a box of old rags would be handy, too*, I thought, as I added the items to my mental list. Housekeeping was never one of my favorite activities, but I almost looked forward to giving this old place a once-over.

I exited the foyer and entered what I would refer to as a drawing room. In the era of this house's heyday, it would have been the room where visitors would gather for a cup of tea and an hour or so of gossip. Now there were only two sofas, a square, glass-topped coffee table, and a few chairs covered with plastic tarps. In the corner, stood an uncovered mahogany grand piano: a fabulous, and, no doubt, expensive Steinway Model D.

Had Mabel been a pianist? I wondered. She'd only been dead for a couple of weeks according to her niece. Yet the drawing room appeared as if it hadn't been lived in for many years. Except for the Steinway piano, which looked as if it'd just been polished moments before my arrival. The pristine piano had sheet music resting against the music rack. It was the notes for a Franz Liszt piece that looked extremely technical and demanding. It was apparent whoever had been playing the piece was a gifted musician. The keyboard and pedals were as shiny as the sheen of the mahogany.

I walked through the drawing room and on into the kitchen. A small gray mouse skittered across the room, startling me. My heart skipped a beat or two, but a loud, shrill, "Get out!" shocked it right back into rhythm. My eyes darted to the origin of the scream. It was Goofus, the cockatoo, who repeated his demand several more times as he rocked back and forth on his perch.

"Well, hello, Goofus," I said. The fidgety bird continued to rock and squawk.

"Go away! Dwop dead, old bwag! Scwam Sam!"

"Now, now," I said softly, trying to calm the bird. If Goofus weren't so unwelcoming, I might have found his habit of adding a "wa" sound to many of his words endearing. Instead, I found it irritating. "Chill out, Goofus. My name's Rapella, not Sam. And I'll scram when I'm good and ready. I've come to feed you, not harm you."

"Go away! Can't eat that! Kill that dwam dog!" Goofus's pink head was bobbing up and down as he rattled on. He had striking plumage atop his head, bands of yellow and red at the base, culminating in white tips. Goofus was of the Major Mitchell's species, Sydney had said. He was noisy, but he was incredibly beautiful. At that moment, however, he appeared to be extremely agitated, like a lunatic who'd gone off his meds. "Vamoose! You be cwuising for a bwuising! Birdie want a cwacker?"

The bird's behavior was so manic, I was afraid to open his cage to put a scoop of the seed, nut, and dried-fruit mixture in his food bowl. I did my best to toss a small scoopful through the gaps in his wire cage. About half of the mixture fell outside the cage, so I refilled the scoop and tried again to make sure a sufficient amount landed in the bizarre bird's food dish. The gravity-fed water bottle hanging in his cage was two-thirds full. *Good enough for now*, I thought.

"Speaking of killing the dog, Goofus, where's your brother, Gallant?"

As if in response to my question, I heard a whining behind me. I turned around and saw one of the largest dogs I'd ever laid eyes on. I froze until the St. Bernard tenderly laid his left front paw on my arm. I patted him on the head, relieved that he appeared as mild as milquetoast; docile and seemingly submissive. I could actually visualize two hyper Yorkshire terriers circling the gentle giant like a swarm of bees, nipping at his lower legs as he stood idly by with the same tranquil look of contentment that was apparent on his furry face right then.

"I like you better than your brother already," I said to the massive dog as I caressed the back of his head. "But you'd make a pitiful guard dog, sneaking up on me like you did. You'd lead intruders right to the valuable jewelry and polished silver, wouldn't you, boy? Can you speak?"

"Ruff, ruff."

"Oh, so you *can* speak. Good boy!"

"Ruff, ruff."

"Can you sit?"

On command, Gallant sat on his haunches. He looked at me pleadingly. I knew he was waiting for a treat in reward for his obedience. I thought back to what Sydney had told me. Gallant's food was in the broom closet beside the refrigerator. I checked the contents of the closet and, although there were no brooms or mops to be found, I found a fifty-pound bag of dog food and several boxes of extra-large dog bones.

I walked back over to Gallant, who was waiting patiently. "You'll have to show me more of your tricks to earn your reward. Can you roll over?"

Gallant remained motionless. He was still gazing into my eyes with anticipation.

"Roll over," I repeated. The dog didn't even flinch. "Okay, boy. We'll have to work on that one. Still, you are a smart fellow, so I am sure you will pick the trick up easily. Can you shake hands?"

Gallant raised his left paw. I shook it and gave him a beef-flavored bone. "Aha! You're a south paw! You're such a sweet boy, Gallant. I wish your brother was as hospitable as you are."

With one clench of his large jaw, Gallant crushed the bone into a zillion pieces. While he made short order of the treat, I filled his bowl with food. Next, I clipped the leash I'd found next to the box of dog bones onto Gallant's collar and took him outside so he could do his duties. There was a break in the precipitation, and I wanted to take advantage of the dry spell.

Before exiting the kitchen, I looked around for a box of doggie doo-doo bags, because I wouldn't feel right not picking up after Gallant. All I could come up with was a quart-sized Ziploc bag. I soon learned the small bag was akin to taking a garden hose to a five-alarm fire. A shovel and wheelbarrow would have been more appropriate for collecting Gallant's calling card. I left the pile where Gallant had deposited it, vowing to collect it the next day when I had something large enough to handle the job.

After I took Gallant for a walk up and down South Hart Street, I noticed the sun was beginning to set on the western horizon. I needed to stop at the store on the way back to the RV park, so I decided I'd wait to investigate the rest of the house when I returned in the morning. I bade farewell to Goofus and Gallant, only one of which had instantly warmed my heart. The smaller of the two scared the holy crap out of me. I wasn't sure I'd ever have guts enough to get within pecking distance of the maniacal creature in the cage.

As I retraced my route to the front door, I heard a moaning sound coming from a nearby room. I knew I should check out the source of the sound. Instead, my instinct was to skedaddle out of the house and race up the sidewalk to the safety of our Chevy truck. I didn't know how or why there'd be someone in the house besides me. Still, I sensed eyes on me as I hurried through the drawing room. Have you ever *felt* someone looking at you? That's the feeling I experienced right then. I chalked up the disturbing sensation to the intense stares of the people looking out from the oval picture frames. When I reached the front porch, I saw no other vehicles on the property, unless there was one parked inside the sad-sack garage.

I had to assume the Heart Shack had not opened up to residents yet. I felt sure they'd do a thorough cleaning of the home before they welcomed guests. It was unfit for human habitation as it stood, and the uneasiness I felt inside the home was overwhelming. Rip would be released from the hospital soon so I wouldn't have to be alone in the house overnight. I had no plans to relocate until then and was having second thoughts about the entire deal.

I'd stop by in the morning, as I'd promised. Maybe my mind was playing tricks on me, and in the light of day the old run-down place would seem more welcoming.

Wishful thinking, as it turned out. Daylight did not make the house any more appealing. It only made the red paint job look more atrocious and the building itself appear more condemnable. The sunlight actually caused the house's flaws to stand out more prominently. I decided to use our cell phone to capture photographs of the property to show Rip when I got to the hospital.

There'd be no time to rest on my laurels, for Rip's release was imminent. I knew the home had once been a place of grandeur, but those days were long gone. Too many moons had risen and set since then. Too many, in fact, since it'd even seen a broom or a dust rag, except for the piano. *There's no way we're moving in this run-down structure until the cobwebs have been removed and the place is sparkling clean, if not nearly sterile. I'll have it spotless before I bring Rip here,* I vowed. *But how? How am I, alone, going to get the house up to snuff in so little time?*

After struggling with the skeleton key, I walked in like I owned the place. I was determined not to let the grime, the eerie sounds, the peculiar photographs of grim-faced people whose eyes seem to follow me as I walked through the room, or even the startling screeches by Goofus freak me out that morning. With my phone's camera, I took a number of photographs in the foyer and the drawing room before I moved on to the kitchen. If nothing else, I'd have "before" pictures to show Rip after the place had been spruced up so he'd appreciate all of the hard work I did to make it livable. I noticed what looked like a tiny pair of needle-nose pliers lying on the marble table when I snapped a photo of the entryway. I didn't recall seeing them the previous day, but I'd been pretty overwhelmed by the home's condition at the time.

"Go away, whinsp!" Goofus squawked as I stepped into the over-sized kitchen. I'm not sure what startled me the most: Goofus's rude but not totally unexpected greeting that reminded me of the scream in my nightmare, or the loud squeaking of the wooden floor beneath my feet.

I figured the bird had meant to call me a wench, rather than a whinsp. Whatever he'd meant to say, I'm sure it was demeaning. I didn't appreciate the ill-tempered cockatoo's name-calling. And I found his speech impediment even less delightful than I had the previous day. If nothing else, it'd become obvious how the two pets' names had come about.

Suddenly I jumped, spinning around like a top, at the feel of Gallant's nose goosing me from behind. I laughed at the surprised expression on the dog's face and reached out to scratch him behind the ears. "Gee willikers, boy! Can't you bark at least once to let me know you're nearby? You'll have me lying in a bed in the cardiac care center, too, if you keep that nonsense up."

Gallant began prancing and pawing at the closet door where his leash and food were stored. I laughed at his playful antics, but as his frolicking became more frantic, it became clear he needed to go to the bathroom, and he needed to go right then. With an empty Wal-Mart bag in one hand, I attached the leash to Gallant's collar with the other and began babbling to take my mind off my nervousness.

"I'm sorry, boy. I'm used to a cat's bathroom habits.

When Dolly needs to go, she just waddles her well-padded behind over to her litter box. Provided the litter's not so overloaded with buried treasures that it offends her sensibilities, she does her duty with no muss, no fuss, and no assistance from her humble servants. Cats may be less devoted to their owners than dogs like you, but they're certainly more self-sufficient. Come on, boy. Let's get you outside right away."

When we returned to the kitchen, the cockatoo was raising a fuss. He called me a "goofball" and told me to get lost. I had a strong suspicion the bird had been called a goofball himself numerous times, because of his similar name. Like most talking birds, I figured he picked up and repeated words and phrases he'd heard repeatedly.

Ignoring Goofus's outbursts, I threw some food in his cage and filled a much larger scoop with dog food for Gallant. After refilling Gallant's water bowl and checking to make sure the cockatoo wasn't in immediate danger of dying of thirst, I decided to check out the remainder of the home. I was particularly interested in the condition of the master suite.

Upstairs, I walked up a long hallway, opening each door as I passed. Every bedroom was identical, simply furnished, and had its own private bathroom. Each room contained an antique armoire, a frameless queen-sized bed, a chest of drawers with a matching nightstand, and a large oval rug. The brand new bedding in each bedroom was in stark contrast to the dreariness of the rest of the house. The rooms weren't spotless, by any means, but they weren't in the state of grime-ridden decay I'd feared they'd be. With a few hours of scrubbing, mopping, and polishing, they could be ready to greet guests.

I continued down the hallway. The floor squeaked, the walls emitted popping sounds, and an occasional thumping clamor echoed from various locations in the building. I steadied my nerves by reminding myself odd noises were to be expected of a home that'd probably been built in the late eighteen-hundreds. The thunderous bellowing sound coming from the attic directly above me was not expected, however, and I stopped so abruptly that Gallant, who'd been trailing behind me, nearly got his nose wedged in the crack of my derriere.

There has to be a reasonable explanation, I told myself. Although there had appeared to be nary a breeze when I'd entered the house, I thought perhaps the sound might be attributed to a random gust of wind reverberating in the open space between the ceiling and the roof. After all, the wood-shake shingled roof was in need of repair, or better yet, replacement. It looked as if a single ember from a bottle-rocket on Independence Day could spark a fire that'd burn the entire tinderbox to the ground.

Yes, that's it! Wind howling through a hole in the roof is all the bellowing sound boils down to, I assured myself when I heard it a second time. No need to panic, and it made no sense at all to let my imagination run wild. It was nothing more than Mother Nature attempting to make me think I was crazy as I walked through the eerie structure.

Half-way down the hallway was the master suite. The majority of the house had that moldy, musty smell that often accompanies nursing homes. Like rugs, elderly folks really should be taken outside and vigorously shaken at least once every two weeks. In sharp contrast, the master suite smelled like an entire can of lavender air freshener had been sprayed into the room.

The bedroom was enchantingly warm and inviting. It had a sitting area with a large picture window that would let in a lot of natural light. I could picture myself sitting in one of the two rocking chairs facing the window with a cup of strong brew and a good book.

The sprawling suite was surprisingly neat, tidy, and dust-free. More astonishing, it was bright and cheery, even with the drapes—which needed to go bye-bye—currently drawn. The bedroom furniture was old, but attractive. The bedspread on the four-poster bed looked brand new, to my delight.

It briefly crossed my mind that Sydney's deceased aunt

could have met her maker while lying in the king-sized bed. After some deliberation, I decided not to inquire about it. After all, what I didn't know couldn't hurt me. Or, at least, couldn't keep me up all night wondering if I was lying in the same spot where Mabel Trumbo had inhaled her last breath.

I took my cell phone out of my back pocket and snapped several more photos. I wanted Rip to have something to look forward to. The master suite offered some very beguiling images; the teal, peach, and yellow bedspread, a vase of fresh-cut flowers on a small round table between the rocking chairs, and an over-sized recliner next to the bed. I was certain the flowers had been placed in the room by Sydney, as a means of welcoming us to the Heart Shack.

Rip would be particularly interested in the leather recliner, if for no other reason than there was a drink holder in the arm rest to accommodate his daily highball, and a remote control on the table next to the flower vase. I was sure the flower vase would be relocated to make room for a bag of barbecue-flavored pork rinds which, to Rip's dismay, I would replace with a bowl of carrot and celery sticks. Mounted to the wall across from the recliner was a flat-screen TV in the sixty to sixty-five-inch range. I knew Rip would be in hog heaven in his new surroundings once we'd taken up residence.

I suddenly realized Aunt Mabel's niece might have to help me build a fire under the seat of the recliner if she seriously expected her patient to leave the cozy chair and go exercise at the cardio rehab facility. I wasn't sure it'd benefit either of us to have the Heart Shack become too comfortable.

Cozy and comfy were not words that would compel Rip to work toward complete recovery, or even compel me to badger him about it. Sydney sounded as if she wanted us to continue to occupy the place until Rip had returned to his former tip-top condition or, for the sake of accuracy, his former sub-par, but reasonably passable, physical condition.

I held up my phone to check the time as I returned to the dining room, but was startled so badly, I dropped it on the wooden floor. I'd unexpectedly come face-to-face, or should I say chest-to-face, with a sprite-like fellow I hadn't known was in the house.

"Top of the morning to ya, me lady!" He managed to say after regaining his composure. I may have been startled, but he appeared shocked to his very core.

The soft-spoken voice belonged to a man who looked to be about a decade older than me. Closing in on eighty was my guess, despite the youthful twinkle in his eyes when he smiled. His Irish accent matched his appearance. In his old and tattered green flannel shirt and faded blue jeans, he reminded me of a leprechaun. At least a foot shorter than my five feet, eight inches, he had an elfin quality to him. I knew instinctively this had to be the caretaker Sydney Combs had talked about with such skepticism. So, it seemed he actually did exist, but why was he still here?

"Good morning, sir. I'm sorry I startled you. You must be the gentleman who used to look after the place," I said after I'd retrieved my phone from the floor and my racing pulse had ebbed. The fellow, whose skin was shockingly pale, seemed to consider his response carefully before finally voicing it.

"Yes, me lady. That I am. And who'd be you?" There was something accusatory about the way the waiflike man spoke, as if he disapproved of my presence. I wanted to ask him why he wasn't at the North Pole making toys with Christmas only seven months away, but was afraid he'd find my facetious question offensive – as I suppose it actually was. He didn't appear to be in a jovial mood, and being insulted wasn't apt to improve it any.

"Good morning. I'm Rapella Ripple." I extended my arm out to shake hands, assuming the elderly gentleman would introduce himself in return. But he didn't. He simply grasped my hand briefly in his own. The handshake was so delicate, like the touch of a feather, and over so quickly, I wasn't positive it'd even happened. It was as if I had shaken hands with an apparition.

"You to be staying here at the Hearty Home?" He asked.

"Yes. I presume we'll be the very first temporary guests of the cardiac center?" I said in the form of a question. I found his reference to the Heart Shack as the "Hearty Home" rather endearing.

"Oh, no, me lady. A many have come, and a many have left, ya see," he replied.

"What do you mean?"

"They take a gander and go away. All of 'em." The little guy shook his head and shrugged, as if totally mystified by their reaction to the place. Had he somehow overlooked its atrocious condition?

"Why?"

I was trying hard not to stare but I couldn't seem to take my eyes off the bizarre gentleman. His unnatural-appearing ebony hair didn't jive with his deeply wrinkled face. It seemed electrified, sticking straight out in every conceivable direction, as if someone had just rubbed a fully inflated balloon on his head. He shrugged again and looked down as he spoke. "I know not why. It be but me and me mates since Ms. Trumbo be kilt, ya see."

I assumed he was referring to Mabel's pets as his mates. "Could it be that folks take a gander and go away because Goofus screams at the visitors, ordering them to vamoose, and Gallant scares the bejesus out of them merely by his size?"

"I think they not liking when Miss Trumbo comes 'a calling, ya see."

"When Miss Trumbo comes a-calling? You know she died of post-operative complications, don't you?"

"I know she die. Not her fault. She be kilt, ya see. But she come back to call on me and me mates. I feed them when she forget. She forget a lot, ya see."

"I'm a bit baffled." To be honest, I was totally flabbergasted by his remarks. Telling the man I was a bit baffled was a gigantic understatement. It was like telling Goofus he was a bit obnoxious.

The caretaker had spoken of Mabel Trumbo in present

tense, as if her spirit was still roaming the halls of the big home. His remarks also indicated that he still resided in the Heart Shack, which made me extremely uncomfortable. "Mabel's niece wasn't convinced you even worked for her aunt, but felt that if you truly did, you'd have moved on following Mabel's death. So, I'm curious, sir. *Do* you still live here?"

"No." I was relieved when he finally responded after a lengthy pause. "But I still keeps me eye on the place, ya see."

"That was very thoughtful of you. But it's no longer necessary now that my husband and I will be occupying the home. My husband's career was in law enforcement, Mister..."

The man looked at me expectantly but said nothing. So I said, "I'm sorry, I didn't catch your name."

The petite gentleman silently stared at his feet. My attempt at prompting him to introduce himself had been unsuccessful. So I asked him outright. "You do have a name, don't you?"

This time he simply nodded. I decided it didn't matter what his name was, but I still wanted to know what he was doing in Mabel's house. He seemed like an extremely odd man. I wondered why he'd inferred that Mabel had died of something other than issues following her bypass surgery. But I didn't want to go there with him. Not at that time, anyway. I wanted to keep our exchange light as I slowly edged my way toward the foyer. I felt ill at ease around him even though I was confident I could roll the little feller in the parking lot if I had to.

It was my curiosity that prevented me from bolting from the room when I finally had the opportunity. Curiosity can be a killer, you know. But, yet, I caved in to the temptation every single time it presented itself, and often regretted it afterward. People often forget the last part of the old proverb, "Curiosity killed the cat", which is, "but satisfaction brought it back". I reckon I just have more cats to resuscitate than most other folks.

"So, why did you stop by? Did you notice someone in the house as you were driving past, and stop to make sure I was authorized to be here?" I tried to sound like I was only making friendly small talk rather than as if I was interrogating him about his trespassing on private property.

The handyman's eyes locked with mine as I waited for a response that never came. The man looked down again and remained mute. The awkward silence continued, which convinced me it really was time for me to vamoose. I needed to head to the hospital, anyway. Rip would be expecting me.

I wanted to speak with Sydney Combs, as well, and tell her about my chance meeting with the caretaker. I also wanted to tell Sydney about the man's fondness for Goofus and Gallant, or his "mates" as he called them. He'd mentioned feeding them whenever that task had slipped Mabel's mind, something that had probably increased in frequency as her Alzheimer's had worsened. Had he stopped by today to make sure Sydney, or someone else, had fed the two animals? I decided not to ask him because it would only delay my departure, if he even bothered to respond. I wanted to put space between us as quickly as possible.

"I'd best be getting back to the hospital to visit my husband," I finally said to break the silence. "Please lock the front door on your way out. Good day to you, sir."

"Same to ya, me lady," he replied in barely more than a whisper.

I rotated my body after I thought I'd heard another voice in the foyer, but saw no one. When I turned back around not more than a second or two later, the caretaker had vanished. Perhaps it was his miniscule size that enabled the man to traverse the wooden flooring without a single board squeaking beneath him. Or it could be that he'd been the caretaker there long enough to know exactly where each foot must fall to avoid the aggravating sound effects. But the fact he could disappear into thin air so rapidly amazed me. I couldn't move half as fast, even if I was being chased by a madman with a running chainsaw in his hands.

I was suddenly having second thoughts again about living in Mabel's house. Clearly, her former caretaker felt it was his right to pop in anytime he wanted. He'd never offered an explanation for stopping by, even after I'd asked for one. Was there a reason he hadn't wanted to share his name or his intentions with me? Had his purpose for entering the house been nefarious in nature, and thwarted by my unexpected presence?

No more than ten minutes earlier I'd been daydreaming about an extended stay in the Heart Shack. But after my unanticipated meeting with the peculiar caretaker, I found myself praying our stay would be short-lived.

CHAPTER 10

"Gotta wonder why old Mabel had a roach clip on the table in this photo you took of her entryway," Rip said as he scrolled through the photos on the phone.

"A what?" I took the photo from him and studied it. "You mean those little needle nose pliers?"

Rip laughed. "I'm pretty sure it's a roach clip, honey."

"Why would a cockroach need a clip?"

Rip laughed again, only this time he laughed hard enough he had to clutch his cushioning pillow to his tender chest. "This clip is used for holding a roach, which is slang for a marijuana cigarette, so the user can smoke it practically down to the end without dropping it or burning his fingertips. See this etched design on the handle of a leaf with all the leaflets? That's a leaf from a cannabis plant. You wouldn't believe how many roach clips I've found over the years while searching suspicious vehicles."

That explained why he recognized the device and I didn't. I was pretty naive about drugs, never having associated with anyone who used them. But I was almost positive the roach clip had not been present in the foyer the first time I visited the house. I handed the phone back to Rip, and he looked through the rest of the photos I'd taken. Once done, he said, "I really don't mind the long commute every day. No sense getting uprooted when we're only talking about a couple of weeks."

As if she were a homing pigeon whose actions were triggered by his remarks, Sydney Combs walked through the door. "Did I really just hear you say 'a couple of weeks', Rip? What did we just talk about? Six weeks of rehab at the bare minimum. Your ticker is repaired and improved. But it's a far cry from being brand new. In fact, two full months would be more appropriate for a guy your age and in your condition."

"What are you trying to say? That I'm old and out of shape?" Rip asked in mock anger. His spirits were high that morning, which warmed my heart.

"Your words. Not mine. But if the pot belly fits—"

"Hey now!" Rip and the nurse both laughed. They'd formed a close bond in a matter of days. Rip had always lived by the motto, "To get respect, you must earn it!" The skilled healthcare provider had more than earned Rip's respect. By convincing my mulish husband to toe the line, she'd earned mine, as well.

"Okay, okay. I give. Even so, I can easily drive back and forth to rehab three times a week for two months." Rip turned to look directly at me. "I know you'd feel more at home in the trailer."

"I've been weighing the pros and cons of moving into the Heart Shack, too," I replied. I glanced over at Sydney after I heard her inhale sharply. She looked as if she'd just witnessed a bunny rabbit pass a milk chocolate Easter egg. "But—"

"But?" Sydney echoed in an alarmed tone.

"But?" Rip repeated a second later.

"But," I repeated, drawing the one-syllable word out like it was twenty-seven letters long. "Not only is the Heart Shack conveniently located, but we can also park the trailer there and save nearly a grand a month. It's kind of a no-brainer."

"It's absolutely a no-brainer!" The nurse agreed emphatically.

"So why did you show me these pictures?" Rip asked, holding up the phone. He was clearly perplexed at my motives. I'm sure he thought my intention was to express to him in photographs why there was no frigging way we could live in the dilapidated eyesore on South Hart Street.

"I just wanted you to see why I'd be spending most of my time there for the next day or two doing some sprucing up." Even though I sensed there was an unspoken motivation for why Sydney seemed to be aggressively overselling the idea of us inhabiting the Heart Shack, I didn't want to insult the lady by indicating the place was a pigsty that'd require an army of worker ants to make livable again. Yet I thought she needed to know the place was not up to snuff. Having one potential guest after another shun the offer of a free, convenient place to reside while a loved one was hospitalized did not make for a positive impression of the heart center's temporary housing facility. Negative word-of-mouth advertising could shut the Heart Shack down before it even got up to speed.

"Sorry it's such a filthy mess," Sydney said. She didn't seem insulted. In fact, she was apologetic and offered to send a housekeeping service in to give the place a thorough cleansing before we moved into it. "I'll see to it the work is underway as soon as possible. There was money allotted for that sort of thing in my aunt's will."

"That'd be awesome. I'd be more than happy to help out as much as I can. I'd do all the cleaning myself if it wasn't so far beyond my capabilities. It's a huge place that's been sorely neglected for quite some time. Not enough hours in the day or enough elbow grease left in this old body to do it all on my own in a timely manner." I felt bad, not wanting to come across as a prima donna who couldn't deal with dust and dirt. "I'm really not so much concerned about the two of us, Sydney. But some of the family members of patients here have stopped by to check the place out and refused to stay. If I had to guess, I'd say they didn't think it was ready for guests."

"What? Who stopped by?" Sydney asked, clearly taken

aback by my remark. "What family members are you referring to? It *isn't* ready for guests yet! There's no way the hospital would allow visitors to stay there until the place has been cleaned, disinfected, and up to their high standards. Not to mention, the contractor we hired to repair the roof, stairs, porch, and other deteriorating areas of the building, hasn't even started on the project. They have to wait until the punch list is approved by the local inspection department, who'd initially wanted to condemn and raze the property."

"I'm glad they reconsidered demolishing it. As far as the potential guests stopping by to inspect the home, I must have misunderstood what the caretaker told me," I replied. Truthfully, I was dead certain I hadn't misunderstood him. But I wasn't as sure that *he* hadn't mistaken the contractors and possible inspectors for visitors who were checking out the place as possible accommodations while their loved one recuperated in the heart center.

"You talked to Aunt Mabel's caretaker?" Sydney asked. "So he truly does exist?"

"Yes, he truly does. I talked to him just an hour or so ago. He stopped by the Heart Shack, startling me when I entered the drawing room. He seemed reluctant to converse with me and wouldn't tell me why he stopped by. Can you tell me anything more about him, Sydney?"

"I've never met the caretaker. Like I said, I didn't really even believe the man existed. What's his name?"

"He wouldn't say, even after I inquired about it. He was extremely cagey about offering any information about himself, for some reason."

"How odd," Sydney said. "I can't imagine why he'd just drop by. Until now, I truly believed he was merely a figment of my aunt's imagination. I thought maybe she'd just concocted him because she enjoyed telling her female friends in the church choir that she had a man living with her. Most of them were widows, or spinsters living alone, you see. Aunt Mabel amused herself by leading them to believe she was living in sin. Now that you've actually met the man, maybe *you* can tell *me* more about him."

"Well, okay," I replied. "Imagine Ernest J. Keebler, the cookie company's head elf, at eighty-years old. He's spritely, moves like a cat, and speaks in a mixture of broken English and Irish brogue. He told me he didn't reside there any longer but still keeps an eye out on the place. The caretaker is a bizarre little fellow. To be honest, he reminded me of a leprechaun."

Sydney gazed at me silently for several long moments, as if suddenly having doubts about my claim to have met her aunt's mysterious caretaker. I could almost hear the thoughts inside her head. *A leprechaun? Really? The mental ward on the fourth floor is accepting new patients, Mrs. Ripple. Perhaps you should check it out.*

I wondered if she was already regretting the offer she'd made us. Nurse Combs probably had enough to do without dealing with a bull-headed heart patient and his whacked-out, hallucinating wife.

Suddenly I was more determined than ever to get the Heart Shack spic-and-span and move into it. I vowed to face my fears and hunt down the man I'd conversed with earlier in the drawing room. If at all possible, I'd snap a photo of him to show Sydney, more as proof I wasn't crazy than anything else. I'd be danged if I was going to let the fellow make me look like a full-fledged fool again. I'd gotten the impression Sydney still believed the caretaker didn't actually exist and thought I, like her aunt, was merely having figments.

Rip chimed in then, as if he too thought I might have spent the last hour or so sniffing Elmer's Glue. "Maybe the guy had lost his lucky charms and was looking for them."

Rip laughed loudly as Sydney tried to suppress a smile. I wasn't amused at all. "Not funny, Rip!"

His sarcastic jibe annoyed me, but even I had to chuckle when he responded in a sing-song voice, "They're magically delicious."

Rip patted my hand to let me know he was only kidding, and said, "Seriously, dear. It was probably just some nosy neighbor snooping around to see what was going on with the property. The new coat of red paint might have piqued his curiosity."

"Yes! That's probably exactly who he was." Sydney said with obvious relief. She was clearly thankful to have Rip supply an answer to explain my puzzling conversation with an uninvited interloper that I thought resembled the cooking-baking elf. "I seriously can't believe there was ever a man taking care of my aunt's property. If there'd been a caretaker, wouldn't the place be in better condition now?"

"You'd think." I responded in agreement, but wasn't convinced the man was nothing more than a nosy neighbor. My stroll down the long hallway had resulted in a symphony of sounds within the walls of the old home. Would a neighbor, unfamiliar with the structure, be able to walk the entire length without a single squeak, creak, groan or thud emanating from the ancient, dried-up woodwork? Even at his diminutive size, I didn't think so.

I'd been told about a possible, albeit unlikely, caretaker who could potentially still be on the premises. So, as anyone else would do, I'd automatically assumed the man who claimed to be keeping an eye on the old mansion was the caretaker. I still wasn't convinced he wasn't. Were my instincts not as spot-on as I'd like to think? Was the curious little fellow who'd inferred he'd been Mabel Trumbo's caretaker merely an imposter?

"Okay, Sydney." I decided there was no sense wasting time trying to convince the no-nonsense nurse that I wasn't having visions or mental issues. "There are several things I'd like to discuss with you that have nothing to do with the man I met today or even with cleaning. For example; all of the door hinges need to be sprayed with graphite, WD-40, or something to eliminate the squeaking sound they make when opened or closed. It's like fingernails on a chalkboard and makes my teeth ache. And that's saying a lot for someone who wears a full set of dentures."

Sydney chuckled at my remark. "I know. I hate it too. Makes the place seem a bit sinister, if you ask me."

"A *bit* sinister? I'm not sure how your aunt stood it. How much did she tell you she was paying this caretaker, anyway?" I'd reverted back to the subject of the puzzling Irish gentleman because I couldn't shake the uneasy feeling I had about him.

"She never said." Sydney suddenly looked as if she'd rather talk about rodeo clowns, tumbleweeds, or even hemorrhoid ointments than her aunt's caretaker. She clammed up and glanced around, obviously looking for an excuse to escape from my prying questions.

"Well, I'll ask him, dear. You can be sure of that. It's a wonder your aunt didn't fall through her own front porch and break a few bones with *this* dude minding the store. 'Ignoring the store' is more accurate from what I've seen so far. The entire place has been woefully neglected for a long time. It's no small wonder the roof doesn't leak, like rain water passing through a sieve. The missing and loose boards on the front porch are nothing but a lawsuit waiting to happen."

"Yes, I know." Sydney appeared embarrassed after my blathering on and on about the pitiful condition of her aunt's home.

I instantly regretted my disparaging remarks, despite the fact I was merely stating the obvious. I hadn't considered the fact that perhaps there was a valid reason the place had not been maintained properly.

After a moment of silence, Sydney continued, "But that's water under the bridge now. The punch list to be handled by Wiley Burke Construction includes fixing the porch and stairs, among many other things."

"That's good."

"Yeah." Sydney looked down at her watch. "You know, I probably should get back to work."

I decided it best to change the subject. It was obvious the current topic was making the nurse uncomfortable, and I had another matter to discuss with her before she wandered off. "My only other concern at the moment is Goofus. He doesn't appear to care for me much."

"Goofus doesn't care much for anyone." Sydney perked up, seemingly relieved the conversation had veered away from the condition of her aunt's home. "He's loud and obnoxious, but basically harmless."

"So he won't bite my finger off if I open the cage to feed him? For a one-pound pet, he's very intimidating."

"Don't worry. He's all mouth and no bite." Sydney laughed and I chuckled along, but wasn't totally convinced the easily agitated bird was harmless. Noticing my unease, the nurse added, "Try singing to Goofus while you're feeding him. It usually calms him right down."

"Um, okay." I could barely stand to listen to myself sing. I was pretty sure Goofus wouldn't be impressed with my crooning, either. "I'm not much of a singer, Sydney. Listening to me sing might have the opposite effect on Goofus. Instead of calming him down, he might choose to use one of those sharp talons on his feet to slash his own throat. Or, worse yet, slash mine."

"Don't be silly, Rapella. It's not like you'll be auditioning in front of Simon Cowell, you know. Goofus is not judgmental at all. He just seems soothed by the rhythmic sound of music."

"Well, if you say so. I'm not sure anyone would describe my singing as rhythmic, or even musical, but I'll give it a whirl. Does he have a favorite song, or genre?" My entire repertoire of memorized songs included no more than about a dozen tunes, most of which came from the soundtrack of the Disney movies that played on our TV all the time when our daughter Regina was a youngster.

"He likes pretty much all music, but for some reason he's partial to the song, 'Who Let the Dogs Out'."

"Okay, great. I'll try that," I replied, as if it was a song I chanted regularly while I soaped up in the shower. I could recite every word of "The Bare Necessities" from Disney's *The Jungle Book*. But I wasn't at all familiar with "Who Let the Dogs Out". I could always Google it, though. Learning how to search the web while visiting the Alexandria Inn the previous summer had opened up a whole new world for me.

Thinking about the inn reminded me that I needed to call Lexie Starr, who, along with her husband, owned the B & B in Rockdale, Missouri. She and Stone would want to know where we were and what was going on with regard to Rip's recent health crisis. Speaking with Lexie always raised my spirits, and my spirits were in desperate need of raising just then.

Before returning to her duties, Sydney assured me the contractors would be starting on the needed repairs in a couple of days, if not sooner. "Hopefully the cleaning crew will be arriving this afternoon, too, or at least no later than tomorrow. Let them know if there's anything special they need to attend to that might get overlooked."

"Will do, sweetie," I responded. There was a lot that needed to be attended to that could *not* be overlooked. That evening, as I sat in the trailer with a fat gray cat who'd be ignoring me like I was nothing but a month-old newspaper lying on the sofa, I was going to consider all that needed to be done at the Heart Shack. I'd make up my own punch list for the cleaning crew and another one for the construction crew. I could then pass on any concerns or suggestions when they arrived to begin work.

I planned to make today's visit with my husband a short one. I was anxious to get started on the Heart Shack and had brought along a mop, broom, and bucket of miscellaneous cleaning supplies from the Chartreuse Caboose. What would have been a year's supply of products for our travel trailer would be lucky to last me until noon in Aunt Mabel's house. Luckily there was a dollar store just a block or so away from the house where I could replenish my supplies if needed.

I wanted be there to oversee the cleaning crew's work. Even though I planned to help, there was a limit to what I could accomplish on my own. My first plan of attack was to fling open all the drapes and let the sun shine in. The interior of the home was dark and gloomy and more than a little spooky. Just brightening the rooms would make the place scads more appealing and, hopefully, make me less edgy.

I'd see about having all the drapes professionally dry-cleaned, as well. There had to be at least a half-century's worth of dust, dirt, grime and spider webs embedded in the heavy fabric, probably accounting for at least a third of their weight. The dry-cleaning fee wouldn't be cheap, but it was a necessity, and it'd be at the heart center's expense. I was always a lot more liberal about spending money when the dough belonged to someone else. In fact, if I could convince the powers that be to replace the drapes with vertical blinds, that'd be even better. The place would not only look brighter, but more stylish. Drapes went out of style with olive-drab shag carpeting and linoleum flooring several decades ago. If the structure was being utilized as a museum, one would want to keep it in line with the era it'd been built. But knowing it was going to be used as temporary housing for the family of heart patients, it should be a cheerful retreat full of light, optimism, and hope.

My husband wasn't very pleasant company after his conversation with Dr. Murillo, who'd been making his morning rounds when he'd paused to speak with Rip. I'd heard the surgeon say, "Your lab work looks normal, which is good. However, physically, you aren't quite ready. Before I kick you out of here, I need to see more cogency, more assiduity, and a lot more sedulity on your part."

Dr. Murillo might as well have been speaking in Mandarin Chinese for all my husband understood of what the surgeon had just told him. I was the one who enjoyed doing crossword puzzles, while Rip preferred to be watching, for the twenty-second time, as Apollo Creed got beat to death in *Rocky IV*.

I'd always found it frustrating when a physician spoke to us in medical jargon instead of layman's terms. In the same vein, there was no logical reason for using hoity-toity words when everyday language was ultimately more beneficial to the patient.

The cardiac surgeon scurried on to evaluate his next patient. Walking beside him, I responded to Rip's questioning look as he slowly made his way around the cardiac ward, grumbling non-stop about the physical anguish he was enduring. "He said you need to get off your ass and on your feet. He wants to see more strength, endurance, and determination. Basically, he wants you to grow a backbone and show some spunk and grit. You refusing to get in as much exercise as they're recommending will only keep you here for a lot longer. And he's not going to be swayed by any begging from you, either."

"Wow! He said all that?"

"Yes, he did."

"The doctor was kind of mean, wasn't he?"

"No, he was being frank."

"Really? Well, then, I don't much care for Frank anymore." Rip laughed at his own wisecrack, but I didn't see any humor in his stubbornness.

"Since Dr. Murillo said you need to get with the program as far as the walking is concerned, I think from now on, whenever you're walking the halls and you feel like you can't go one more round, you should suck it up and walk another two rounds."

"Are you trying to kill me, woman?"

"No, I'm trying to save your life. As they say: no guts, no glory."

"I don't want glory," he muttered, as he turned to shuffle back toward his room. He then made another attempt at levity that I didn't find funny, either. "What I want is a cheeseburger in my gut."

"Well, you can want in one hand, and you-know-what in the other, and see which fills up first. The fear of losing you took ten years off my life. We are not going to go through all of this for you to turn right around and see how fast you can plug up your arteries again."

"It took sixty-nine years for those arteries to plug up, and—"

"And, it will take me about sixty-nine seconds to go speak to your nurse. I'm thinking what you need is a booster dose of

Nurse Combs." I knew Rip was only joking with me. I had witnessed a new determination in his attitude after the devoted nurse had got hold of him. I'd watched her tear him a new one without ever raising her voice or losing her patience. I had silently applauded her every word.

After listening to him complain about his "low-fat, low-sodium, zero-taste supper" the previous evening, Nurse Comb had explained, in no uncertain terms, that bypass surgery lowers the risk, but does not prevent, heart attacks. "The same waxy build-up, called plaque, that blocked blood-flow through the arteries to your heart can block the carotid arteries leading to your brain and cause a stroke. It can also block the blood flow to your legs and cause an excruciating condition called PAD, or Peripheral Artery Disease. In addition, it can block the blood flow to your kidneys, causing RAS, or Renal Artery Stenosis, and eventually renal failure."

"Right now I'm suffering from STD. Nobody seems to care about that," Rip mumbled.

"What?" Sydney asked, looking as befuddled as I felt. I knew if Rip had an STD, he didn't get it from me. The nurse asked, "You have a sexually transmitted disease?"

"No, not hardly. I'm talking about STD, as in starving to death. I've noticed you medical folks prefer to speak in acronyms, so I simplified it for you." Rip was clearly amused by his pun. When neither Sydney nor I cracked a smile, Rip added, "Man, this is a tough crowd today."

"You are not starving to death, Clyde." The nurse's use of his given name had made Rip sit up and take notice. Sydney looked over her glasses at Rip as she spoke. "If you ate what the kitchen staff brought you, you wouldn't feel hungry all of the time. I realize the meals here are not prepared by Cordon Blue chefs, but it's not as unsavory as you'd have us believe. The nourishment is critical to help rebuild your strength."

"Yes, ma'am." It was clear Rip's stand-up routine had reached its conclusion when he responded sheepishly before the nurse continued lecturing him.

"You would not care for thrice-weekly dialysis treatments, Mr. Ripple. You have my word on that. By making a number of healthy lifestyle changes, all of the painful and potentially fatal conditions, like the renal failure I just described, can be avoided."

He had taken note of her warnings that previous evening and vowed to do all he could to prevent further damage to his circulatory system. It was the nurse's dire predictions of what would likely occur should he spurn the idea of exercising that finally got him up on his feet and moving. However, he still wasn't moving enough to satisfy Dr. Murillo and was discouraged by his surgeon's words of chastisement. His disappointment had him acting childishly, and I thought the threat of fetching the nurse to give him another round of reprimands might be effective. And it was.

"Should I go fetch Sydney Combs and see what she thinks about it?" I asked my defiant husband.

"Oh, please, no. Don't get Nurse Ratched on my case again! I will do what I'm told. I promise." He often kidded Sydney, comparing her to the wicked nurse in Ken Kasey's *One Flew Over the Cuckoo's Nest*.

I knew Rip had had high hopes of getting to go home that afternoon, and I felt sorry for him when I sensed his disappointment. Following his exchange with Dr. Murillo, I could almost see the wind being sucked out from under Rip's wings. It was like someone had stuck a hat pin into an inflated balloon. The good-natured manner he'd been displaying when I'd first arrived spewed out of him like a whoosh of helium being released. He turned and walked sullenly back to his room, and I followed quietly. He plopped himself down on the side of his bed a little more forcefully than he should have.

"Umph," he exhaled loudly. He snatched his pillow to put pressure on his sore chest, and said, "I think no matter what I do, they'll have me chained to this bed for another—"

Before Rip could get fully invested in his most recent

pout-fest, I interrupted. "As much as I'd love to stick around and chat, darling, I need to get busy making our new accommodations ready for you. You'll be out of here in no time, as long as you are vigilant about getting up and walking the halls as often as possible. In the meantime, I want to make the Heart Shack clean and comfortable. It will help make your recovery process easier."

"Don't you want to stick around to watch Dr. Murillo yank these drainage tubes out of my chest? He said they're coming out this afternoon. A fun time will be had by all, I'm sure."

"As enjoyable as that sounds, Rip, I really need to get to cleaning as soon as possible."

"Well, okay, but—"

Not letting him voice another objection, I leaned over and kissed Rip on the mouth. "Sydney said having the tubes removed was not as bad as it sounds. Just man-up, dear. I'll be back this evening to sit with you for a while. Behave now, and do what the medical staff advises you to do. Unless, of course, you want to be chained to that bed this time next week."

"Oh, horse feathers!" Rip's retort was loud enough to be heard at the nurse's station three doors down the hallway.

"Shush," I said, my finger against my closed lips.

"She's right, Sir Whines-a-Lot," Sydney said, as she dashed into the room. I swear the woman had the room bugged, the hearing of a red-tailed hawk, or possessed an extraordinarily keen sixth sense. "Keep it up, Clyde, and I will personally chain you to that bed. Turns out, police officers aren't the only people who have handcuffs. And don't bother asking me why I own a pair." She laughed, winked at me, and patted Rip's feet to let him know she was only messing with him. She'd quickly learned that using Rip's given name, which was printed on his hospital wrist band, was a reliable way of putting a peck of prickly burrs under his saddle.

She turned and grabbed her stethoscope off the window ledge next to Rip's bed, where she'd set it after checking his blood pressure earlier, and sprinted back out of the room, all without missing a step. Obviously, she'd been in the process of taking another patient's vitals when she realized she'd left her stethoscope behind in Rip's room.

As usual, I wanted to applaud the nurse's remarks. Knowing a clap of my hands would not sit well with my husband, I flashed a smug smile at Rip instead, and dashed out of his room before the cranky sourpuss could utter a grumpy response. I had grimy floors to mop, daunting drapes to take down, and a dust mite killing spree to go on. And, although I didn't know it at the time, I was about to have a murderer to hunt down, as well.

CHAPTER 11

When I walked into the foyer of the Heart Shack a few minutes later, I came face-to-face with Sydney Combs. Or so I thought. We stared at each other in silence. She appeared as shocked as I felt.

"Who are you?" The woman's voice was anything but welcoming.

"Huh? What do you mean, who am I?" Now I was just plain dumbfounded. How could the gal not recognize me? I'd just spoken with her a few minutes ago. It was as if it were she who'd been inflicted with Alzheimer's rather than her aunt. "How in tarnation did you beat me here? You were talking to another patient when I passed by her room on my way out of the cardiac ward."

"I think you're referring to my sister, Sydney."

"Oh." It suddenly occurred to me then that the woman in front of me was wearing a jogging suit rather than hospital scrubs. Sydney had mentioned in passing that she had two siblings, a sister and brother, but failed to mention her sister was an identical twin. If not for the fact Sydney couldn't possibly have changed and beat me to the Heart Shack, I'd have been certain she was playing a trick on me.

"So you and Sydney are twins, I see. How nice. If you're anything like your sister, and I assume you are, I adore you already. Sydney has made my life so much easier by getting my husband to toe the line. If not for her, I don't know what—"

I ceased talking abruptly when I realized Sydney's twin was stoically staring at me with her hands on her hips and an impatient look on her face. I'd been rambling on to give myself a chance to recover from the shock of feeling as if the woman I was praising had magically teleported herself from the hospital to the Heart Shack's foyer.

Finally, the woman replied. "I'm Adelaide. Adelaide Combs. Who are you, and why are you here?"

"It's nice to meet you, too, Adelaide." My response came off as sarcasm, just the way I'd intended it. Her behavior was disrespectful. I'd given the girl no reason to treat me rudely. Despite my irritation, I swallowed hard, took a deep breath, and forced myself to speak in a friendly fashion. If possible, I didn't want to get off on the wrong foot with Sydney's twin. Sydney was delightful, but her sister appeared to be a different story.

"I'm Rapella Ripple. Sydney offered us a room here at your Aunt Mabel's home while my husband, Rip, completes his cardio rehab. In return, we'll be taking care of Goofus and Gallant. I also plan to assist in the clean-up of the home to get it ready for guests. And getting this place up to snuff so the Heart Shack can open up for guests will be quite an undertaking, as I'm sure you're aware."

"Heart Shack?" Adelaide asked. Her voice was intensely brusque. "What in the world are you talking about?"

"Didn't you know?" I was surprised by her apparent lack of knowledge about the future of her aunt's home. Were the sisters not on speaking terms, or had Sydney simply preferred not to discuss the situation with Adelaide? It didn't bother me to let the cat out of the bag. "After your aunt left her home here to the cardiac center, they decided to name it Heart Shack and use it as temporary housing for families who have a loved one recovering from heart surgery or other cardio-related issues."

"Are you for real, lady?" Adelaide asked. It was plain she

was hearing about her aunt's endowment to the cardiac center for the first time. She clearly thought that, following her aunt's death, she was now part-owner of the property in a three-way split with her siblings. "If I'd known that, I might have done things differently. Was this clever scheme my sister's idea?"

"Um, well, I don't know the details. However, I would not refer to it as a 'scheme'. If it was Sydney's inspiration, it was a darned good one. It'll be a godsend for us, and many others, I'm sure. You see, Sydney offered us the master suite for the duration of our stay. However, while most of the guests will be staying here at no cost, with nothing required of them in return, Rip and I will be earning our keep. In my case, I'll be investing plenty of blood, sweat, and tears in exchange for a convenient place to stay. Rip, on the other hand, may not be able to contribute much more than keeping the couch on the screened-in porch from levitating off the floor, but I assure you I'll be donating enough elbow grease for both of us."

"Are you done?" Adelaide asked. Her cheekiness was unnerving, but I was not going to let the bad-mannered twit rattle me. When I hesitated to reply to her caustic question, she repeated it. "Well? Are you done?"

I was aware that her 'are you done?' referred to my babbling, but I replied as if I thought she meant with the cleaning project. "Hardly, Miss Congeniality. It should be apparent to you that there's a lot of work to be done around here. I assume, as Aunt Mabel's great-niece, you're planning to roll up your sleeves and pitch in. So when can I expect you to begin? There'll be guests arriving soon, and we need to get the place in order quickly."

After staring at me without a single blink for at least ten seconds, she turned toward the front door as if to depart without answering my question. Her face was crimson. When she snatched her purse off the marble table in a fit of fury, I noticed the roach clip was no longer there. I could tell Adelaide had a big fat bee under her bonnet and more than a few bats in her belfry. As she opened the door, she said, "Don't hold your breath waiting for any so-called 'guests', lady. My brother and I might have something to say about that plan. So you can take your stupid, old, nosy-ass somewhere else and mind your own stinking business! Tasman and I will see to it that no one connected with the heart center ever steps foot in our house. Along with my sister, it's their fault my Aunt Mabel is not with us today."

"Good luck with that, Adelaide. But, don't forget that karma can be a real you-know-what, and will come back to bite you in the butt when you least expect it." Because of her nasty, mean-spirited name-calling, I felt compelled to get the last word in, which I did because her "whatever" response to my remark about karma simply didn't count.

I went back inside before the vicious woman could spout any more nonsense. I peeked out between the kitchen curtains and watched Adelaide reach into the mail box and pull out a bundle of grocery flyers, magazines, and envelopes. Using the rusty, wrought-iron table on the front porch, she sorted through the envelopes. The final envelope caused the woman to suck in her breath dramatically and her eyes to widen in anticipation. After studying the enclosed folded sheet of paper for almost a full minute, I read her lips as she exclaimed, "I can't believe this." She then swiftly reinserted the paper in the envelope, crammed the envelope into her purse, and stuffed the rest of the mail back into the box.

In an obvious rush to get to her car, an older red and silver Mini-Cooper, her feet only touched two of the six steps leading from the porch down to the sidewalk. Luckily for her, those were the only two treads on the staircase still securely attached to the stringers.

Being the naturally inquisitive type, I was dying to know who the sender was of the envelope she'd confiscated. If for no other reason than that I could tell Sydney when I spoke with her later on that evening. I'd always considered myself a good judge of character, and Adelaide didn't have to beat me over the head with her pitchfork for me to recognize which of the Combs' sisters was the evil twin.

Clearly there was an unresolved issue between the two. And, as presumptuous as this may sound, I already knew whose side of the fence I was on.

I scrubbed the foyer floor until it shined while mulling over my uncomfortable encounter with Adelaide Combs. Afterward, I sprayed the walls with a wood cleaning and protecting solution and polished them to such a luster that the knots and natural grain of the wood were visible. I was down on my knees polishing the baseboards when there was a rapping on the door. I pulled myself up to my feet, but there was no one on the front porch when I opened the door. Whoever had knocked was obviously very impatient. In case there was someone walking around the side of the house looking for the property owner, I stepped outside and hollered, "Who's there?"

When no one answered, I went back inside and resumed my work. Impressed with the welcoming appearance of the foyer—following two hours of laboring over it—I decided to take a break. I wanted to drive to the hospital for an abbreviated visit with Rip and, if possible, speak with Sydney. My next project would be dealing with the drapes. Before the task could begin, though, I needed to get permission to take them down to either have them dry-cleaned or removed from the premises to make way for new vertical blinds.

I was hoping to get the go-ahead to drag the drapes to the curb and deposit them in the dumpster that'd been delivered in advance of the construction crew's arrival. The dark draperies throughout the house played a huge part in its dark, dank, and gloomy ambiance. They also probably harbored untold numbers of scary hazards; toxic byproducts of cigarette smoke, rodent waste, pesticide residue, mold spores, skin cells, and harmful, man-made chemicals known as PCBs. They were simply dreadful and needed to be banished from the Heart Shack, along with Adelaide Combs and the freakishly weird caretaker.

* * *

With that objective in mind, I locked up the house and walked to the truck. After starting the Chevy, I turned on the radio and headed for the hospital.

"The body of local philanthropist, Mabel Trumbo, is slated to be exhumed on Thursday. Due to a recent anonymous tip, detectives are now looking into her death as a possible case of foul play." After I heard the female voice on the radio, which was tuned to the local news station, I cranked the volume up and pulled the truck to the curb. I was disappointed when the lady said nothing further other than, "More on the story tonight at six on the local news broadcast. This is Alexa Bancroft, reporting for KEX5 News."

I put the transmission into park and reached in my purse to grab a pen and a pad of paper. I wanted to write down the details of what I'd just heard before I forgot them, which usually took no more than a minute—or two, on a good day.

I wondered if the Combs twins had heard the new development regarding their aunt's death. Could the exhumation been the disturbing news in the letter Adelaide had confiscated? Maybe the mysterious man I'd met inside the home that morning had been on to something. He'd seemed convinced some form of malevolence had been involved in Mabel's death. Had he been the anonymous tipster? It seemed likely to me. But who was he, if not the caretaker? Would a nosy neighbor get involved to that extent? It was possible, of course, but didn't seem likely.

I could hardly wait to get to the hospital to tell Sydney what had just been broadcast on the news in the event she hadn't already heard. The light at the only intersection between the Heart Shack and the hospital was changing from yellow to red when I coasted through it in my rush to reach the heart center. In my defense, I had glanced both ways and was convinced I could shoot the gap while avoiding contact with both the UPS truck approaching from the west and the black SUV nearing the intersection from the east. In my opinion, the light-running incident was explicitly warranted—a no harm, no foul kind of situation. The soccer mom in the SUV who flipped me off must have felt differently.

CHAPTER 12

A s you can imagine, after risking my life at the corner of Ninth and South Weller Streets to get to the hospital in record time, I was a little let down to find Sydney and Adelaide conversing when I arrived, clearly already in the know about the breaking news. They were having an animated discussion at the nurses' station as I approached. It was like watching a young lady argue with her own reflection in a mirror. If not for the identifying nurse's outfit, I couldn't have told you which twin was which. As I got within earshot, I heard Sydney say, "I gave her permission to stay there, and you should be as appreciative of her willingness to help out around the place as I am."

"Are you for real?" Adelaide asked.

"Besides, I'm the interim manager of the Heart Shack until the center hires someone to be in charge of the place full-time. Mrs. Ripple's presence there should be of no concern to you or Taz."

I slowed my pace substantially as I neared the pair. It was not only to enable me to eavesdrop on more of their conversation, but also to avoid knocking down a silver-haired heart patient who was walking the hallways of the cardiac ward.

"Yeah, whatever," Adelaide said. The evil twin was an absolute snot. Her attitude made me want to throw her over my knee and wear out a belt on her behind. "What's with the sudden decision of the authorities to exhume Aunt Mabel's body?"

"I don't know why, but they've suddenly decided to do an autopsy, Adelaide," the anxious nurse in the pastel pink and light blue scrubs said. "If there was any indication of foul play surrounding Aunt Mabel's death, they should have performed the autopsy before the embalmment. It's ludicrous for anyone to believe her death was related to anything but her open-heart surgery. Whoever called in the anonymous tip doesn't know what he or she is talking about. Do you know anyone who might've done that, Addie?"

"How would I know?" Adelaide answered defensively. "I guarantee you, calling in an anonymous tip's the last thing I'd do. I want this entire ordeal over with and my share of the money deposited in my nearly empty account as soon as possible."

"Why doesn't that surprise me?" Sydney replied in a sad, resigned voice.

"But maybe they *should* be checking into her death," Adelaide ignored her sister's remark and continued in a scathing tone. "I'm not convinced the medical examiner's ruling was correct. After all, Aunt Mabel had a professional nurse, who studied cardiac care extensively, as her in-home caretaker following her bypass operation. Assuming her nurse had a clue about what she was doing, Aunt Mabel should've been the least likely patient to die of complications."

"What are you implying, Adelaide?"

"Well, you're the one who bought her groceries, planned her meals, and fed them to her. You were also responsible for filling her pill box with her prescribed medications, and taking her vitals. You did nearly everything for her. Just saying."

Adelaide's implication was clear. Anger had taken the

place of sadness in her tone as Sydney mimicked her sister's last comment. "Just saying? Just saying what? You're absolutely right I did nearly everything for our aunt, who for years raised us like she was our own mother. All with no help from you, and very little from Tasman! But I share no responsibility whatsoever in her death, Addie! All the training, knowledge and skill in the world can't ensure a patient's ultimate outcome is positive. There are any number of complications that can occur following open-heart surgery, regardless of the quality of care the patient is receiving. I was super careful when I filled her medication box, too. So don't be tossing any accusations at me. I think she most likely threw a clot. And, by the way, Dr. Murillo concurred with my conclusion."

"How would you know? You weren't even there when she passed! Neither was the doctor, for that matter. If you *had* been present, maybe you could've saved her life. She really needed someone with her 'round the clock."

"I *did* hire a day nurse to care for her when I couldn't be there."

"Maybe that wasn't enough. She couldn't remember shit, you know."

"Alzheimer's is a terrible disease, not one that should be ridiculed with snide remarks like the one you just made, Addie," Sydney said to her obnoxious sister.

"Whatever," Adelaide repeated. Her one-word reply made me want to slap the self-satisfied smirk off her face. And wear out a second belt on her behind, as well.

"And, furthermore," Sydney continued, "I have a job and bills to pay, so I couldn't be with Aunt Mabel 24/7. There was probably nothing I could've done anyway. And by-the-by, where were you when our aunt needed someone to keep an eye on her after the operation? Not helping, that's for sure! At least Tasman agreed to watch her on Sundays, when I had a twelve-hour shift and the nurse had the day off. Even though I was leery of leaving her in Taz's care, with Aunt Mabel not trusting him much, at least he gave me a much-needed break. It would've been nice to have you to spell me now and then, too. I hardly got any sleep and sorely needed help in taking care of all of the arrangements for her health care, and, ultimately, her funeral."

Adelaide obviously had no intention of taking ownership of one iota of blame. She sneered as she turned Sydney's words back on her. "Well, *by-the-by*, who gave you the right to make all of the decisions regarding Aunt Mabel's estate after her death?"

"Aunt Mabel did! She gave me power-of-attorney! Me! Not you or Taz! I had nothing to do with the contents of her will, Addie. However, she did leave me in charge of executing it. That doesn't mean I wouldn't have welcomed some assistance. But I haven't noticed you or Tasman offering to help out."

Sydney was royally pissed, and I admired her angry retort. Score one for the more responsible of the two sisters, who were mirror images of each other in looks, but seemingly polar opposites in every way that truly mattered.

"Seriously, Sydney? You live within twenty minutes of Aunt Mabel. Tasman and I live in Yakima and Tokeland, both almost three hours away. Doesn't mean we shouldn't get equal say, even if we didn't actually do any of the leg work. More importantly, we deserve an equal share of the remainder of her estate. In fact, Tasman and I plan to put the brakes on letting her house go to the heart center. With a little fixing up, we could all make out like bandits on the sale of that place."

"And that, in a nutshell, is all you two care about, isn't it? I'm not going to let you stop the transfer of the house to the heart center, Addie. And that's all there is to it! I plan to fulfill Aunt Mabel's final wishes exactly in accordance with her last will and testament. Besides, she didn't have much in the way of valuable possessions or belongings. Even upscale furniture is not worth much after it's been used."

"What are you talking about? She possessed something extremely valuable—if we can only find it."

I wondered what valuable possession Adelaide referred to. The Steinway piano was worth a substantial chunk of change, but it was hardly difficult to locate.

"Or so the story goes," Sydney replied. "There may be no truth to it. However, everything she did have, other than her property on East Hart Street, will be split three ways in equal proportions, I can assure you. So you can take your phony concerns about her cause of death and go back to Yakima."

"Tasman and I both want to know something. Were you behind her decision to leave her house to charity? After all, you are an employee of the heart center, which just happens to have been her most fortuitous beneficiary. She didn't leave a dime to my employer or Tasman's." Adelaide was livid. It was as if a volcano had erupted inside her when she next spewed out, "Be honest, Sydney! It was your idea, wasn't it? You influenced her to make that decision and alter her will before she died, didn't you?"

"Seriously, Addie?" Normally unflappable, Sydney had raised her voice and was practically hissing when she responded. "You truly expected her to leave her home to the First Cut Hair Salon where you've worked for no more than two years? Then, there's Tasman. Is he even employed right now? Last I heard, he'd been let go from the fast-food restaurant for smoking weed on the job."

"You should have stayed out of it, Sydney. Aunt Mabel would have probably left her home to the three of us. We deserve that money, not people she'll never even know."

Sydney shook her head in disbelief at her sister's malevolence, as did the rest of us witnessing the contentious exchange between the twins. "As I've already told you, Addie, I had nothing to do with the contents of the will. But, had she not left the house to the cardiac center, I suppose you think I should have been the one to do all of the work, seeing that the house was restored and in good-enough condition to put on the market. The magnitude of your greed and sense of entitlement is unbelievable."

"That's not the point!"

"Then what *is* your point?" Sydney hollered. She appeared startled by her own vehemence. She froze as her gaze scanned the area, suddenly aware that two of her fellow nurses, the silver-haired patient in the hallway—who, along with his walker, had come to a standstill—and I were all captivated by the heated exchange. It was as if all four of us were hanging on the sisters' every word. Lowering her voice substantially, she spoke directly to Adelaide. "Get out of here, Addie! Go home! I have patients to tend to, and I can't discuss this with you here at the hospital. Besides, I'm not stupid, you know. I know the reason you've come here is to try and—"

I couldn't make out the rest of the nurse's comment. I couldn't tread any slower without walking backwards, and Sydney had finished her statement in a whisper. I nearly lost my balance trying to make out the last few words. They sounded like, "wind the wold", which made no sense to me. Nor could I make them make sense by playing with similar words in my mind.

However, whatever she *had* said had clearly had a powerful effect on her sparring partner, who wadded up the envelope she'd been clutching and threw it to the ground. Adelaide then turned and stomped off toward the elevators in a red-hot fury.

Crapola! I said to myself as I held my breath in anticipation. *What the bloody hell is in that envelope?* My curiosity about its contents was now so overwhelming, I had to resist the urge to snatch the legal-sized envelope up off the floor and race down the hallway to the public restroom so I could lock myself in and read it.

But I had to accept that whatever was inside the mysterious envelope was between the sisters. And Tasman, too, of course, who I hoped had more sense and compassion than Adelaide. Just then, Sydney picked up the crumpled envelope and tucked it into a corner of the "COW" next to her.

I watched as the crimson-faced nurse scurried down the hallway, pushing the COW, or WOW, in front of her as she headed toward the very restroom I'd wanted to lock myself in. I figured she was going to hide out in there long enough to let the built-up steam inside of her diffuse while she examined whatever was on the paper that had so intrigued me. The temperature in the tiny room would probably be a good ten degrees higher by the time the overheated nurse exited.

As much as I wanted to see the expression on Sydney's face when she came back out of the restroom, I was even more anxious to tell Rip everything I'd witnessed and experienced since I'd last seen him.

When I arrived at Rip's bedside, however, I discovered my parade had already been rained on. He was sitting on the side of his hospital bed, breathing harder than usual, as if he'd just returned from a lengthy walk down the hallways of the cardiac ward. Before I could even greet him, he burst my bubble.

"On the news this morning, they reported that they're initiating an investigation into the cause of Sydney's great-aunt's death. They have reason to suspect there was more to it than initially met the eye. They kind of implied that malpractice by hospital staff or nursing care negligence might've been responsible. But they also said they couldn't rule out foul play by someone outside the medical field. Crazy, huh?"

"Yeah. Crazy." My crestfallen expression and unenthusiastic response went unnoticed by my oblivious husband. I'd forgotten he'd had the TV on every waking moment during his hospital stay, and most likely when he was asleep, as well. "Did they mention what had occurred to stir up this hornet's nest?"

"Apparently someone was upset about the medical examiner's ruling and took their concerns to the police department. Sydney doesn't seem too happy about the development. And who could blame her?" Rip said. "Knowing about my law enforcement experience, she was in here earlier asking me questions about exhuming bodies and why they might have decided an autopsy was necessary two weeks after Aunt Mabel's burial. I explained there was no statute of limitations on murder, and that if the authorities were to exhume her aunt's body twenty years from now and found evidence of foul play, the perpetrator would be brought to justice just as if he'd committed the murder that very day."

"Why was she so upset?"

"She said her aunt's death had been a cut-and-dried case of heart failure due to complications following her double bypass. Understandably, she doesn't want to see the hospital's reputation or her own being dragged through the mud. Again, who can blame her? She was an emotional wreck when she discussed the situation with me."

"I suspect she's under a great deal of pressure and had a lot of angst she needed to get off her chest. I just witnessed a blowup between her and her twin sister."

"Her twin sister? Sydney never mentioned having a twin," Rip said. He appeared genuinely surprised.

Cool, I thought. *I actually* do *have some interesting information to share with him.* I'd assumed she'd mentioned being a twin to him in one of their many conversations and he'd just forgotten to tell me. As it turned out, Rip had no inkling about Sydney's siblings, which delighted me! I knew I had piqued his interest when he picked up the TV remote, muted the sound, and smiled. "So, tell me about Sydney's twin. I can tell you are busting at the seams to share what you've learned."

"Yes. I am, indeed. Adelaide Combs, who's an absolute holy terror, is Sydney's identical twin. Other than their clothing, I can't tell them apart. I guarantee you, if the two were standing here naked, side-by-side, you wouldn't be able to distinguish between them, either."

Rip raised his eyebrows. For once, I couldn't decipher his expression. Was he wondering why I was so worked up, curious about why Sydney hadn't mentioned her twin to him, or simply visualizing the two young, good-looking women naked? I decided it was the latter when he responded, "I'm not sure my initial reaction would be to try and distinguish between the two."

I shook my head. "Dirty old man! Seriously, Rip. It's almost freaky how identical they are. Physically, anyhow. Personality-wise, there seems to be no resemblance whatsoever."

"Really? Isn't that unusual for identical twins?"

"Very unusual. Or so I've heard."

"What was their spat about?" Rip asked.

"What else? Money. Adelaide also implied that Sydney might have had a hand in their aunt's death, which is hogwash. Sydney is not only an outstanding nurse, she's one of the warmest, kindest, most caring people we've ever met. Don't you agree?"

"Absolutely," Rip said. "But that doesn't mean there's not a side to her character we aren't privy to. We can't judge her totally by her nursing persona. She does have a controlling manner that might make it difficult to be in a close relationship with her."

I considered Rip's remarks for a few moments. While I tend to look only at the positive side of people I'm fond of, Rip delves deeper into their character. His career in law enforcement forced him to interact with people from all walks of life. During his tenure on the force, he'd dealt with the best of folks for certain. But he'd also come face-to-face with just the opposite: the worst of humanity, the scum of the earth, the dregs of society, and downright evil sociopaths who have no consciences whatsoever. Knowing what makes a person tick and, more importantly, what might make them come unglued to the point they might be dangerous, was crucial to how he approached any given situation. I trusted his instincts.

"You're right, honey. I just feel bad for Sydney. Particularly if she's done nothing more than try to fulfill Aunt Mabel's final wishes and do what she thinks is best for everyone involved. Adelaide indicated Mabel might have owned something of value, but Sydney sounded skeptical about that. I can't see her trying to screw her sister and brother out of a single dime, can you?"

"No, Rapella, I can't." Rip had heard me use a zillion clichés over the years, and he employed one of my most oft-used ones then to make his point. "Remember, you can't judge a nurse by her scrubs any more than you can judge a book by its cover. I could never have predicted that a male Olympic decathlon gold medalist would one day transition into becoming a woman, for example. And I'm not saying I have a problem with the Olympian's choice. Live and let live, as far as I'm concerned. I'm only saying things happen every single day that surprise and even shock me. Things I never could have imagined occurring, *do* occur, and on an incredibly frequent basis. There are a lot of people in the world who are remarkably skilled at putting on a front. In other words, there's only so much credit you can put into a gut feeling you have about someone. You always have to be prepared for the unexpected."

"Yeah, I know. I just don't want to see such a sweet gal adversely affected if this whole thing blows up in her face."

"Neither do I, honey. But if Cindy has nothing to hide—"

"Good grief, Rip. Her name's Sydney."

"What's the difference?"

"The first syllable is pronounced 'sid', not 'sin'." I tried to think of a way to help Rip remember the nurse's name and decided applying his bucket list to the equation might do the trick. "You know how you're always saying you want to visit Australia before you croak? If we were there on vacation, would we be more apt to visit the town of Sydney or the town of Cindy?"

"Well, Sydney, of course. But what's that got to do with anything?"

"Never mind." *Maybe,* I thought, *I should ask Dr. Murillo if he's sure he'd performed a triple-bypass operation on Rip and not a partial lobotomy.* But then I recalled that Rip had had difficulty remembering names even before the cardiac surgery. If you were to ask him about the tools in his tool box, without a second's pause, he'd tell you he had thirteen screwdrivers, eleven kinds of pliers, three hammers, and twenty-seven wrenches, each with their own specific function—which he'd be delighted to elaborate on if you'd only inquire. He could also remember every phone number he'd dialed in the last ten years and who'd won the Superbowl for the last twenty.

But ask him the names of his two grandchildren, and he'd have to think about it. Not remembering names was just one of his quirks, I guess. Lord knows I have a quirk or two myself. "Go on with what you were saying, Rip."

"Now that you've interrupted and corrected me, I don't remember *what* I was saying."

"You said, 'If Cindy has nothing to hide' before I broke in to gently remind you the nurse's name is Sydney," I said to prompt Rip's recollection.

"Oh, yeah. That's right," Rip said. I wanted to smack the remote control out of his hand when he came out with his next remark. "So, anyway, if Cindy has nothing to hide, and doesn't deserve to have the truth behind her aunt's death blow up in her face, she should come out of this situation just fine. One way or another, it will work itself out."

Rip wrapped his arms around my waist and gave me a warm embrace. As he hugged me, he simultaneously cranked up the volume on his television, and said, "Look how young Al Pacino was in this movie."

I knew Rip's abrupt change of topic was designed to take my mind off an issue that was bothering me. And on a day like today, I welcomed the distraction.

However, once the distraction had worn off, the niggling notion would rear its ugly head again. I knew it, and so did Rip. The idea I might be able to spare Sydney some unjustifiable grief would pop up in my mind—right out of the blue—numerous times in the next couple of days. Niggling notions had a way of doing that, you know.

CHAPTER 13

I returned to the Heart Shack and spent the rest of the afternoon cleaning. I was hungry and sore from hours of toiling, and looking forward to returning to the Chartreuse Caboose for a tequila sunrise, a bowl of chili, and some rest. And in precisely that order, I might add. On my way back to the RV park, I stopped at the cardiac center to make a brief visit with Rip. After a short chat, I walked out of his hospital room and nearly ran right into Sydney, who'd just exited the next room down the hall. I heard her say as she walked out the door, "Be right back. I need to go start an IV on a new patient."

I smiled at Sydney. She nodded in response, clearly preoccupied. As I passed the room she'd just exited, I looked in and saw she'd left her computer-on-wheels behind. I could see the top of the envelope Adelaide had crumpled and thrown on the floor sticking up from behind the computer screen. Knowing Sydney would be busy with the IV insertion for a few minutes, I knew I'd have time to look at the contents of the envelope. But with two patients occupying the room, I'd have to look as if I was supposed to be there and had every right to mess around with items in and around the computer.

Despite knowing I was putting myself at risk of being

caught red-handed by pretending to be a cardiac center physician, it was the best idea I could come up with on short notice. I'd seen a hamper next to a room marked "soiled laundry".

I walked briskly down the hallway to the over-flowing hamper and sorted through its contents until I found a plain white jacket that looked like the one several of the doctors who'd visited Rip's room had been wearing. It was too large for me, but it'd have to do.

I told myself I'd have to remember to take a long shower when I returned to the trailer that evening to make sure I removed any trace of bacteria or fungi from my body after pawing through all of the dirty sheets, towels, and gowns. Back at the room where Sydney had left her COW, I noticed her stethoscope hanging from a hook right inside the door. I wrapped it around my neck and breezed into the room as if I was the director of the entire hospital. I'd seen the patients' names on a dry-erase board mounted on the wall just outside the room, so I turned to the patient in the first bed and said, "Good afternoon, Mrs. Quigley. How are you feeling today?"

Stupid question to ask, I soon discovered. I should have said absolutely nothing and acted as if I was in deep thought, concentrating on a critical matter that could only be addressed from Sydney's rolling computer cart.

"We're the Biggs. Mrs. Quigley's in the other bed. Who are you?" Mr. Biggs asked, speaking for his recuperating spouse. "I don't believe we've met before."

"I'm Doctor, um, well, Dolittle. Dr. Dolittle." I was afraid they'd recognize the name Ripple from the dry-erase board outside Rip's room, and I hadn't taken the time to come up with a fictional name, so I'd said the first thing that came to mind. Past experience has taught me that's a dangerous thing for me to do.

"Dr. Dolittle?" The man asked. "Your name is actually Dr. Dolittle, as in the movie where the doctor can communicate with animals?"

"Yes. Ironic, huh?" *Not only is it ironic,* I wanted to say to Mr. Biggs, *but it's appropriate, too, because I planned to do as little as possible while impersonating a physician. Would you have been less inquisitive had I'd chosen the second name that came to mind—Dr. Pepper?* I laughed, and added in a joking manner, "And, I really do have a fascinating chat with my cat every day."

After a polite chuckle, the man said, "Well, Dr. Dolittle, my wife seems to be having trouble breathing. What should we do?"

"Well, uh, Mr. Biggs, if I were you, I'd call a nurse. On second thought, I'll go get one for you as soon as I finish my current task. It will only be a minute or so."

"Didn't you say you were a doctor?"

"Yes. But I didn't say I was a good one." I meant this to come off humorously, but the couple both looked at me as if wondering if they should call security, or pull on the cord that told the nurse station that a patient needs urgent attention. So, I quickly continued. "Just kidding, folks. Nurse Combs will be right back to assist you. I'll let her help you since you're her responsibility and I don't want to step on anyone's toes around here. You know how territorial these nurses can be."

"Well, all right. I guess we'll just have to wait for her."

"It shouldn't take long."

I was relieved to see Mr. Biggs was content with my response. Mrs. Biggs wasn't saying anything, but that might have been because she wasn't getting enough oxygen to her brain.

I pulled the envelope from beside the computer and withdrew the paper inside. I'd intended to scan the document, return it to the envelope quickly, and dart right back out of the room. I hadn't expected to have any interaction with either patient or their spouses. I should have realized that was nothing but a pipe dream. After waiting hours to speak to a doctor when he made his rounds, I knew from personal experience that the first thing you do when one finally enters your room is to start shooting questions at him.

"Is my wife still scheduled for a chest x-ray this afternoon?" Mr. Biggs asked.

Before I could think of a response, a male voice shouted from behind the curtain dividing the two beds. He'd obviously been listening in on my exchange with the Biggs couple. "Dr. Dolittle! Come quickly. My wife needs help getting up to go to the restroom."

Oh boy! I thought. If I help the recent heart surgery patient shuffle across the room to the john, at a likely "glacier-melting" speed, I'll never get out of this room before Sydney returns. But what else could I do? Once again, before I could come up with a response, Mr. Quigley spoke again.

"Too late. Clara just soiled herself. Oh, good Lord," Mr. Quigley said. He sounded as if he was trying not to gag. "It's all over her and the bed."

My first thought was not something I'd want to repeat, but the four-letter "s" word would have been quite appropriate. Then I realized the patient losing control of her bowels was actually a stroke of luck because now Mrs. Quigley wouldn't need assistance getting to the restroom. That smelly ship had already sailed. So I did the only thing I could at that point. I said, "I'll send a nurse in right away to clean up the mess and put fresh linens on the bed. She can also tell you, Mr. Biggs, what time your wife's x-ray is scheduled."

And then I bolted as if I'd just discovered a suicide bomber in bed two. I re-hung the stethoscope on the hook on my way out, and then ripped off my jacket and tossed it into the hamper as I tore up the hallway. I darted into Rip's room just as Sydney walked out of a patient's room three doors down.

"I thought you left," Rip said.

"I did, but then I saw the envelope I told you about on Sydney's COW and I brought it in here to read." He didn't need to know the details of my acquisition. He was recovering from major surgery and should be under as little stress as possible.

"You took the envelope off her cart? Don't you think that's kind of an invasion of her privacy, Rapella?"

"Yes, of course it is, dear. And I'm not proud of myself for doing it. But what's done is done. Now hush up for a moment so I can scan through it quickly." As I spoke, Rip looked at me like I'd just stolen the crown jewels from the Tower of London.

The letter was from the hospital's board of directors, informing the family of Mabel Trumbo that her death had been brought under review due to a re-evaluation of the results of the medical examiner's report. There was a lot of legalese and medical mumbo-jumbo I didn't understand, but I got the gist of the letter. Mabel's death had officially been classified as a pulmonary embolism, but there was reason to believe there may have been negligence on the part of the cardiac center's medical staff. They specifically mentioned failing to inform the patient of critical post-operative precautions and/or giving her the wrong medications and/or food items. I read the important parts of the letter out loud to Rip. "All staff members involved with the patient prior to her death will be brought before the medical board for questioning."

"Do you think that will include Sydney?" Rip asked.

"I think that goes without saying. After all, she's the surgeon's personal nurse, and was responsible for the patient's at-home care after her aunt left the hospital. Do you think it's possible Sydney did something wrong? Screwed up her aunt's medications or something? Sydney was under a lot of pressure with so much on her plate, between her job here and taking care of her aunt." Even as I spoke, I couldn't quite wrap my head around the situation. The very thought of Sydney being found guilty of negligence in the death of her beloved aunt made me shudder.

"I suppose it's possible. I sure hope not, for Sydney's sake. She's too good a person and nurse to be dealt a hand like that. You better get that letter back where you found it right away, Rapella. Sydney might walk in here at any moment."

"Yeah, I know." I folded up the letter and returned it to the envelope. "And, hey, I'm impressed you got Nurse Combs' first name right three times in a row."

"Before I spoke, I imagined myself on vacation in Australia," Rip said with an impish grin. "Don't you realize I am keenly focused on every single thing you say to me?"

Yeah, right. Of course you are, dear. I didn't have time to respond, so I just stuck my tongue out at him. On my way out of his room, I pretended to wade through the load of bull crap Rip had just dumped on me.

As I stepped into the hallway, I saw Sydney wheeling her COW toward me. Rather than concocting an elaborate scheme to return the envelope to the cart, an envelope Sydney might have already noticed was missing, I decided a simple approach was the best. I approached her just as she reached the nursing station.

When she looked up at me, I handed her the envelope. "I found this on the floor just outside the room next to Rip's and saw it was addressed to your family, so I wanted to make sure it was returned to you."

"Oh, thank you, Rapella. I must've dropped it." She folded it in half and shoved it in the front pocket of her scrubs. "Did you happen to see a woman go in or out of that room just a short while ago?"

Uh-oh! Time to wing it. "Yes, I did. I saw a female physician leave the room just as I exited Rip's."

"What did she look like?"

"Oh, I'd say she was about my height and weight. And she had salt and pepper hair like mine, but was probably seven or eight years younger than me. She was heading in the direction of the elevators when I saw her. Why do you ask?"

"I was just wondering who she was. No biggie." Sydney looked concerned, and I knew why. She was probably wondering if someone from the medical board was looking for her, or even interviewing patients about the care they'd received from her. I was quick to change the subject.

"I'll be heading back over to the Heart Shack in a couple of minutes. Anything special you'd like for me to do?"

"No, Rapella. You're doing more than enough already, and I really do appreciate you." Sydney impulsively reached out and gave me a quick hug. "Thanks for seeing that this envelope got returned to me. It's kind of important."

I'd say it's very important, dear, I wanted to reply. Instead, I said, "No problem, sweetie. It was the least I could do." *And, being that it was I who stole it from you in the first place, it really was the very least I could do.*

CHAPTER 14

It was three-twenty when I returned to the Heart Shack for another few hours of scrubbing and mopping. With so much to do and so little time to do it, I didn't have the luxury of letting grass grow under my feet. Walking up the sidewalk, I again felt eyes following me—all the way to the front door this time. I turned to find a woman in the yard adjacent to Mabel's staring at me. The house next door was not nearly as old, but much smaller than the Heart Shack, and the lawn was meticulously manicured. It was as if it'd been trimmed with a pair of surgical scissors.

Feeling uncomfortable, I turned toward the door and pretended to be checking for mail for a few moments before turning back around to see if Mabel's neighbor was still staring at me. She hadn't moved a muscle. Her gaze was still fixed directly on me. She was petite and had a tanned and deeply wrinkled face befitting a woman I estimated to be in her middle seventies who enjoyed yard work. If she could claim to be five feet tall, it was only because of the army boots she wore. The boots boasted higher heels than seemed appropriate for gardening.

With her deep-set eyes still fixed on me, I felt uneasy again and immediately turned away. My first notion was to quickly enter the house so I might avoid any interaction with her. I didn't need yet another reason to feel on edge every time I was on the premises of the bright red Heart Shack. With my back to the next-door neighbor, I hastily fiddled with the skeleton key to unlock the front door which only made my fingers quiver clumsily and the task more difficult.

But suddenly a thought caused me to do an about-face. It had just occurred to me that a short woman in my age bracket, if not a few years my senior, might possibly be the spouse of the man Rip had tried to convince me was the nosy neighbor I'd encountered earlier in the day. Shoving the key ring in my front pocket, I turned around and walked toward the neighbor. Her eyes remained fixed on me and she stood as motionless as the garden statue next to her.

Walking briskly as I approached her, I waved good-naturedly. To fill the awkward silence, I said, "Good afternoon, neighbor!"

"Neighbor?" Her voice was not exactly friendly. She appeared to be distrustful, as if concerned I might be up to no good.

"Yes, ma'am." With forced cheerfulness, I added, "Temporarily, anyway. The former owner's niece is a friend of mine, and—"

"Sydney? Or the other one?" There was a semblance of fondness in her voice as she mentioned Sydney's name. The tone she used to ask the second question indicated otherwise. It seemed as if she and I shared a negative opinion about Adelaide.

"Yes, Sydney. I can honestly say I don't consider Adelaide a friend."

The neighbor didn't reply. So I stuck my hand out and introduced myself. When the lady shook my hand without introducing herself in return, I asked, "And you are?"

"Just fine, thank you."

"That's nice. But what I meant was, what is your name?" I was pretty sure she'd known what I meant and was being intentionally evasive, like the caretaker had been earlier. As Yogi Berra would have said, it was like déjà-vu all over again.

"Itsy."

"Itsy? As in itsy-bitsy?"

She looked at me as if I'd just claimed to be an alien visiting from the recently demoted space object named Pluto. After scrutinizing me for several long, uncomfortable moments, she finally replied. "Itsy, as in Itsy Warman."

"Oh." I was stymied by her antisocial behavior and decided to attempt a few pleasantries and then leave her to her flower-planting. "It's nice to meet you, Ms. Warman."

"I go by Itsy."

"Very well. I see you enjoy gardening, Itsy."

"Who said I enjoyed gardening? These flowers ain't gonna plant themselves, you know."

So much for pleasantries, I thought. Her response had been terse, but when I laughed at her remark, she smiled, exposing darkly stained teeth. I'd soon learn Itsy had a hankering for a wad of chaw now and then.

"No, I reckon they ain't," I replied with a chuckle. Now that this woman named Itsy was being a little more amicable, I thought it'd be a good time to segue into a conversation about the man I'd met in the drawing room. "Am I to assume then that your husband doesn't have a green thumb?"

"Who said I had a husband?" This time she slapped the side of her dirt-smudged jeans and laughed heartily. Her guffawing was so contagious that soon we were both snickering so much we had tears running down our cheeks. The woman laughed so hard, she nearly gagged on a swallow of black saliva which she hacked up and spat onto the ground in front of her.

"No husband, huh? Want one?" I asked, trying not to appear disgusted by the lady's unladylike habit. Itsy's dour mood had turned on a dime, and I wanted to take advantage of her new light-hearted demeanor. "I got a husband I'll sell cheap. It's an older, restored model, but hopefully it's still got a few years' worth of use left in it. Just recently been rewired, in fact."

My silly response set us off again. When we both finally quit our raucous cackling, Itsy smiled broadly. "Thanks, but no thanks. I don't need no stinking husband telling me what to do. Too set in my ways from being on my own so long."

Still giggling, I said, "Okie-dokie, Itsy Warman. I can't fault you for wanting to maintain your independence."

After nodding her agreement, Itsy said, "Welcome to the neighborhood."

"Thank you. I'm looking forward to moving in. Right now I'm trying to blow the cobwebs out of the old place."

"Good luck with that. A blow torch might be your best bet. Mabel wasn't much for housework, and Ridley wasn't either."

"Ridley?"

"Never mind."

"Who's Ridley?"

"It's not important."

"Was Ridley Mabel's caretaker?" It'd been obvious Itsy had tried to backtrack after mentioning the man's name, but I was like a dog with a bone now. I wasn't giving up easily. "What's Ridley's last name?"

"I've already said too much." Itsy shuffled her feet nervously after replying. I stared at her expectantly for several long moments, until she finally added, "Okay, yes. Ridley Wickets was Mabel's caretaker. But you didn't hear it from me, and that's all I'm saying about him."

Itsy's reluctance to expound on the caretaker was perplexing. I might've been determined to find out more about the Ridley she'd mentioned, but Itsy was even more determined not to share any additional information about him with me. Still, my intuition told me he was the Irish bloke I'd run across in the drawing room that morning. I didn't want to alienate the neighbor, though, so I asked her about her recently deceased neighbor.

"It sure was a shame about Ms. Trumbo's death, wasn't it? Were you two close?"

"Not really. Didn't cotton to her much."

"Why didn't you care for Mabel?" I consciously tried to sound conversational, rather than prying, but her response convinced me my effort had failed.

"I had my reasons."

"Yes. I'm sure you did. Even so, it's sad she died of post-surgical complications."

"The fact I was often annoyed by the woman doesn't mean I believe she died of natural causes." Itsy spoke in a huff, with her arms folded across her chest as if affronted by my causal comment. I couldn't swear to it, but I thought I saw a tear well up in her right eye, which made no sense to me at all, given her distaste for her late neighbor.

"Why do you believe her death wasn't from surgery-related complications?"

"I have my reasons," she repeated. Itsy clammed up abruptly and I suspected she'd said all she intended to say about the matter. But after considerable contemplation, she continued. "Never really trusted those Combs kids. They're a greedy lot, except for maybe Sydney."

"Are they from Australia?" I hadn't detected an accent from either twin, but the twins' names were both that of major Australian cities. And I realized their brother could have been named for the little island of Tasmania which was located in the Tasman Sea, off the southern edge of the "down-under" country.

"No. All three were all born in the states," Itsy replied. "It was their grandmother, Rosalyn, who spent her childhood in Australia. Their mother, Norma Jean, named them in her grandma's honor. The family lived nearby when Rosalyn, who was Mabel's older sister, was killed by a shark while swimming off the coast of Oregon."

"Yikes! How tragic!"

"Yep. Good way to spoil an enjoyable day out on the water, ain't it?"

"I'd say so." Where the siblings were from was neither here nor there as far as I was concerned. I had more important fish to fry. I didn't have a lot of time to waste jabbering with Itsy Warman, so I felt compelled to ask, "So you truly believe one of Mabel's kin could've had a hand in her death? Ridley seems to agree that she didn't die of natural causes. The local homicide detectives must think so, too. Or at least they have some reason to believe foul play might have been involved."

"Where'd you hear that?" I could tell by Itsy's reaction and the quizzical look on her face, she had no clue what I was talking about.

"Didn't you hear on the news? They're planning to exhume her body. They may have already done so. I'm sorry. I thought by your earlier comments you already knew about it."

Itsy looked as if she'd just seen a ghost squat down and relieve himself in the middle of her flower bed. "Why? Did they say why they wanted to exhume her body?"

"The reporter said it had to do with an anonymous tip."

"Did they say who the anonymous tipster was?" Itsy asked.

"Um, no. That's kind of the point of being anonymous."

"Oh, yeah. Guess you're right." Itsy appeared flustered. "I'm happy to hear they're reevaluating Mabel's cause of death. Even though I never believed it, I'd heard they'd officially concluded she'd died of complications. Wasn't that what the medical examiner supposedly determined?"

"I think it was the assumption at the time. But I got the impression from the news report that an autopsy was not initially performed after her death. The family didn't request one, and being that Mabel had just undergone open-heart surgery, complications following that operation was a natural assumption. To verify the initial determination, they've decided to do an autopsy, or at least to the extent one can now be performed."

"That's crazy. Kind of disrespectful to disturb a body after it's already in its final resting place. Whatever. Not my problem. I suppose if someone took Mabel's life deliberately, they need to pay for their actions. As exasperating as she could be, I still believe justice should be served."

"Absolutely!" I agreed emphatically. "If Mabel's death truly was a case of neglect, or even a homicide, it's not for certain it was at the hands of a family member. It could've been anyone. Maybe even someone who lived in the neighborhood." As soon as the words were out of my mouth, I realized they'd sounded like I was questioning Itsy's innocence. After all, she'd just admitted to having issues with Mabel.

Itsy's amicable expression morphed into one of distrust. I knew I'd probably want to converse with her in the future, so I didn't particularly want to piss her off at our first encounter.

"Those purple iris bulbs should multiply quickly," I said, faking a sudden interest in her flower-planting project. "What a beautiful border they'll make along your driveway in a year or two. Do you dig your bulbs up in the fall and store them inside over the winter?"

Itsy's tenseness gradually eased and we chatted a few more minutes about flowers and a few other mundane subjects, such as what time the mail carrier normally delivered the mail on South Hart Street and the upcoming postage rate increase.

"I just purchased an entire roll of the 'forever' stamps," I said. "I wanted to stock up on them before the price went up again."

"At this stage in our lives, isn't that kind of like buying green bananas?"

I laughed at her quip and bade her adieu, telling her I looked forward to visiting with her again once we'd gotten settled into the Heart Shack. I expected her to echo my sentiments.

"Silly name for an old house, if you ask me," Itsy said instead before we parted ways.

CHAPTER 15

◆

A knock on the front door caught me off-guard. I'd been about to step up onto a chair in hopes of being able to reach the drapery rods to bring them down.

"Anybody home?" A deep, gravelly voice resonated from the foyer. It was a warm, friendly voice that made me not hesitate to welcome the visitor.

"In here!" I replied. I'd been expecting a representative from the local inspection department and assumed that's who'd come calling.

I nearly choked on my own saliva when a tall, well-built man with wide shoulders walked into the drawing room. With dark hair, piercing blue eyes, a chiseled chin, and a broad, white-toothed smile, he was the most attractive human being I'd ever laid eyes on. This epitome of masculinity could grace the cover of *Playgirl Magazine*. I know I'd buy two copies myself: one to gaze at and the second as a spare, in case my eyes burned a hole through the first one. "Howdy!"

"Good afternoon, ma'am." He glanced at the wobbly wooden chair next to me. "Looks like I arrived just in time to lend a hand. Standing on that chair's probably not a good idea for someone your…"

"Age?" I supplied the word when he stopped short of finishing his remark.

"No, that's not what I was going to say," he replied, without further clarification. With a grin, he added, "It doesn't look safe for a person of any age to stand on."

When I returned his engaging smile, I could tell I had a goofy grin on my face. Even though the man was obviously younger than my daughter, there was no escaping the magnetic effect of his devastating charm and appearance, no matter your age. My gaze locked with his. Looking away was like trying to let go of a live electric wire.

Trying not to sound like a blooming idiot, I introduced myself and explained why I was there. He acted as if he was genuinely engrossed in what I had to say. When he didn't respond with his own introduction, I asked, "Are you here to approve the punch list so the Wiley Burke Construction crew can commence with the repairs?"

"No."

The man's response wasn't very informative so I stared into his bluer-than-blue eyes and waited patiently for him to elaborate on why he *was* there. I was beginning to feel uncomfortable about the man's unexplained presence.

Appearing uneasy himself, he finally said, "I just dropped by to see how things were progressing on the house."

"Why?" I asked wearily. His justification seemed to me to be contrived.

"Well, you see," he began hesitantly, "for a number of years I took care of a lot of the handyman projects here for Mabel. I guess you could say I have a personal interest in the preservation of this historic home."

"Really?" I asked, dumbstruck by his explanation. Did that mean the tiny Irish man I'd met wasn't the real caretaker Sydney had been doubtful even existed? Recalling what she'd told me earlier, I had to wonder if the widowed church choir ladies had actually met Mabel's houseguest. And, if so, had they truly believed this was the gentleman their friend was "shacking up" with? *In her dreams, maybe*, I thought. I asked the uninvited visitor, "Are you saying you were the caretaker here?"

"Um, yeah, I guess so."

"So, you must be the Ridley Wickets the neighbor lady told me about," I stated matter-of-factly.

Before he could confirm or deny my statement, it occurred to me that he could assist me with the draperies. "As the caretaker here, Mr. Wickets, you should be able to point me toward a ladder so I can pull down all of these dreary drapes."

"I wasn't actually Mabel's caretaker, per say."

Oh, dear! I thought. I stepped back and glanced at the opening into the foyer, judging the distance I'd have to cover to make an escape if it were to become necessary. If he wasn't the caretaker, who was he? The possibilities that rushed into my mind were terrifying. Visions of Ted Bundy, the physically attractive but monstrous, serial-killer from the seventies, zipped through my mind. I subconsciously reached for the fireplace poker.

Studying my anxious expression and defensive reactions, he took the brass poker out of my hand and spoke in a comforting tone. "It's okay, ma'am. I *was* hired by Mabel Trumbo to do some handy work. However, I was just a friend willing to help out on occasion, rather than an actual caretaker."

Tomayto, tomahto! I thought with relief. I was relieved to know it was just a distinction without a difference. What Mabel called a caretaker, out of a sense of superiority, perhaps, Ridley modestly referred to as a friend helping out.

"I see." I chuckled and asked, "Did you know she referred to you as her caretaker to her friends?"

"Well, you see, there was a misunderstanding about that which I never had the heart to bring up with Ms. Trumbo. I met her one day, several years ago, at a church function. Mabel asked me if I knew of a handyman she could hire to do a few chores for her. Since I live nearby, I offered to help out and told her I wouldn't accept payment from her because it was the neighborly thing to do."

"How thoughtful! That was very generous of you." I was relieved to discover that Ridley Wickets was not the devil in disguise, as I'd momentarily feared. Evidently he *was* the Mr. Wickets Itsy had mentioned, but not an actual caretaker. I no longer worried I might be a serial killer's next victim. In fact, instead of being a monster, the man was an absolute angel.

"It was no big deal really. But Mabel said she wouldn't feel right asking me for any assistance in the future if I didn't accept payment for my services."

"I can understand why she felt that way," I said in Aunt Mabel's defense.

"I could too. So I told her that for twenty-three dollars, I'd take care of the items she needed repaired around this place."

"Twenty-three? That seems like an unusual amount."

"It was. I deliberately made it an odd amount so she'd think I'd carefully calculated what my expenses would be. I suppose what transpired afterward was my own fault. I should've been more specific about the terms of our agreement." He laughed, clearly not troubled about the misunderstanding.

"So, Mabel accepted your offer, assuming you meant repairs needing done right then *and* any that might pop up in the future. And for the rest of her life you were at her beck and call. Am I right?"

"Yep! Something like that." Ridley chuckled again. "But, it's not as bad as it sounds. Living alone gets rather lonesome, so I enjoyed fixing things around here. She never asked me to do anything that was a major project. I did, however, repair a few things that Mabel wasn't disturbed by but concerned me greatly. For instance, a gas leak in her stove and an electrical short in the lamp next to her bed."

"Did you consider replacing the dangerously loose and deteriorated boards on the front porch and steps?"

Mr. Wickets looked down, as if ashamed. I hadn't meant to imply he should have done even more for Mabel Trumbo than he'd so generously volunteered his time, effort and resources to do. Twenty-three bucks would barely cover the cost of a hammer and box of nails these days, much less all the other expenses the repair jobs must have entailed over the years. Before I could clarify my remark, Ridley explained.

"Every board of the porch and stairs needs to be replaced. I was planning to begin that project when, all of a sudden, Mabel passed. The place needs a lot of work, as I'm sure you've discovered. It's a money pit, to be totally honest, and I could only afford to do so much."

"I'm sorry if I sounded critical. I certainly didn't mean it that way. I feel like you deserve a medal, Mr. Wickets." I detected an uneasy expression on the man's face after my last remark, but chalked it up to the fact he was the kind of stand-up guy who didn't want to be rewarded for his humanitarian efforts.

"Truly, I didn't mind helping out at all, even when at times it seemed as if she needed something fixed nearly every day. I suppose she was lonely, too, and welcomed the company, if only for the few minutes it took me to change a bulb, replace a furnace filter, or knock down a spider web."

"Well, it was extremely kind of you. I can only imagine how lonely I'd be if I lost my husband, which I nearly did recently when he experienced a cardiac episode." If I'd been in Mabel Trumbo's shoes, I might have found something that needed fixing every other day, too, just for the pleasure of this kind man's company. He would've been a nice treat for the aging eyes, as well.

However, even as tight as I am, I wouldn't have felt right not paying the man for his labor and the necessary materials. And I don't mean twenty-three dollars. I mean what he actually earned for his work. "I suppose she enjoyed telling people she had a tall, handsome caretaker on the payroll, too. Don't you think?"

"I don't know about handsome, but I suspect so." Ridley replied with a wry grin. "I recall a number of times being introduced to one of her lady friends after she'd call me over to look at some insignificant thing. Like the time she had a drawer pull in dire need of tightening. When I arrived, I was suddenly the center of attention at a luncheon she was hosting for our church choir. Involvement with the church was the one exception to her otherwise reclusive lifestyle."

Ah-ha! I thought. Mabel's friends *were* familiar with her so-called caretaker. They all attended the same church. The two "least likely to cohabitate" parishioners must have been the most popular subject of the church's gossip grapevine if the bulk of the choir believed Mabel's story.

Before I accidentally made an inappropriate comment, I motioned toward the Steinway in the corner. "That explains the beautiful grand piano. By the looks of the music sheet displayed on the rack, which is one of Franz Liszt's 'Hungarian Rhapsodies,' she must have been a gifted pianist."

"Yes, I suppose so, although I never heard her play it. The Steinway used to be a fixture at the Sacred Heart Catholic Church, until several years ago when the elders decided to upgrade. The remarkable acoustics of the cathedral were ideal for a Quimby pipe organ. We had a host of bake sales, car washes, a pie-eating contest, and a few other money-making events to raise the funds to purchase one. We also raffled off the piano. There were 1,626 tickets sold, bringing in nearly seven thousand dollars to go toward the new organ. And Mabel, who had only purchased one raffle ticket, had the winner."

"Wow! How lucky was that?"

"Yeah. Lucky." Ridley's tone was a mixture of ruefulness and sarcasm.

He looked away, but I caught his reflection in a framed mirror next to the fireplace. I was almost certain he'd rolled his eyes. I had to wonder if he'd hoped to win the Steinway himself. He might have bought a lot of the tickets to increase his chances, and still lost out to a lady who'd bought only one. And how often does that seem to be the case when you hear about some fortunate soul winning a huge lottery prize? Then again, maybe he thought the raffle was a foolish way to dispose of a piano whose worth was probably four or five times what the raffle collected for it. As I'd been trying to assess his expression in the mirror, I had tuned his voice out. Now I turned my attention back to Ridley as he continued to talk about the magnificent new instrument.

"The sound is absolutely amazing. If you and your husband get an opportunity to come—" Ridley stopped abruptly, as if he'd suddenly realized he was about to give away state secrets, and switched to another topic. "So what were you contemplating when I entered the room a few minutes ago. Anything I can do to help?"

Even though the screeching halt of his explanation regarding the church's pipe organ nearly made my neck snap back from the sudden about-face in momentum, like a Lamborghini going ninety to nothing in the span of two seconds, I chose not to ask what he was about to say. Instead I winked and asked, "Could I interest you in a twenty-three-dollar contract to do a little handy work around the place?"

"I am at your disposal, ma'am, but your money is no good with me," he responded. He followed his remark with a deep bow.

"Actually, I just need a ladder so I can reach the drapery rods. I'm sure I saw one out in the garage. Could I impose on you to carry it in here for me?"

"Absolutely. But I know the location of a sturdier one upstairs, which I'll go fetch."

"Thank you. I want to brighten up this dark and gloomy room with something that will let light in, like vertical blinds if I can get the cardiac center's approval."

"Blinds would look nice. With nice window coverings, this room will be cozy once the furniture is all uncovered. I'll get the drapes taken down for you, and then I'd best be on my way."

"Thanks. I'd appreciate it, Mr. Wickets."

The helpful gentleman appeared to be contemplating a response, but after a few seconds he shook his head and walked toward the staircase.

When he returned with the ladder, I decided to quiz him. Aware now that the elfin-like Irish fellow I'd encountered that morning was not actually Ridley Wickets, I was both curious and concerned about his true identity. Who was he if not the man Mabel thought of as her caretaker? Before I could question him, though, he began to quiz me.

"I know you haven't been around here much, Ms. Ripple, but have you seen anything, or anyone, that seems out of place?" Ridley asked nonchalantly as he positioned the ladder next to the window.

"Oh! Have you come across the leprechaun too?"

"The leprechaun?"

"Well, he's not an actual leprechaun, but he sure resembles one." I raised my hand to my chest to indicate the height of the little Irish guy. "Have you not seen an odd little guy around the neighborhood who's about this tall and speaks with an Irish brogue?"

With neither a yay nor a nay, Ridley asked, "Did you converse with the man?"

"We spoke briefly after he nearly scared the life out of me right here in the drawing room. He moves silently, like a cat. Well, most cats, I should say. Dolly, my sixteen-pound tabby, couldn't sneak up on a mouse if her life depended on it. It'd be like a twenty-year-old sloth trying to run down a two-year-old cheetah."

I noticed Ridley wasn't laughing along with me. Instead, he appeared impatient, as if totally uninterested in my cat's weight issues.

"Did he mention why he was here? Did he tell you his name? Or what the nature of his relationship with Mabel was?" Ridley's inquiries were more in the nature of an interrogation than a run-of-the-mill interest in the comings and goings of the Heart Shack, but they convinced me he'd never met the Irish intruder.

"Everything about him was unusual. As a matter of fact, he pretended to be you. He insinuated he'd been the caretaker around here for a number of years. Why do you ask?"

"Just wondering why he was here. I guess it's just second nature for me after keeping an eye out for Mabel for some time. I really have no clue why the guy you met would pretend to be me. But I wouldn't worry about him, if I were you. I certainly wouldn't make any effort to track him down and question him."

"Do you think he might harm me? Should I call the local police?"

"No. I don't believe for a moment that he's dangerous. He's probably just a nosy neighbor," Ridley said, echoing my husband's opinion. "I'll look into it for you."

"Thanks." I felt better knowing this handsome, capable man was going to try to identify the trespasser. "By the way, Ridley, I'm Rapella Ripple. My husband, Rip, and I will be staying here in the Heart Shack for approximately two months while he recovers from heart surgery."

Ridley shook my outstretched hand firmly. "Welcome to the neighborhood, Rapella. Heart Shack's kind of a silly name for this place, don't you think?"

Another déjà vu moment, I thought. His words had nearly mirrored Itsy's from my conversation with her less than an hour earlier.

After Ridley stacked all of the drapes in a neat pile on the floor, he said, "There you go, Ms. Ripple. You're all set to turn this gloom-and-doom room into a neat and sweet retreat."

"You're a poet and didn't know it, Mr. Wickets," I replied with a smile. "I am most appreciative of your kindness, and your long reach."

"Happy to help." As he spoke, he withdrew a wadded-up slip of paper out of his front pocket. He straightened the strip of paper out as best he could and wrote "564-555-0206" on the back of it. "Here's my number if you need any help. Also, if you do hear anything new about Mabel's death, please drop a dime on me. I heard they're exhuming her body to perform an autopsy. Anonymous tip, or not, it seems a little disrespectful to me. Not to mention, totally unnecessary. Regardless, we had a special relationship, and I'd like to be kept in the loop."

"I'll make sure you're kept up to date. I was glad to hear the real story about Mabel's caretaker. Her niece, Sydney, will be interested to hear the truth too."

Ridley's face was unreadable. I was usually good at interpreting expressions, but this was an exception. I'd been about to inquire about his relationship with Mabel's next-door neighbor, but something in his demeanor stopped me. He may not want to share details with me any more than Itsy had. I'd try to wring it out of the woman the next time I had the chance to chat with her.

"Well, I'll let you get back to your work." Ridley realigned the neatly-folded stack of draperies while speaking, as if he was either nervous or afflicted with OCD. "I'll probably drop in and check on you now and then in case you need some help with something or just need a fellow with a long reach—if that's all right, of course."

"If that's all right?" I repeated his last few words in disbelief. "Mister, you are welcome to stop by any time you feel like donating a little elbow grease to the cause."

Ridley picked up the ladder and started to walk toward the staircase, but then stopped and turned back to face me. "Your last remark reminded me of something I'd been meaning to do. Every door in this house needs to have its hinges greased. If I don't take care of lubricating them right now, I'm apt to forget. Mind if I take care of that little chore tonight? Otherwise, the squeaking sound every time a door is opened or closed will drive you crazy within a week."

I wanted to let him in on a little secret. Stopping the doors from squeaking was but a drop in the bucket when it came to everything about this house that was driving me crazy. But I was all for having him silence the nerve-wracking squeaks. "That'd be awesome! I put a can of graphite spray in with my cleaning supplies this morning."

"Graphite can coat the floor with a black powder, which can do a number on light carpet, like that in the bedrooms. The stain left behind is nearly impossible to remove."

"Well, in that case, there may be a can of WD-40 under the sink. Let me go see if—"

"No, no. This would be a good opportunity to try out some plumber's grease I just bought. It's very light and stable enough not to run off the hinges like some of the lubricating oils. I've heard plumber's grease lasts significantly longer than silicone spray, which is also a good option. On the other hand, silicone spray is less sloppy. Automobile grease will also—"

"Whoa!" I interrupted him because I didn't have the time or patience to sit through a long drawn-out dissertation on the pros and cons of different lubricants. "You don't have to justify your choice. I trust you to make the correct one."

"Okay, good. Then plumber's grease it will be."

"That'd be great. I think I saw a container of that stuff under the kitchen sink."

"On second thought, I believe silicone would be the best option."

"Don't have any of that, I'm afraid." I didn't care if the handsome, but incredibly indecisive, gentleman used a fistful of grease off one of the axles under our Chevy truck. I just wanted to be able to mark that time-consuming task off my to-do list.

"I have some. I'll run home to fetch it and be back in a while."

"Sounds good. I'll be here another couple of hours, most likely."

"Oh, really?" Ridley looked at his watch as he spoke. The wheels in his head seemed to be working overtime. No doubt he had a stressful job like so many other people. His next remark convinced me that my assumption was correct. "Actually, I won't be able to get back until later. I almost forgot I have a work-related meeting I need to attend in about forty-five minutes."

"If you don't mind me asking, what do you do for a living?"

Apparently he did mind me asking, because he simply replied, "Let's just say I have a very powerful boss who is always looking over my shoulder. He doesn't miss a single thing."

I was a little flustered about why he didn't just say whether he was a teacher or an attorney, or even a Chippendale dancer, which did not seem to be beyond the realm of possibility. But I didn't have time to dwell on it. "I assume you still have a key?"

"Well, no, not anymore. I tossed it after Mabel passed, not expecting to have a need for a key to the place again."

"Then I'll leave mine under the welcome mat when I leave."

"Not a good idea. It's the first place a burglar would look, Rapella."

We agreed to hide the key ring behind a bristly briar bush alongside the front steps. I'd leave it there for him when I left, and he'd return it to the same spot after he'd finished up his hinge-greasing project.

"Thanks again, Ridley," I said.

"My pleasure. I'll return the ladder to the store room and then see myself out."

After he'd ascended the stairs with the step-ladder, I withdrew the piece of paper Mr. Wickets had written his phone number on and noticed it was a sales receipt from a pharmacy for a refill of the same depression medication Rip had taken for six or seven months after his retirement. Our decision to become full-time RVers is what had helped him get off the costly drug. I refolded the receipt and placed it in my wallet for safekeeping in case I needed to contact the man in the future.

As I was looking around, trying to decide where to start, I noticed a pair of sunglasses lying on the fireplace mantel which I assumed had been left behind by Mr. Wickets. He must've been holding his shades in his hand when he'd first entered the room, because I recalled being so mesmerized by his startling blue eyes that a bulldozer could have scooped up the sofa and driven off with it for all I'd have noticed. I placed the sunglasses in a more prominent place so he'd see and retrieve them when he left that night after completing his hinge-lubricating project.

I went back over the events of the day in my mind while I

ran a dust rag over the furniture. As I uncovered all of the furniture and piled up the plastic tarps to put on the curb on my way out, I felt an overwhelming compulsion to dig further into the truth behind Mabel's death, not only for Sydney Combs sake, but to satisfy my growing curiosity, as well.

As my last chore for the evening, I needed to feed the two animals and take Gallant outside for a walk. I'd Googled the song Sydney had recommended, and found the lyrics to the song by the Baha Men group. But I couldn't figure out how repeating the words "Who Let the dogs out? Who? Who?" over and over could be sung in a calming, melodious manner. Or in any manner, for that matter.

I sang "Poor Unfortunate Souls" from The Little Mermaid soundtrack instead, and was thankful when Goofus instantly stopped squawking and bobbing. As if he'd just been shot with a tranquilizer dart, the bird became completely still. One might have thought he was playing the mannequin game, a silly trend that was currently sweeping the nation. I gently opened his cage and reached inside to fill his water bottle and food bowl. I was relieved to come away unscathed. After I closed the door and ceased my off-key warbling, Goofus hollered, "Tanks you!"

I was offended by the bird's sarcasm. I knew without a doubt it was not a "thank you for singing to me," but rather "thank you for stopping that god-awful noise before my ears began to bleed".

While I walked Gallant, I thought back to my conversation with Ridley Wickets earlier in the evening. On more than one occasion, he'd deliberately stopped short of telling me something he'd suddenly thought better of. *What had he not told me?* I wondered. *And, more importantly, why?*

What could the man possibly have to hide? What did he know that he wasn't sharing with me? Did he also have a reason to suspect there was more to Mabel's death than met the eye?

I'd have to find a way to entice him back to Mabel's house while I was there, I decided. I could call him in the morning to thank him for taking care of the squeaky door hinges. If I couldn't come up with something to coax him over by then, there was always the possibility of a drawer pull in the kitchen in desperate need of being tightened. If that ploy worked for Mabel, maybe it'd work for me, as well.

After I brought Gallant back inside and gave him a treat, or what I like to refer to as poop pay, I started to gather my things to depart. As I was picking up the last of my cleaning supplies, the lights began to flicker. They went on and off in a pattern. It was as if someone was trying to communicate with me in Morse code. There were three long time-periods of light in the middle of two groups of three really short periods. It was like dit-dit-dit, dot-dot-dot, dit-dit-dit in flashing lights rather than sound.

Suddenly I realized the blinking pattern spelled S.O.S. in Morse code. Did someone need help? If so, who? Then it hit me like a wrecking ball. *Maybe it's me who needs help*, I thought. *Like at a psychiatric hospital, perhaps.*

I thought back to what the leprechaun look-alike had said earlier. "She comes to call on me and my mates." Could it be that Mabel truly had been murdered and was now haunting the house? Had she come to call on me, asking for my help in seeing that whoever had taken her life was arrested and punished for their crime? Or was I losing my mind and starting to imagine things? I could have just dreamt I met and chatted with the little elfin guy. It would have been one unbelievably vivid dream, but I might have been under more stress than I realized. Maybe an appointment with a psychiatrist wasn't such a bad idea.

To appease my vivid imagination, I grabbed the fireplace poker off the tool rack on the hearth once again and went from room to room, covering the entire bottom floor. I found nothing to explain the flickering lights. I decided the long, stressful day really was causing my mind to play tricks on me. I convinced myself the flickering was due to nothing more than a short in a wire. Ridley had said he'd fixed electrical shorts in the house before but I had no clue where the breaker box was.

The idea the wiring in the house could be older than I was, and the fact that burning to death due to an electrical fire wasn't on my bucket list at the moment, made me wonder if it was too soon to call Ridley and ask him to check it out while he was working on the hinges that evening. But I was afraid he'd think I was a bigger pill than Mabel had been, so I ignored it.

With the brass poker in hand, I walked up the stairs as quietly as possible, tip-toed softly down the hallway, and glanced into each room. There was no way to prevent the creaks in the floorboards, so sneaking up on an interloper was out of the question. I stopped abruptly when I detected the sound of music. I recognized the tune as *The Dance of the Sugar-Plum Fairies*. It sounded like the song was being played using bells.

At that point, a person who was playing with a full deck of cards would've flown down the stairs and out the front door. But as if I had a pair of jokers missing, I was compelled to find the origin of the sound. I followed the musical bells all the way down the long hallway to the farthest bedroom. When I walked in, I saw a tiny ballerina figurine twirling inside an open music box that was sitting on the top of a chest of drawers. I picked up the music box to see if I could determine how it could suddenly begin to play of its own accord and found an index card lying across the bottom. YOU DON'T BELONG HERE was written across the card in bright red lettering.

I gasped at the message, which felt like a direct threat to me. I dropped the card like a red-hot poker. The real poker, still in my left hand, suddenly felt like an inadequate weapon. What troubled me the most was its resemblance to the nightmare I'd recently had. How do you defend yourself against an unknown, unseen, opponent?

I then glanced inside the music box to see if anything else was in it and discovered the gold and jade ring Rip had recently purchased for me. Trying not to faint in fright, I lifted my right hand and saw a bare ring finger. Then I recalled I'd taken the ring off to protect it from the strong, abrasive, chemicals I'd used for cleaning. I'd set it on the marble table in the foyer where the roach clip had once been, which I realized now was a foolish thing to do. Next time, I'd put it in my pocket where it'd be more secure. After the traumatic recent events, the ring had much sentimental value to me, I was so thankful to have it back in my possession, even if I hadn't even been aware it was missing.

After slipping my ring on, I turned and ran down the hallway. When I reached the top of the stairs, the house suddenly went dark, as if someone had thrown the main breaker to the building, another odd reminder of my bad dream. Not wanting to make a misstep and go ass-over-appetite all the way down the staircase, I sat on my rump and slithered down the stairs like a snake. I dropped the fireplace tool on the floor as I dashed through the drawing room, snatched my purse off the piano, and was out of the house in the space of five seconds. It was as if the missing pair of jokers had been returned to my deck, and I had come to my senses when I'd read the note and found my ring. I couldn't get out of that house quick enough. That note was definitely a personal threat. Someone wanted me gone—like yesterday!

Whoever was in the house could've easily made off with the expensive piece of jewelry and my purse as well, but robbery evidently wasn't their intent. Scaring me off the property was!

There are no such things as ghosts, I told myself as I hurried to the truck. *And there are no such things as haunted houses. Man, do I need a stiff drink when I get back to the Chartreuse Caboose. Two would even be better.*

On the drive back to the RV park, I couldn't shake the notion that no one else had been in the house that evening except for me and Ridley Wickets. Who besides the handy man could have snatched my ring off the table in the foyer, placed it in the box, and activated the ballerina and music? I tried to recall hearing him exit out the front door, and couldn't. Perhaps he'd not actually left when he'd told me he'd show himself out. Had I completely misjudged the man and his intentions?

The truth behind Mabel Trumbo's death was getting curiouser and curiouser, and my increasingly persistent compulsion to do some personal investigating was becoming difficult to ignore.

CHAPTER 16

Sydney Combs stopped me early the next morning when I passed by the nurse's station at the cardiac center on my way to see Rip. "Do you know who was looking through my aunt's file cabinet in the Heart Shack last night?"

"No," I replied. "But I do know someone was there and tried to scare me into leaving. Successfully, I might add. I'm not certain it's safe for me to return."

"What?" Sydney looked genuinely alarmed. "What happened?"

I explained the incident with the jewelry box that had nearly caused my heart to stop. Sydney claimed to have no idea what or who was behind my terrifying experience. She was confident it was connected to her own troubling experience earlier that morning, however. "Oh, my! I'm so sorry you were frightened like that, Rapella."

"Me too. So what were you saying about your aunt's file cabinet?"

"I stopped by the house after my shift ended to see if you were still there. When I walked into the storeroom, I discovered all of my aunt's file folders had been rifled through. Can you think of anyone who might've done that?" By the tone of Sydney's voice, I had an uneasy feeling she thought I might have been snooping through her aunt's stuff.

"The only person I can think of who might be responsible for both issues would be Ridley Wickets. He stopped by—"

"Who?"

"Ridley Wickets was your aunt's caretaker."

"He stopped by the Heart Shack again?"

"Yes, but it was the real caretaker this time, Sydney, not the Irish imposter."

"What?" Sydney looked at me as if I'd just told her the real caretaker reminded me of Alice Cooper, complete with a Hawaiian lei made out of tulips, who'd I'd discovered tip-toeing through her aunt's storeroom the previous night. Stunned, she repeated herself. "What?"

"It appears the real Ridley Wickets is a very charming, handsome man in his forties, I'd say. He was as confused as I was about the little guy who reminded me of a leprechaun. We chatted and Mr. Wickets seemed very kind and thoughtful. Helped me out a bit by—"

"I don't understand," Sydney said. I wanted to tell her she'd understand better if she'd let me finish and quit interrupting me. Instead, I bit my tongue and listened as she continued. "Why would he try to scare you away? Why would he snoop through stuff in the basement storeroom? He lived there for a number of years and could've pilfered through my aunt's things any time he pleased. I'd have thought he would've moved out after my aunt's passing."

"According to Ridley, he never lived in the home to begin with and—"

"No, I'm almost certain Aunt Mabel said he occupied a spare—"

"Ridley explained to me that he had just stopped by your aunt's house on occasion to repair, replace, and restore things that needed attention. His said his rates were quite reasonable. She paid him a grand total of twenty-three dollars for several years' worth of on-call service. Didn't she ever mention his fee to you?"

"No. For whatever reason, Aunt Mabel was very evasive about her caretaker, but insisted he wasn't merely a fabrication. She never even told me his name was Ridley Wickets. Did he indicate the purpose of his visit yesterday?"

"I got the impression it was primarily for nostalgic reasons. He's interested in seeing the house preserved. After we chatted, he helped me take the drapes down. He then volunteered to take care of all of the squeaky doors in the place, and naturally I jumped all over his offer. He had to leave for a work-related meeting, but I hid the key ring you gave me so he could come back to lubricate all of the hinges after I left. As you've probably noticed, they squeaked like a mouse with its tail caught in a door jamb. I have no idea why Mr. Wickets would be looking in her file cabinet, though."

"Had to leave for a work-related meeting, huh? Yeah, right. The guy was obviously scouring through those files for a reason, Rapella."

"Do you think that's why he wanted to frighten me off? With me out of there, he'd be free to sort through her files. You can be sure, dear, that if and when I see him again, I'll ask him about it."

"Please do. I'd like to know what he was searching for. He doesn't have permission to sort through anything in Aunt Mabel's house, or even be alone in it."

"Of course not! I'm so sorry I let him use the keys you entrusted me with."

Thinking back to our exchange, I recalled Ridley being surprised to find someone in the house. Had I temporarily thwarted his plan to scour through Mabel's files, and then handed my key over to him like some addlebrained numbskull so he could come back later and pilfer at his leisure? And if that was the case, had Ridley found whatever it was he'd been looking for? If so, what was it?

I decided not to bring it up with Sydney. For one thing, I felt embarrassed by my naivety, if that's what truly had occurred. But, I also found it difficult to believe Ridley was the kind of individual who'd snatch up my ring and put it in the music box, along with a threatening note to frighten me. If he'd wanted access to Mabel's files, he already had it. After all, I'd given him my key to the place, and assured him I'd be gone by the time he returned.

I couldn't convince myself the reason behind Mr. Wicket's visit was sinister or amounted to diddly-squat, and I didn't want Sydney getting the police department involved. Not yet, anyway. I wanted to delve into the matter myself a little before turning it into a great big, and possibly unnecessary, hullabaloo.

"Well, I'm not buying his lame excuse," Sydney said emphatically. I almost wished I hadn't even mentioned Ridley's visit. The girl had enough stress to deal with already. Her voice rose as she continued. "To sneak in like that, the man's obviously up to no good. I'm not happy about his trespassing at all! If Ridley Wickets stops by again, please ask him why he was going through my aunt's files and tell him his services are no longer needed. Make sure he knows he's not welcome in the house anymore."

"Um, okay. I'll do that." I was uncomfortable about the idea of banishing him from the house or grilling the nice gentleman as to why he'd gone through Mabel's stuff uninvited. I couldn't be positive it had even been him who'd scoured through the file cabinet. Having helped Mabel out with repairs around the home for several years, he surely wouldn't feel like an interloper when he walked in uninvited. I wouldn't have. "By the way, Sydney, what did you need to see me about last night when you stopped by?"

"I, uh, well, um, I just wanted to make sure you were getting along okay. Didn't want you overdoing it or anything."

"I'm not, but thanks for your concern. I'll admit, though, that I'm hesitant to go back to the house now that I know someone doesn't want me there."

I noticed Sydney looked away as we talked, as if she were unable to meet my eyes. I wasn't sure I was buying her story any more than she professed to be buying

Ridley's. How could Sydney have noticed the file folders had been disturbed unless she'd gone down to the storeroom herself? What was she hoping to discover down there? She hadn't mentioned to me she'd be stopping by. Although I didn't want to even entertain the notion, I had to wonder if she might have been behind the music box incident. Could there be a reason she was already regretting her offer to let us stay there? I shook my head. *Don't be silly, Rapella*, I thought. *You're letting your imagination overtake your good sense.*

"If Mr. Wickets left the keys behind the briar bush as promised, I assure you I won't let the keys out of my sight from now on."

"Thanks, Rapella. I wouldn't worry too much about the note you found. Whoever left it had every opportunity to harm you if that was their intention. But they didn't, so they're obviously just trying to scare you away. I'm sure that's all there is to it."

"That's all?" I asked. "Isn't that enough?"

"Don't let them get to you. You have every right to be in my aunt's house. It's the note-writer who doesn't belong there." As Sydney walked away, I noticed a look of apprehension on her face, as if she was carrying the weight of the world on her shoulders. I hated that she was under so much pressure. I vowed to get the truth out of Ridley Wickets soon, if only to help alleviate her stress. And mine, too, of course.

After a brief visit with Rip that afternoon, who was scheduled to be released the following day, I reluctantly headed to the Heart Shack to take care of Goofus and Gallant. I was relieved to find the keys exactly where Mr. Wickets had agreed to leave them.

As I walked into the kitchen, Gallant ambled over to have his head caressed. He was happy to see me. Goofus, however, was just plain rude.

"Don't need your help!" Was my greeting from the annoying cockatoo. "Schwam! Go home!"

"If I go home, Goofus, who's going to feed your unappreciative ass?"

"Unprissy ass! Shut up, Goofus. Stupid bird. Unprissy ass. Woo-hoo."

"It's unappreciative, not unprissy. Do you have to repeat everything you hear, Goofus?"

"Stupid bird! Stupid bird! Woo-hoo! Go away, dumb dog!"

I heard Gallant whimpering behind me. I patted his massive head as he drooled all over my shoes. "Don't take it personally, Gallant. You are a sweetheart, but your brother is a bad, bad boy!"

"Bad boy. Bad, bad boy! Can't eat that. Scwam Sam!" The bird chanted behind me.

I calmed Goofus down by humming a Disney tune I'd remembered from when Regina was a child. While he was momentarily chilled out, I filled his water bottle and food bowl. When I finished the task, I stopped singing.

"Scuse you!" The bird repeated several times before banging its head against the cage.

Excuse me? I knew my singing was dreadful, but Goofus didn't have to be boorish about it. Just in case, I checked to see if he had blood running out of his ears.

"You really are a bad boy, Goofus!" I said, staring straight into the bird's beady eyes. "I have a mind not to feed you again until you apologize."

"Unprissy ass! Don't need you! Vamoose," was the bird's unconcerned response.

"We'll see about that! You know, maybe I *should* feed you, Goofus—to that Doberman pinscher that lives across the street!" I turned to snap the leash on Gallant's collar, knowing he was anxious to get outside to relieve himself. "Let's go, Gallant. Your brother needs a time out."

"Dwop dead!" I heard as Gallant and I went out the kitchen door to the backyard.

After a restless night, I headed to the hospital early the next morning. At the nurses' station, Nurse Combs informed me that Dr. Murillo would be making a final assessment about Rip's release when he made his rounds around eleven. She also told me that both the construction crew and the cleaning crew were slated to begin work that day. She'd asked if I'd be around to let them into the house, and I'd assured her I'd make certain I was.

"Good," she said. "I'll stop by on Thursday to see how the work's going and check in on my favorite patient."

"Okay," I replied, and then jokingly added, "I'll warn him!"

In the meantime, I'd see if I could locate Ridley Wickets so I could supply some answers for Sydney when she stopped by later in the week. I'd track down the Irish fellow too if at all possible.

CHAPTER 17

I'd been understandably nervous when I returned to the Heart Shack that morning. But the house was quiet, and there was nothing amiss that I could detect. While I waited for the workers to arrive, I descended the dark staircase off the kitchen to the basement. The wooden steps were unstable and creaked eerily. I took Gallant with me for peace of mind and we finally found the storeroom in a remote corner of the basement. It was not easily accessible.

I was taken aback at the state of disarray in that dank, musty room. Every drawer in the file cabinet had been emptied, along with the contents of a roll-top desk and two storage cabinets. Clearly, someone had gone through everything with a fine-toothed comb. It looked as if a tornado had roared through the basement overnight.

I knew it was possible that someone other than Sydney or Ridley had participated in the frantic search that had left the room in such a mess. It wasn't inconceivable that the leprechaun, who could appear and disappear without warning, had been behind it. Then again, it might've been the owner of the disappearing roach clip, who was probably Tasman. It could've even been the individual who'd left the intimidating message in the music box. Were he and the roach-clip owner one and the same? Did Ridley scour through Mabel's stuff after pulling off the music box prank? Or, God forbid, was Sydney responsible for the nasty note, as well as the chaos in the storeroom?

Suspense and intrigue were mounting. But one thing was certain; whoever had trashed the storeroom had obviously been on the hunt for something that meant a great deal to them.

Gallant suddenly began to growl. I pulled him closer to my side and tightened my hold on his collar. Whether it was an intruder that'd caught his attention, or simply a marauding mouse, I wasn't hanging round to find out. I practically drug the huge canine up the rickety stairs to the main floor.

I soon realized the search hadn't been limited to the out-of-the-way storage room. Someone had gone through closets, cabinets, and drawers in other rooms, as well. It was less evident in those rooms because the searcher had been more cautious about putting things back in order before going on to scour another area.

What did Aunt Mabel have in her possession that someone was determined to locate? Was there a rush to find the item because the heart center was soon to take legal possession of the house? Was the item worth a great deal of money? Could it be desired only for sentimental reasons? Or was there another motivating factor—perhaps sinister in nature—that caused the person to be desperate in their efforts to find and seize the item in question? Maybe the house contained evidence of a misdeed the perpetrator did not want discovered. Could that frantic person be afraid that if left behind, this incriminating item might fall into the wrong hands?

These questions whirled through my mind like a 35 mm film spinning on a reel in an empty movie theater as I straightened up the master suite in preparation for Rip's arrival. Still pondering who was behind the rummaging, I returned to the main floor. I walked through the drawing room and, as before, I felt eyes following me to the front door. A chill ran down my spine. It didn't stop until it reached my socks.

* * *

"Hallelujah!" I heard my husband say as I neared the door to his hospital room.

Dr. Murillo stood at Rip's bedside when I entered the room. "Okay, Rip. I'll have a nurse prepare your discharge papers while you get dressed. It might be an hour or so. The cardiac ward is full and two nurses are off sick, including Nurse Combs. The rest are scurrying about trying to keep up with the work load."

"Hello, Dr. Murillo," I greeted the surgeon. "No big hurry. He's been here for a number of days. What's another hour or two?"

"Easy for you to say," Rip said jokingly. He then directed his attention toward the surgeon. "I hope Nurse Combs is not seriously ill. She's been very inspirational to me."

"That's nice," the surgeon responded absentmindedly.

"Sydney stopped by my room earlier this morning," Rip said. "She must have fallen ill afterward."

"I guess so." Dr. Murillo answered in a distracted manner, as if his head nurse's health was neither here nor there. He was simultaneously reading a chart in his hand and glancing at a text on his phone. As hectic as his pace routinely seemed to be, Sydney probably could have called in with mad cow disease without it penetrating the surgeon's concentration.

"Take care of yourself, Mr. Ripple. I'll see you at your follow-up appointment next week. I've got to continue my rounds right now, but you have my card if a problem arises. Don't hesitate to call." With that, Dr. Murillo turned and briskly fled the room.

"Thanks for everything, Doc," Rip called out as the surgeon closed the door behind him.

An hour and a half later, Rip was transported to the front door of the cardiac center in a wheelchair. When he reached the sidewalk, Rip lifted his arms dramatically, exclaiming, "Free at last, free at last! Thank God Almighty, I am free at last!"

I laughed at his playfulness. "Wait here, Mr. King. I'll go get the truck and pick you up at the curb."

"Hey look, Rapella! There's Brandy with my cup of coffee!"

I looked in the direction he'd indicated and saw the hospital volunteer Rip had put the fear of God in when she refused to bring him a hot cup of the caffeine-laden beverage. She was sipping the hot beverage from a Tervis tumbler.

"That's not her name. It's—"

"Oh, yeah. Now I remember," Rip cut in. "It's Candy, right?"

"Close enough," I replied with a sigh. I knew he'd gotten confused about the young lady's name again because of her candy-striper status, but since he'd probably never need to know or use her name again, I decided not to waste my breath reminding him that her name was Jasmine. I thanked the nurse's assistant who'd wheeled Rip down to the front door, and Rip expressed his appreciation, as well. I was thankful the assistant was back inside the building before my husband's next remark.

"Speaking of coffee, now that I've been sprung, there's nothing to stop me from stopping at the first convenience store and scoring a steaming cup of hot brew."

"Actually, honey, there *is* one thing to stop you."

"What's that?"

"Your wife."

We could hear a loud clamor emanating from the Heart Shack when we turned the corner on to South Hart Street. It did my heart good to know the construction crew was on the job and the cleaning crew was due to arrive soon.

Rip's eyes widened at first sight of the bright red, rambling mansion. He opened his mouth to speak but nothing came out.

"Cat got your tongue?" I asked him playfully.

"It's even more shocking in person than in the photos you showed me. Kind of overwhelming, isn't it?" Rip said as he stared at the structure in awe. It was as if he'd just seen a mirage in the middle of the Sahara Desert and was waiting for it to disappear.

"Yes. It really is. I'm not sure the red paint job was the best idea in the world, but no one could say it doesn't make an impact."

"That's for sure. Speaking of a cat having my tongue, where's Dolly?"

"She's coming with the Chartreuse Caboose this afternoon."

"Oh, gosh. I'd forgotten about the trailer. I guess I need to go hook it up and drive—"

"Nope," I said.

"But, Rapella, you've never hooked the trailer up before."

"Relax. It's all taken care of. Dave and Cindy Miller, the couple parked in the site next to us at the RV park, offered to tow the trailer here this afternoon."

"That's very thoughtful of them. We should treat them to dinner somewhere."

"Got it taken care of, honey. They already have plans for this evening, but they'll be joining us here for supper in a couple of weeks when they come into town for Dave's overnight sleep study test at the Neurology Institute."

"Sleep study?"

"Yes. Don't you remember the test that checks for sleep apnea, a condition you told Dr. Herron that you considered hogwash when she recommended you have one performed? Dave may have sleep apnea, just as you likely do. It'd be a crying shame to go through all of this cardiac surgery and rehab only to stop breathing in the middle of the night because of some 'hogwash' condition you refused to be evaluated for."

"Get back to the Muehlers," Rip instructed. I just shook my head and didn't bother to correct him on the couple's name.

"They should arrive with Dolly and the Caboose around four. And, honey, you don't need to be going out to a restaurant quite yet. Your recuperation has really only just begun. Which reminds me, I'll be driving you to your first rehab session this afternoon at two."

"Say what? *This* afternoon? Are you kidding me?" Rip looked flabbergasted, as if I'd just told him he needed to put a new roof on the house before sundown. "Wow! There really *is* no rest for the weary, is there? You'd think they'd give me at least one day to get settled back into real life before forcing me to—"

"Forcing you to do what, Rip? Forcing you to do what's necessary to recover fully so you can go on with your life and be physically capable to participate in all of the things you enjoy doing?"

"Aha! I think I just figured out what was wrong with Nurse Ratched today. You swallowed her, didn't you? I can actually hear Sydney every time you open your mouth to speak."

"Yes, that's exactly what happened, and don't you forget it! Now let's get cracking. There's no time to rest on your laurels. You've got a two o'clock appointment you can't afford to be late for. I'll be dragging you kicking and screaming to the truck if I have to. There is a bit of good news, however."

Rip perked up instantly. "Really? What's that?"

"You got Nurse Combs' first name right for once."

"Oh, joy." And with his disgruntled response, Rip perked down just as quickly as he'd perked up.

I got Rip settled into the recliner in the master suite and went down to the kitchen to prepare a casserole so it'd be ready to pop in the oven later on. Not knowing how long the rehab session would take, I didn't want to put it off until after our return, particularly with the Millers dropping off the trailer around four. I took Gallant outside so he could take care of business, and fed both pets. For once, Goofus was quiet. He looked as if he was brooding, but I knew he was probably shaken up by the commotion and noise of the construction workers. I thought about recording the racket on my phone so I could play it every time I had to open up the sassy bird's cage.

"No worries, Goofus. They'll be done and out of here in

a couple of days. And I'm not going to sing to you this morning."

Now I realize it's harder to judge a bird's demeanor by his expression than it is a person's. But the look on Goofus's face was clearly one of gratitude. As I closed the door to his cage, I said, "Listen here, brat! I don't enjoy listening to you any more than you like listening to me. You should be thankful I'm not letting you starve to death. You don't want to die of STD, like Rip thought he might, do you?"

"Go away, bwat!" Goofus said softly while remaining still. "Prissy ass."

"You're exasperating, but you're certainly a quick learner."

"Go away, you old bwag! Don't need your help!"

"Did you just call me an old bag?" I asked the cheeky cockatoo.

"Old bwag. You old bwag."

"Okay, fine. Why don't you feed yourself tomorrow then? And, while you're at it, you dumbass bird, feed your brother, too, and let him outside to take a big dump."

"Take a wump! Take a wump! Dumbass!"

Although his speech impediment had kicked in on the word *dump,* he somehow managed to enunciate the similar word, *dumb*ass, precisely. I instantly regretted my poor choice of words and told myself I'd have to be more careful what I said around Goofus. He had no filter to prevent him from repeating any phrase or word he heard. *A person could get into big trouble by saying the wrong thing around him,* I thought.

"You old dumb—"

I slammed the kitchen door behind me before the insufferable cockatoo could finish his insult.

CHAPTER 18

"I'm going to run to the store, honey," I told Rip a few minutes later. He was engrossed in an old *Gunsmoke* rerun he'd probably seen a dozen times before. "I need to pick up a few things so I can put together a salad for tonight."

"Shush," Rip said suddenly, pointing at the television screen. "Breaking news regarding the autopsy results of Mabel Trumbo's body."

"—body exhumed Monday," the news reporter was saying as I turned my attention to the television. "Autopsy reports indicate an abnormally high level of Vitamin K in the body of the late Mabel Trumbo, who'd recently undergone double-bypass surgery at a local cardiac center. The philanthropist had bequeathed her 1882 Victorian mansion to the center to be used as temporary housing for the families of heart patients. Her death has been determined to be associated with this suspiciously high Vitamin K level." The reporter turned to a renowned heart surgeon. "Dr. Gupta, can you explain to our viewers the significance of the results and how it relates to Ms. Trumbo's death?"

"Simply put, Vitamin K helps the blood to clot. That being said, having a very high level of Vitamin K works against the blood-thinning medications normally prescribed to bypass patients. Pulmonary embolism, the official cause of death, or COD, has not changed from the preliminary findings. Ms. Trumbo died from a blood clot in the lung. Sheriff Watts of the Seattle Police Department stated in a press release that foul play had been ruled out, but Ms. Trumbo's death is being investigated as a possible case of medical malpractice on the part of hospital staff."

"Thank you, Dr. Gupta," the reporter said, turning to face the camera. "Callie Barnes will look at our weather for the week when we return from these messages."

I picked up the remote control to lower the TV's volume. As usual, the sound was too loud for us to carry on a conversation because my husband refuses to wear his hearing aids. I was afraid one of the neighbors from four or five houses down the street would complain about the noise. "Why would those results be considered a possible case of medical malpractice or negligence, particularly if the cause of death remained the same?"

"Beats me. It's Thursday, isn't it? Didn't Sydney tell you she'd be stopping by this afternoon to check in on the cleaners and construction crew?"

"No. Today is Wednesday. But I'll ask her about it tomorrow. In the meantime, here's your lunch." I set the plate down on the side table next to the recliner. I was proud of the dish. "It's got to be good. I found the recipe on an app called YUM."

"YUM? Are you joking?" He stared down at the plate, as if waiting for me to laugh, pull another plate of food from behind my back, and say, "April fools, honey. Here's your Big Mac and fries. I'll be right back with your chocolate shake."

"I'm serious, Rip!" I tried to contain my irritation. After working diligently to produce a healthy meal for him, he was looking at the food as if he'd watched me scoop it up out of Dolly's litter box.

"What is it?"

"A grilled salmon filet on a bed of steamed couscous, topped with a brown butter sauce."

"On a bed of what?"

"Couscous. Small steamed balls of semolina. It's a staple food throughout much of North Africa. Like I said, I found it on an app called YUM."

"Steamed balls of what? Oh, YUM." Rip's voice reeked of sarcasm, with a heavy dose of skepticism thrown in for good measure.

Grilled salmon had never been his favorite, although he'd eat fried crappie all day long. He'd always been a meat and potatoes kind of guy, but was open to almost anything as long as it was cut from a farm animal, fried in oil, drenched in cheese, wrapped in bacon, or had "double cheeseburger" in its name. He wanted nothing to do with fancy sauces and creams, casseroles consisting of twenty or more ingredients, especially unpronounceable ones, and he absolutely turned his nose up at anything seasoned with cilantro or garnished with sprigs of parsley. I won't even start on how Rip felt about rice cakes, tofu, hummus, and seaweed. I knew getting him to try new recipes that were designed to be heart-healthy was not going to be an easy task, but I'd hoped I wouldn't have to fight him every step of the way.

Rip grumbled a few unrepeatable four-letter words. "Do you seriously expect me to eat this salmon on a glob of salmonella balls?"

"Semolina, not salmonella."

"What's the difference?" Rip asked in disgust.

"Well, for starters, semolina is not a potentially lethal bacterium."

"Thank you for small favors."

"Oh, for gosh sakes, Rip! Bag the bitching and just try it. You might actually like it. And you're going to have to start getting used to eating food that doesn't shoot straight for an artery like a well-trained homing pigeon. I'm trying to keep you alive, whether you like it or not."

"Well, at the moment, I'm not sure I like you trying to keep me alive."

Feeling unappreciated, I slammed a second door in the

space of ten minutes, before another insufferable individual could finish his insulting retort.

Keeping Rip alive might be an even harder challenge than I'd anticipated. You know what they say, don't you? You can lead a stubborn mule to water, but you can't make him drink. Or something like that. I'm sure the same theory goes for bull-headed husbands and couscous.

When I returned to the house with four bags of groceries, the cleaning crew had already called it a day, and the construction crew was packing up their tools. It was nice not to have to be wary of falling through the front porch as I carried the bags into the house. All of the bad boards had been replaced.

"Can't eat that, skid," Goofus said as I walked into the kitchen toting the groceries.

"Behave yourself, silly bird. Besides, this food's for me and my husband, not you."

"Scwam Sam. Can't eat that, skid."

"I think you mean kid, Goofus. And I must admit I prefer that to the 'old bag' you called me earlier."

The bird continued his talking and squawking as he danced around the cage. He was making up for lost time after being uncharacteristically quiet because of the construction racket all day.

After I finished putting away the groceries, Gallant strolled into the kitchen. I caressed his muzzle as I clipped the leash on to his collar.

Before the two of us could exit through the back door, the old-fashioned rotary phone on the counter rang. I picked it up and said "hello". All I could hear in the background was the sound of someone breathing. I repeated the greeting a couple of times in case the caller hadn't heard me, but to no avail. I told the caller what he could do with himself and slammed the phone down angrily, convinced it'd been some young punk making prank calls to random phone numbers.

"Okay, Gallant. Are you ready to roll?"

"Ruff! Ruff!"

* * *

We fell into a comfortable routine the following week. Rip hadn't been released to drive yet, so I drove him to rehab Monday, Wednesday, and Friday mornings, and encouraged him to do his assigned daily walking and exercises on the off days. Throughout that week, the construction crew completed their numerous projects around the place. They didn't touch the garage, but the supervisor of the crew told me there were plans to eventually raze it and put up a multi-vehicle carport in its place.

Throughout that first week of our residence in the Heart House, the cleaning crew labored hard to get the place sparkling. The dust bunnies had been relocated and the new vertical blinds brightened up the drawing room considerably.

It was now a very comfortable place for me to spend the evening hours with a good book and a quart jar full of tequila and orange juice, while Rip alternately exercised, ate, slept, and watched crime shows in the master suite. The first two he did reluctantly and with a great deal of grumbling, but the latter two he managed splendidly without complaint.

I'd spent much of the first few days in the bedroom watching over him, until he began to balk at my constant hovering.

"You don't need to watch over me like I was a knife-wielding toddler in a room full of exposed electrical outlets. Kick your feet up, honey. Get some rest before you end up in the same boat I'm in. Who's going to look after me if you're laid up? Besides, I've got my sidekick here now to keep me company." As he spoke, he caressed the head of the huge grey and white fur ball sprawled out across his lap. Dolly purred loudly and contentedly in return.

So, I did as he suggested. I did sneak upstairs and look in on him every hour or so, just to make sure he didn't need something, and to ensure that Dolly hadn't parked herself atop his slumbering face and suffocated him.

But for the most part, I enjoyed the peace and quiet and some alone time. I especially reveled in the huge space available to me. Our entire home on wheels would fit in the drawing room, with a duplicate one parked beside it. The Heart Shack consisted of more square footage than every house I'd ever lived in put together. I don't think I'd have wanted to be responsible for the upkeep of a structure this large for any length of time, but I could definitely handle it for a couple of months.

The only things that troubled me about the house were the odd sounds and unusual occurrences that defied explanation. For example, the previous day I brought a pitcher of sun tea into the drawing room and set it down on a trivet. I filled a glass with tea and took it upstairs to Rip. When I returned to the drawing room, the pitcher was empty. There was no evidence that the remaining tea had leaked out of the pitcher. It was just gone! Convinced someone was playing a trick on me, I searched the house, only to find out Rip and I were the only ones in the building.

Another eerie event was the morning I'd found Gallant sitting on the front porch whining to get inside when I'd first gone downstairs after waking up. I distinctively remembered taking him out to do his duty before I'd gone to bed the previous evening. I let Gallant in, unnerved about how he'd gotten outside. I'd then gone upstairs to dust and vacuum, put freshly laundered sheets on the bed, and scour the toilet and lavatory in the master suite. When I went downstairs forty-five minutes later, I could hear Gallant pawing at the back door, wanting inside again.

Several thoughts crossed my mind. Was someone trying to scare us away, perhaps the same individual who'd instigated the music box prank? Secondly, was there a great big doggy door somewhere in the house I hadn't discovered yet that would allow Gallant to come and go as he pleased? If so, wouldn't a doggy door big enough to allow Gallant to pass through be an open invitation to burglars, intruders, and other animals? What would keep a family of rabid raccoons from moving in and taking up residence in the Heart Shack? But the thought that bothered me the most was that I was honestly beginning to believe I was going cuckoo for cocoa puffs. I felt like I was one hallucination away from needing to be institutionalized.

In the event it wasn't merely my imagination in free fall, knowing someone had twice entered the house undetected, let Gallant outside, and then departed without letting him back in was upsetting. The lovable pooch could have wandered off and become hopelessly lost, been dog-napped by someone who wanted a massive St. Bernard to spend hundreds of dollars feeding, or been injured by a car or another animal, like that aforementioned rabid raccoon family.

Even more disconcerting was the notion Rip and I could've been axed to death as we slept, and never known anyone had been in the house until we woke up dead the next morning. And waking up dead was not something I'd signed up for when I'd accepted Sydney's offer. I'd have to ask her about who else might have a key to her aunt's house.

I was slowly getting accustomed to the unexpected noises, intermittent electrical outages, and oddities of that nature, but the day I saw a rubber dog toy fly horizontally across the room when there was no other living creature in sight, was the day I nearly called Sydney and told her Rip and I would be moving on. Immediately, if not sooner!

Rip had tried to convince me Gallant had tossed the toy while playing with it, but if the dog could sling a toy like that, he should have been signed to the Seattle Mariners pitching staff. I'd never seen Gallant tossing a toy around as if he were a rambunctious puppy. He typically exhibited about as much get up and go as Rip did. Finally, Rip calmed me down by reminding me I'd been under more pressure than normal, and the mind can do unimaginable things when it was stressed to the max.

And then the mysterious piano-playing began.

CHAPTER 19

◆

"**R**ip! Wake up!" I whispered to Rip one night as he lay in the bed beside me, sawing great big redwood logs. When I failed to rouse him, I shook him several more times. "Wake up!"

"What's wrong?" He mumbled, letting the fog clear.

"Listen."

I could clearly hear music emanating from the bottom floor.

"Listen to what?"

"Someone is playing the piano." I wasn't surprised Rip couldn't hear it. The music was barely audible to me, and I didn't have a hearing impairment that prevented me from hearing high tones like he did.

I could tell Rip thought he'd been awakened from a sound sleep in order to listen to a figment of my imagination. "I don't hear anything. You were having a dream, Rapella. Go back to sleep."

"I was not dreaming. I hadn't even fallen asleep yet. I've been tossing and turning since I came to bed. I'm telling you, Rip, there's someone playing the piano downstairs. I'm going to go see who it is."

"No. You're not going downstairs if you think there might be an intruder. I'll check it out if it'll make you sleep better." Rip groaned as he sat up in bed. I felt bad, knowing it was an effort for him so soon after having his chest split open like a watermelon on Independence Day. But I felt it was an emergency, possibly even a life-or-death situation.

As Rip leaned over to put on his slippers, he moaned a time or two before saying in a mocking manner, "I can't count the number of middle-of-the-night calls I responded to during my law enforcement career where an intruder, burglar or, on occasion, a serial killer, had broken into someone's home to play classical tunes on their piano."

"There's no call for sarcasm, Rip. If I'm not mistaken, someone's playing the Hungarian Rhapsody piece by Franz Liszt that was on the music rack of the Steinway."

"You're not familiar with 'Who Let the Dogs Out', but you recognize a Franz Liszt number?" Rip can be very persnickety when awakened from a sound sleep in the middle of the night.

"Are you going to check it out or not? I'm quite capable of doing it myself if you don't want to be bothered." At that point, I was actually hoping it *was* a serial killer pounding the ivories. Naturally, I wouldn't want the dude to hurt Rip. I only wanted to prove to my husband I hadn't gone bonkers.

"There was no one at the piano or anywhere else downstairs," Rip said when he returned to the master suite about fifteen minutes later. "I checked every room so you wouldn't make me go back down a second time."

"I heard the music stop before you even got to the staircase. Whoever was playing it obviously heard us talking and escaped out the front door before you made it down there. I understand your desire to practice caution while descending the stairs, but an intruder could have finished the song, made himself a peanut butter and jelly sandwich, eaten it while watching an old *Honeymooners* episode, and still escaped the house with his walker before you got to the drawing room. That's why I wanted to go down rather than ask you to do it."

"I wish now I'd let you," Rip grumbled. "I'm in no condition to be chasing down imaginary piano-playing villains."

"I think 'chasing' is a bit of an exaggeration." I knew I was being overly snippy. But knowing someone had let himself into the house without our knowledge was alarming and Rip's refusal to believe me had me seeing red. "Besides, it wasn't my imagination! I swear. Whoever the intruder was, he or she was talented enough to be a concert pianist."

Rip looked at me as if I'd just told him I was planning to travel to the planet Antarea with a group of aliens I'd found encapsulated in cocoons at the bottom of a friend's swimming pool. Purely to humor me, he said, "Okay, dear, whatever you say. Regardless, I've ascertained we're alone in the house now, so get some sleep."

Where's a piano-playing serial killer when you need one?

After coffee the next morning, I calculated I had just over an hour before I needed to take Rip to his Wednesday morning therapy session. I put Gallant on a leash and was going to walk him up the street to a dog park about three blocks away. I needed the exercise and knew he would benefit from it too.

"Good morning, Itsy! Beautiful day, isn't it?" I called out to my neighbor as Gallant and I headed down the sidewalk to the street.

"Yes, it is," Itsy replied. She was pulling weeds in one of her flower beds that were so small they were barely visible to the naked eye, as if they'd only germinated an hour ago. "At my age, every day I wake up is a beautiful day."

"I guess you're right. You're up and at it bright and early this morning. No wonder you have the prettiest front yard in the neighborhood."

"Thanks. I won the 'yard of the month' award three times in the last two years. Unfortunately, your crabgrass-ridden lawn is an absolute hell hole, and your obnoxious weeds are trying to invade my yard."

"You mean noxious?"

"Yeah, they're that too." Itsy laughed, but I could tell she found the infringing weeds maddening. She began to choke, then leaned over to spit a mouthful of black saliva into her flower patch. I watched with concern. She smiled, and said, "Tobacca's a natural fertilizer, you know."

I nodded in response, wondering how she kept from upchucking her entire cheek full of "tobacca".

"Yes, of course it is, Itsy," I said. "When Sydney stops by today, I'm going to ask her if the heart center would consider buying some gardening tools and a few plants. It's really not *my* lawn, but if they'll pay for the necessary items, I'll donate my time and trouble to make it look better."

Itsy nodded. Then she pulled her gardening gloves off and stood up. "Did you hear about Mabel's autopsy results on the news last night? It looks to me like the medical board's going to point the finger at Sydney, as if she was to blame for her aunt's death due to negligence in her nursing duties."

"Yes, we watched the news last night, too. Rip and I know from personal experience that Sydney couldn't be a finer, more conscientious care-giver. I hate to see the girl's life turned upside down for something she's not responsible for, don't you?"

"Yeah. I don't particularly trust Adelaide and Tasman, but I've always liked Sydney. I can't believe she's to blame in any way."

I had to agree. With years of experience and substantial training in cardiac care, how could Mabel Trumbo's vitamin K level have reached the excessive level the autopsy report had indicated while under Nurse Combs' care? On the other hand, how could Adelaide or Tasman have been involved in their aunt's death if the official cause was pulmonary embolism?

I couldn't put the pieces together. Yet. But I was determined to try, for Sydney's sake. If Rip came through this cardiac episode in one piece, as it appeared he would, I had the nurse to thank more than anyone else, with the exception of Dr. Murillo. "You may be on to something, Itsy. I hadn't considered the possibility of Sydney's siblings trying to frame her; intentionally killing their aunt in such a way it'd appear as if it was due to Sydney's negligence as their aunt's primary care giver. They seemed to think they were in line to each inherit a third of the proceeds from selling their aunt's house, and obviously feel it's Sydney's fault they won't get a dime out of it."

The expression on Itsy's face prompted me to inquire about the extent of the deceased woman's estate. "Do you know if she had a lot of money invested that the Combs' kids stood to inherit? Did she own anything else of great monetary value they might have believed they had coming their way?"

"Possibly," Itsy said. After a long pause, she added, "But I can't say for certain. I don't honestly know what she had in her possession."

I thought it an odd answer, but I didn't press the lady further, as she appeared to be in deep thought. The possibility of a frame-up was something to mull over. I was happy to discover I had a neighbor who liked to gossip. I'm not a rumormonger myself, of course. But that doesn't mean I don't like being kept in the loop.

"By the way, Itsy, did you happen to see anyone coming or going from Mabel's house last night?"

"No. And I was sitting out on my front porch until about eleven, like I often do on mild evenings. Why do you ask?"

I started to tell her about the piano-playing I'd heard in the middle of the night, but decided better of it. I didn't want the nice neighbor to think I'd recently escaped from the funny farm, so instead I asked, "Did you happen to be sitting out on your porch the night before Mabel passed away?"

"Yep. I remember that night well. It was a Sunday. Tasman had been looking after Mabel all day because the day nurse was off on Sundays, and Sydney had a long shift at the heart center. I saw Sydney stop by, probably on a break from work, around five. Tasman came out of the house about ten minutes later. He raced up the sidewalk to his car like the place was on fire and cases of fireworks inside the house were about to light up the sky. He looked stoned, as usual."

"Are there cases of fireworks inside the house somewhere?" The thought troubled me. I wasn't sure I wanted to be living in a house that might turn into a Fourth of July display at any given moment.

"Nah. I just meant he had skates on in his rush to leave."

"Tasman had skates on?"

"It's just a saying, Rapella. Good grief. I'll try to be more literal so you can keep up," Itsy shook her head in frustration, as if she was trying to communicate with someone who was dense as a vat of mercury. And here I thought *I* was the master of clichés and colloquialisms. Itsy used phrases I'd never even heard before. I shook my head, and asked, "Is that all you saw?"

"Yep. Just after Tasman drove away, I went inside to get a bite to eat. I didn't see what time Sydney left."

"Do you reckon Tasman had something to do with his aunt's death—after Sydney left, I mean? Like you said, I'm sure she just stopped by for a quick moment to check on Mabel, and then had to get back to the hospital to finish her shift. Or, maybe she spelled Tasman just long enough for him to run an errand. Sydney indicated she never felt comfortable leaving him alone with their aunt, but she didn't have much of a choice."

Itsy shrugged. "Yeah, he could've played a part in how Mabel gave up the ghost, I guess. Iffen, that is, there turns out to be something amiss about how she kicked that oxygen habit of hers. Whatever the case, Mabel's using a stepladder to pick dandelions now."

Itsy definitely had a colorful way with words. As I grimaced at her gallows humor, Itsy leaned over and pinched the blossom off a dandelion. It was as if the yellow weed reminded her of the euphemism about being deceased.

I didn't want to ask her about whether or not Mabel had actually been on oxygen, lest she think I was still having trouble keeping up with her. "Speaking of ghosts, Itsy, did Mabel ever mention anything about her house being haunted? Did she say anything about odd, unexplainable things going on like flickering lights, unusual noises, or disappearing leprechauns in the drawing room?"

"Not that I recollect. She certainly never mentioned anything about disappearing leprechauns. Mabel was one egg short of a carton but even so, she wasn't *that* much of a nut job. I'm kind of starting to wonder about you though."

"That makes two of us! Three, if you count my husband. You sure didn't care for Mabel very much, did you?" I asked.

Itsy shrugged again. "Let's just say we had our differences."

"Like what?"

Without answering my question, Itsy knelt down to resume her weeding. "You best be getting along, Rapella. I've got work to do. Besides, old Gallant there looks like he's about to drop a load, and I don't want him dropping it here. I'm very particular about how my lawn is fertilized."

I decided to walk Gallant in another direction. Ridley had indicated he went to the same church as Mabel, Sacred Heart Catholic Church on Falmouth Street. It was farther from the Heart Shack than I'd anticipated, but we came to it just as I was about to turn around. Gallant and I continued a little farther so I could make out what was on the sign in front of the ornate building.

The sign read "Join us for Wednesday evening mass. Wal-Mart is not the only saving place." It was nice to see the powers-that-be at Sacred Heart displaying a sense of humor. We walked to the other side of the sign, the side facing the traffic coming down Second Street. "Honk if you love Jesus. Text while driving if you want to meet him. Wednesday night worship 7:00."

"Oh, crap!" I said out loud, after discovering Gallant had

done just that right next to the church sign. I'd forgotten to bring a bag to clean up after Gallant and felt bad about him defacing the church's manicured lawn.

I read the sign again as I urged the dog to hurry up and finish his business. Today was Wednesday, and there'd be a service at seven that evening. I wasn't Catholic, but there was no reason I couldn't attend the seven-o'clock worship service. Rip would be perfectly content to spend the evening staring at the boob tube in our room while I was gone.

I thought that by attending the service, I might get an opportunity to speak with Ridley Wickets again. I'd called him a couple of times in the last several days and left messages. As of yet, I hadn't received a response. The sunglasses had disappeared from the fireplace mantel where I'd left them, but not until a couple of days after Ridley had visited the house. I assumed he'd stopped by one day when I'd left the front door unlocked and retrieved them without sticking around to say hello.

I'd promised Sydney to ask the caretaker if he'd been rooting around in her aunt's basement, and if so, why. So far the opportunity to ask him hadn't presented itself. If he was in attendance for mass that evening, I hoped to engage him in a conversation afterward.

"Come on, boy! Let's get going so we can be home before Rip and I need to leave for his rehab session. Besides, we need to get out of here before someone drives by and sees where you just deposited your church offering."

"Ruff! Ruff!"

CHAPTER 20

W hen Gallant and I turned the corner onto South Hart Street, I recognized the red and silver Mini-Cooper parked on the street in front of the Heart Shack. Curious as to why Adelaide Combs had come calling, we picked up our pace. The St. Bernard, who Sydney told me was approaching eleven years old, had one speed—and it wasn't "warp".

When Gallant began to pant, I slowed down to let him catch his breath. "I'm sorry, boy. I keep forgetting that in dog years, you're about nine years my senior."

When we walked into the foyer, I was surprised to see a thin, wiry man with long dirty-blond hair sorting through the stack of mail I'd stacked on the marble table. I was even more surprised to see him wearing the sunglasses I'd thought belonged to Ridley Wickets. "Hey, buddy. Do those sunglasses belong to you?"

He stopped thumbing through the collection of envelopes and stared at me as if expecting me to break into a song and dance routine. "No, lady, they belong to Elton John but he's letting me borrow them. Who'd you think they belonged to?"

I've always heard that dogs are good judges of character, so I believed Gallant when he moved closer to my side and began to snarl and display his intimidating eyeteeth. He then growled in a deep-throated timbre. I reached down to grasp his collar, which would have done little to stop him should he have decided to pounce. When the fellow took a step toward Gallant, the dog cowered and scooted in behind me, as if he feared he had a brutal beating coming. I wondered if the man had abused him in the past.

"Chill out, Gallant," the man said. "Hey, boy! It's just me, dude."

"And who might you be?" I asked. I'll admit I was acting a little proprietary for someone whose name was not on the deed to the house, or even the electric bill the scraggly dude held in his right hand.

"Part owner of this place," he answered defensively. "So, who are you and what are you doing here?"

His response made it clear he was the twins' pot-smoking brother. By the condition of his teeth, marijuana likely wasn't the only substance he was abusing. To me, he had a definite meth-head appearance. As he glared at me, Tasman inhaled deeply, resulting in a whistling from his nose. It was as if the nasal septum between his nostrils was perforated. I'd heard this happened to cocaine addicts on occasion. Could this be the case with Tasman? I may not have recognized the true purpose of the roach clip I'd found, that undoubtedly belonged to him, but I was well aware of the fact that marijuana was a gateway drug to more powerful narcotics. If Tasman was addicted to street drugs like meth and cocaine, why in the world would Sydney ever entrust her aunt's well-being to his care?

I listened to Tasman's nose whistle again before responding. "My name's Rapella Ripple, and I have every right to be here."

"Did Sydney hire a dog walker?" He asked.

"What difference would it make if she did?"

"Ain't really none of your business, old lady, but Sydney is getting paid by the estate to take care of the animals. Me and Addie's money shouldn't go toward paying someone like you."

"Well, it isn't, you insolent little twerp. Sydney isn't paying 'someone like me' to walk Gallant." I tried to skirt past Tasman but he blocked my passage. The sensation of being trapped unnerved me. "Please step aside and let me pass."

Tasman put his hands on his hips and didn't budge. The creepy smile on his face displayed both his rotting teeth and a tongue piercing. His threatening demeanor was disturbing. The long period of silence made me even more uncomfortable.

I glanced at the vase of lilac blossoms on the table. I'd added them to brighten up the entrance, but that didn't mean the glass jar couldn't also be utilized for clocking rude little bastards on the head, if the situation called for it. As I was debating my next move, Tasman finally spoke.

"You didn't tell me why you're here, old lady."

"My husband and I are temporary residents of what's now being referred to as the Heart Shack." In case, like his sister Adelaide, he was unaware that his aunt had bequeathed her home to the heart center, I went on to explain the nature of my presence, which only seemed to inflame him more. It was like tossing gasoline on a smoldering fire.

After getting a few graphic expletives out of his system, Tasman calmed down enough to respond to my explanation. "Adelaide told me about the so-called Heart Shack."

"There's nothing 'so-called' about it, numb nuts!" I decided I could participate in offensive name-calling just as easily as he had.

"Adelaide's checking out my aunt's will to see if it's even legal. Sydney's stupid heart center may have to take a flying leap if we have anything to do with it, you stupid old bag."

"Good luck with that!" My patronizing tone clearly hit a raw nerve in Tasman, who sneered at me as he spat out more ugly words. "You can drop dead for all I care, lady."

Drop dead? Old bag? Could Goofus have picked these

cruel phrases up from this jerk? I could see the little creep calling his aunt nasty names just as he had me, even after she'd given him a home when he and his sisters were orphaned.

"You need that horrid-looking mouth of yours scrubbed out with a bar of soap, young man. What makes you think your aunt's will might be invalid?"

"Cause Adelaide said so."

"Cause Adelaide said so?" I mimicked his words as mockingly as I could. "Is she the brains behind this money-grubbing duo? It's obvious you aren't."

"What's it to you, lady?"

"You are an ungrateful brat! You're fortunate your aunt was kind enough to put a roof over your head." *I'd like to put something over your head too, buddy boy, and it ain't a roof,* I thought, but managed to resist saying. I hadn't liked this disrespectful prick at first glance and had no problem telling him so. "I'm appalled by your attitude. Why, I wouldn't be surprised if you didn't intentionally—"

Just then one of the twins joined us in the foyer, who I knew by the scowl on her face was Adelaide. It was probably a good thing she'd interrupted me. I was about to accuse her despicable brother of doing something vile that I had no proof whatsoever he was guilty of doing.

My habit of treating suspects as though they were guilty until proven innocent had sent me on more than one apology tour in the past. The last thing I wanted was to feel obliged to issue an apology to some brazen piece of work who'd call me an old lady and a stupid old bag. I turned my attention to the leader of the money-grubbing duo as she began to spout her own brand of nonsense.

"Aunt Mabel was coerced into changing her will before she died of mysterious causes," she said matter-of-factly as Tasman stood next to her, nodding his head like a bobble-head doll. "I'd bet my life on it."

"And I'd love to take that bet, young lady. I don't know where you got the notion she was coerced into anything, but I do know her cause of death was not mysterious. The medical examiner listed your aunt's official cause of death as pulmonary embolism. What's mysterious about that?" I wasn't going to mention the recent autopsy results in case she hadn't already heard about them. I didn't want to give Adelaide the satisfaction of knowing Sydney could potentially be held responsible for their aunt's high Vitamin K level, which may have ultimately led to her death. I truly felt Sydney would be cleared of any responsibility in Mabel's passing.

I glanced from Adelaide to Tasman. This time I stopped just short of accusing the pair of murder. "Does either of you two know something about her death, or have a personal reason you should be turning yourself over to the police department?"

Neither looked pleased about my last question, not that I expected they would. I'd intended it to be a remark that would stick in their craws—and hopefully chokes the crap out of both of them.

"I don't know why I'm even wasting my breath talking about my aunt's death with you. It's none of your concern to begin with. Just feed and walk the damn dog and stay out of our business." With that retort, Adelaide clutched her brother's arm and led him out of the foyer, through the drawing room, and on to the kitchen. I was but a few steps behind. After huddling together and conversing in low whispers, they walked toward the staircase leading to the basement.

I would have liked to follow them to see what they were up to. Were they on a mission to continue raiding their aunt's storeroom? Unfortunately, I didn't have the time for it. Rip was due at rehab in ten minutes.

Sure enough, I could hear rummaging through boxes and drawers in the storeroom directly below the kitchen as I rushed to feed the two pets. I fed Gallant and gave him his poop pay, despite the fact he'd earned it in a most sacrilegious manner by relieving himself on church property.

"Can't eat that skid! Get outta sear!" Goofus chanted. He

seemed even more manic than usual as he bobbed his head and paced from one end of his perch to the other and back again.

I began to sing softly, but Goofus only became more frantic. I decided to wait to interact with the crazed bird until he'd calmed down. I wanted to pull the same number of fingers out of his cage that I poked in. Although I'm ashamed to admit it, I once briefly considered ways I could eliminate the feathered nuisance while making his demise look like an unfortunate accident. I swallowed hard when I realized that the same kind of wicked deed might have done Mabel in.

At Rip's very first rehab visit on Monday of the previous week, he'd had to walk around the facility for ten minutes before walking on a treadmill for five and ride a stationary bike for another five. Rip's therapist, Ethel, was nearly as old as Rip and was a strict drill master. She pretty much wiped the floor with my poor husband, and didn't take "no" or "I can't" for an answer. I adored Ethel just as much as I did Nurse Combs.

Rip was exhausted by the time he dragged his bone-weary keister back to the truck. When he'd exited the building that first day, he'd looked as if he'd scaled Mount Everest—and died just before reaching the apex. Truly, he'd looked like death warmed over, which I don't feel guilty saying now that I know he's going to be all right.

With each session after his first one, Ethel had increased his walking and the time on each apparatus by one minute. This morning, at his sixth rehab session to date, he'd been instructed to walk for sixteen minutes and do eleven minutes on the two pieces of exercise equipment. By the incredulous expression on Rip's face when Ethel gave him his instructions, you'd have thought she'd insisted he run a full marathon and then tack on another five miles as a celebratory victory lap.

Following today's session, Rip didn't have enough oomph left to lift his own feet into the truck. I had to hoist

him into the passenger seat and strap him in like a toddler.
He was dead weight and unable to offer much assistance.
Getting the right hold on his body to lift him, without
collapsing with him on top of me, had taken numerous
attempts. I'm sure it'd been a comical scene for the folks
coming and going from the facility. We might have even
gone viral on YouTube that evening, because I swear I'd
seen a young man videoing us with his cell phone.

Rip wasn't adjusting as quickly to the therapy as I'd
anticipated. I felt sorry for him because I had witnessed the
effort he was expending. But I had to set my feelings aside
and continue to nudge him along. The outcome was too
important to let him skate by without pushing himself as
much as possible.

When we returned to the house, he slowly climbed up the
stairs to rest in the recliner, mumbling the entire way. I was
wishing Goofus was making a racket instead of being
uncharacteristically silent, so his carrying-on would drown
out Rip's complaining. Rip had finished his second full
week of rehabilitation therapy, yet for some reason, the
decrease in remaining rehab sessions and the decrease in
bellyaching were not occurring proportionately—not that
I'd ever seriously thought they would.

Once I knew Rip was safely up the staircase, I gathered
all of the ingredients I'd need to prepare supper. I'd invited
Dave and Cindy Miller to join us for dinner that evening
before they headed over to the sleep lab to get Dave set up
for his sleep study. I wanted to use the time to get a head
start on things.

I chopped up the head of lettuce, radishes, green bell
pepper and a cucumber for the salad I aimed to serve with
my chicken enchilada casserole. I placed the vegetables in
an airtight container and put it in the fridge to stay fresh
until the four of us sat down to eat.

While Rip rested upstairs, I took Gallant out for a long
walk. Upon returning, I read a couple of chapters of the
book I was immersed in, then I puttered around in the

kitchen, setting the table and creating a centerpiece out of lilac blossoms, and several roses Itsy had snipped off one of her bushes for me.

I went upstairs just before five to rouse my sleeping husband because the Millers were due shortly.

"Rip, wake up. We'll be having dinner soon. Cindy's bringing sugar-free apple tarts for our dessert, which is so thoughtful of her."

"You didn't tell me Nurse Combs was joining us for supper."

Clearly Rip hadn't pictured himself down-under before he'd replied, as I'd instructed him to, because he'd mistaken the nurse's name for Cindy again. I exaggerated the enunciation of the first syllables of the two names as I responded. "Not SYDney, CINdy. Cindy is Dave Miller's wife's name."

"Who's Dave Miller?"

"Jeez Louise, Rip. He's the guy who owns the fifth wheel that was parked next to our trailer at the Sunset RV Park. Remember? They towed the trailer here for us so I wouldn't have to do it by myself."

"That was very kind of them, but there would've been no need for you to handle it alone, honey. I could have done it."

"No, you couldn't have. There was no way you could've tackled that job so soon after your operation, honey. You weren't even released to drive until yesterday. Sydney warned you to build up your strength and endurance, but to go about it in baby steps for a while. You've done well in your efforts to not overdo it. Maybe too well, in fact."

"What do you mean by that?" Rip asked.

"Nothing, dear. Now get up so you can make your way down before the Millers arrive."

"All right. I'll have to remember to thank Dale," Rip said. I just shook my head as I watched Rip reach for his shoes, but couldn't help groaning at his next remark. "That was really thoughtful of the Muehlers to help out and tow the trailer here for us."

"Oh, my! You know, it might be best if you just avoid using either one of their names tonight. Dave's about forty, I'd say. Call him 'son' like you do every other fellow at least a year younger than yourself. And you can call Cindy 'dear', 'sweetheart', or any of the other terms of endearment you use when you can't remember a lady's name."

"Will do, darling," he agreed.

Sometimes when Rip used one of his go-to terms of endearment on me, I wasn't sure if it was because he loved me, or because he couldn't remember my name without thinking about it for a few seconds. I was certain this habit had less to do with memory impairment, and more to do with inattentive listening. He never forgot the names of the Three Stooges, or the Dallas Cowboys team members, or every single actor in the cast of *The Godfather*. It was selective hearing; he only heard what he wanted to hear.

"As tired and wrung out as I am right now, Rapella, I'd be just as happy to avoid talking at all tonight. You can do most of the conversing at supper. Okay? You usually talk enough for both of us anyway."

I smacked him on the shoulder. "Get a move on, Buster! I think I just heard a noise downstairs."

I hurried to greet our guests. I'd heard the sound of steps above us during my exchange with Rip. I'd assumed Tasman and Adelaide were in the attic, searching high and low for anything they might be able to get a buck out of in a local pawn shop. When I reached the bottom of the stairs, I could hear activity still in the basement. It seemed as if they'd split up in order to cover more ground. I'd never seen such a pair of self-absorbed, bad-mannered weasels in my life.

I nearly bit my tongue off when I ran into Sydney as I turned to go into the drawing room. The noise had come from her rather than the Millers. When I'd called Sydney earlier in the afternoon to schedule Rip's follow-up appointment with Dr. Murillo, I'd been told she was out on sick leave again. I was beginning to worry her illness might be serious.

She'd told me she'd be stopping by tomorrow, which was Thursday, to check on Rip, as she had the previous Thursday. However, today was Wednesday. I hadn't heard her come in and didn't expect to see her until the next day. Her hair was pulled back in a ponytail, and the knees of her old faded blue jeans were smudged with dirt. She had a bulging Wal-Mart bag dangling from her right hand. *Where was that plastic bag of yours when I wanted to put something over your brother's head?* I wanted to ask.

"Sydney! It's good to see you. We were concerned when Dr. Murillo told us you'd taken sick leave again. I hope everything is okay and you're feeling better."

"No worries. Don't tell anyone at the center, but I was fibbing about being ill. I hate to waste vacation time on something like having the flu. It'd be better spent on lounging on the beach of some Caribbean island."

I laughed and said, "I hear you! Are your siblings still here?"

"Yeah, unfortunately. They're still seething about Aunt Mabel's decision to leave her home to the cardiac center. They're accusing me of forcing her hand in the decision, which is pure bull-crap. It's bad enough I have to go before the medical board. They both deny making the anonymous call to the police department about doing an autopsy, but I'm not buying it. I'd say Addie did it, if I had to place a bet on it. Taz usually just follows her lead."

"Yes, I met your charming brother earlier. We didn't exactly hit it off. I thought I heard you say your aunt also had a day nurse. Are they planning to question her, as well?"

"I think so. The day nurse, Patricia Lankston, is as sweet as they come. She's a retired hospice nurse and as far as I'm concerned, there's a special place in heaven for people who take on that heart-rending job. Patricia was hired to make sure Aunt Mabel didn't fall going to the bathroom, choke on a grape, forget to take her medications, or anything like that when I couldn't be here. But Patricia was informed of all of the basic discharge orders before she started. My auntie was beginning to struggle with memory issues, you know. It was getting to the stage she needed 'round-the-clock care. In fact, we were looking into assisted living facilities for her to move in to as soon as she had, at least moderately, recovered from her bypass surgery."

I wondered who she'd meant by "we" but decided it wasn't my place to inquire. Before I could respond to her comments, there was a loud thumping sound echoing up the staircase from the basement. It seemed clear now that all three of the Combs siblings were scouring the house. "Are you and your siblings trying to remove all of the personal items from the house before the cardiac center takes legal possession of it?"

"Yes."

"Uh. Okay." Sydney's response did not reveal anything I hadn't already figured out for myself. While I had the girl's attention, I thought it was a good time to ask about Mabel's next door neighbor. "Sydney, are you familiar with the lady who lives next door?"

"Itsy Warman?"

"Yes, that's the one."

"Itsy's a hot mess, if you ask me. She and my aunt had a love/hate type of relationship from the day Itsy moved in next door. And it stayed that way until Aunt Mabel took her last breath."

"What was their issue? Itsy appears to be a touch on the eccentric side, but seems to be basically harmless."

"Most likely just a jealousy thing. I think Aunt Mabel kind of lorded it over Itsy because she had a bigger house than Itsy, a personal caretaker, and was a merry widow rather than—egad!—a lowly spinster." Sydney chuckled after her facetious remark and the dramatic look of horror that had accompanied it. "They might as well have been roommates so they could squabble with each other without having to walk next door. But it was one of those deals where they couldn't live with each other, yet they couldn't seem to live without each other either. I always felt a sense of relief, knowing Itsy was right next door if Aunt Mabel needed help with anything, or just someone to keep her company. It was Itsy, in fact, who first discovered her body after she passed unexpectedly. The two ladies might deny it, but they cared more for each other than either of them would let on."

I knew Sydney was correct. I'd noticed Itsy's eyes cloud up when she spoke about Mabel. It was that love/hate relationship between the two that I thought might make Itsy the perfect ally in helping me determine the truth behind the woman's death.

How would Itsy feel about attending Wednesday mass with me this evening? I asked myself after Sydney had ended our conversation to resume her plundering. I was sure dinner would be over and our guests would have departed by six-thirty, so I gave the neighbor a quick call and made arrangements to meet up with her at our truck at six forty-five.

CHAPTER 21

◆

"Why are you dressed like you're going to an inaugural ball? Didn't you tell me we were just going to a church service?" Itsy asked as she climbed into the truck that evening and eyed my black and gold dress I'd purchased prior to our Alaskan cruise.

"Yes, I did tell you we were going to a Wednesday evening worship service. So why are you dressed like you're about to compete in the pumpkin-seed spitting contest at the King County Fair?"

"I'll have you know I'm wearing a brand new outfit," Itsy said in defense of her denim dungarees and Miller Lite t-shirt.

"You call that an outfit?" I asked. I could suddenly picture the type of banter between Itsy and her recently deceased neighbor. Like the conversation we were currently engaged in, it was probably a tit-for-tat exchange that was not intended to be mean-spirited, but rather entertaining in nature.

"I have a shirt that says, 'The Devil Made Me Do It'. Would you have preferred I wear that instead?"

I laughed at Itsy's remark. "You know, it might've been fun to watch all the parishioners' reactions to it. We have a few extra minutes if you'd like to go back in and change."

"No, thank you. Now, what was the purpose of all this again? Neither one of us is Catholic, so what's the point?"

"I just want to speak with Ridley Wickets if he's at the service tonight," I explained.

"Oh?"

I turned to look at my companion, wondering how well she knew Mabel's caretaker. But I didn't want to sound too inquisitive. I could sense she was already curious about my intentions. "I appreciate you going with me. I'd have felt conspicuous going alone. And, like misery, discomfort loves company."

"No problem." Itsy's expression and demeanor made it clear she was having an intense debate with herself, as if uncertain how much to say about the man who helped her neighbor out on occasion. After an involuntary and nearly imperceptible shrug, she said, "I never knew Ridley to be a church-going fellow. He rarely left the confines of Mabel's house. It was like he was a vampire, or an albino whose eyes were sensitive to the sun. Haven't seen him since Mabel died, though. Until you told me you encountered him in the drawing room, I'd assumed he'd moved on. I'm not certain how safe that'd be for him, though."

I was mystified by Itsy's comments, but we were about to enter the church and I didn't want to discuss it right then. I glanced over and was relieved to see she didn't have any tobacco in her mouth. Her choice of clothing was bad enough without her walking into the cathedral with a Bible in one hand and a spittoon in the other.

When we walked into the main chamber, I could hear the beautiful tones of the Quimby pipe organ resonating throughout the cathedral. As Ridley had stated, the acoustics in the massive room were incredible. I leaned over and whispered to Itsy, "Did you know Mabel won the Steinway piano that the organ replaced in a fund-raising raffle?"

"*Won*? Yeah, right."

Again, I wasn't sure what to make of Itsy's response, which was reminiscent of Ridley's, but I didn't have time to inquire about it. I noticed that everyone knelt at the end of their chosen row before they took a seat. They bent their heads and made the sign of the cross, moving their hand vertically and then horizontally across their chests with their right thumb touching the first two fingers of that hand. I didn't know if that was expected of everyone in attendance, or only those of Catholic persuasion. Either way, the straight skirt of my dress was so form-fitting, it wouldn't allow me to kneel down without giving a free peep show to the young usher standing a few yards in front of me.

I grabbed Itsy's wrist and pulled her behind me into the pew the usher indicated. We'd been seated just three or four rows from the back of the cathedral, which was ideal. It'd allow for a better chance of spotting Ridley Wickets if he happened to be in attendance that evening. As it turned out, there wasn't a viewpoint in the entire room that wouldn't have worked just as well.

We listened to a few more hymns while the choir accompanied the organist in perfect harmony. The pews steadily filled until there didn't appear to be an empty seat in the sanctuary. Suddenly, bells rang out. The humming sound of many people talking ceased instantly.

A voice filled the chamber from the lectern and reverberated around the cathedral. "Let us begin in the name of the Father, and the Son, and the Holy Ghost. May the grace of our Lord Jesus Christ, the love of God and the communion of the Holy Spirit be with all of you. Welcome, my friends. Let us pray."

I froze. My mouth gaped open like a blow-up doll. I caught Itsy's eye and whispered, "What in tarnation?"

Itsy glanced around, and then leaned over and asked, "What's your problem? Did you think they'd start the service by passing out garlic sticks and goblets full of Chardonnay?"

I didn't appreciate Itsy's sarcasm and couldn't understand why she wasn't as astonished as I was. "Why didn't you tell me Ridley was a priest?"

"Ridley? What are you talking about?"

"If the priest standing up there at the pulpit is not Ridley Wickets, who is he?"

"Beats the holy hell out of me," she replied.

"Shush!" I glanced around and noticed glares from a number of worshipers sitting around us. I guess they didn't appreciate Itsy's charming way with words as much as I did.

Itsy glanced around too and then leaned toward me and, in a much softer voice, said, "I've seen that man going in or out of Mabel's house on a few occasions. When I asked her about him, Mabel just said she knew him from church. She didn't mention his name, and I didn't care to know it, anyway!"

"You never attended church with Mabel?" For some reason, I was surprised they didn't attend services together.

"Hell no," Itsy whispered. After I shushed her once more, she continued. "On the rare occasions I attend church, it's usually not a Catholic one, and one of the people attending the service is carried out the back door in a pine box."

As Itsy made the inappropriate reference to a funeral, I saw her reach into a bag of fresh chew tobacco. I slapped her hand, and whispered harshly, "Put that back in your pocket! You can't chew that in church!" Itsy grimaced, shook her head in disgust, and returned the half-full package to her rear pocket.

I was afraid to ask Itsy another question because a lot of her responses seemed to have the word "hell" in them. I felt this was very inappropriate for conversations taking place during a mass. I shook my head at Itsy's behavior and prayed she'd sit quietly throughout the rest of the service without causing a scene. I felt her fidgeting for quite a while and was relieved when she finally stopped moving.

Having no former experience with Catholic services, I marveled at how many times the crowd repeated the words, "Thanks be to God." I was trying to pay attention to the Biblical readings, but my mind was too occupied with other things. In particular, I was curious as to why the Catholic priest had lied to me, trying to pass himself off as a caretaker named Ridley Wickets. At one point, I leaned over and whispered to the woman on the other side of me.

"Do you happen to know the priest's name? He's quite impressive."

Although the elderly Hispanic woman didn't act as though she wanted to engage in chit-chat in the middle of the mass, she reluctantly replied, "Father Cumberland. He's been the cleric here for almost twelve years. Now please be quiet."

"Yes, of course. Thank you."

I turned the opposite way to pass the information on to Itsy, only to discover she was sound asleep, her head listing to one side, nearly touching the shoulder of the man seated next to her. I shook her arm gently, and whispered, "Itsy, wake up!"

"Huh?" She jerked her head up, trying to orient herself. After a few moments, she asked, "Waddaya want?"

"The priest's name is Father Cumberland."

"Good for him. You woke me up to tell me his name after I made it clear I didn't care?" The volume of Itsy's voice had increased and people were beginning to stare.

"Keep your voice down, Itsy. We need to lag behind after this service is over. I want to speak to the priest."

"Okay, fine. Wake me up when it's over."

I was content to let her snooze throughout the remainder of the mass, and told her to rest her head on my shoulder rather than that of the obese man next to her. In my defense, I didn't know she was going to begin snoring loud enough to wake the dead. She snorted so thunderously during a pause in the reading of scriptures, Father Cumberland stopped speaking and everyone in the crowd turned to fixate on the two of us in the back of the sanctuary. A few of the worshipers couldn't refrain from snickering.

Before long, everyone, including the priest, were chuckling in amusement. I'm sure my face was as red as the carpet runner dividing the two long rows of pews. And to think I'd been concerned I might look conspicuous if I were to attend church alone that night.

The laughter continued until I elbowed Itsy hard enough to rouse her, and she sat up in the pew, and shouted, "What the (bleep)?"

The resounding, perfectly enunciated f-bomb was not well received by the crowd, to put it mildly. For several long moments after Itsy's outburst, it was so quiet in the cathedral, you could have heard a termite choking on a sliver of wood inside a wall of the hallowed building.

"Good evening, Mr. Cumberland. Would you like me to call you Father, or Ridley?" I asked the priest after the service had concluded. Itsy had gone outside for a chew as I'd waited in a lengthy line for my chance to converse with the priest. He was obviously a popular spiritual leader of the Sacred Heart Church.

"Hello, Mrs. Ripple. It was nice of you to join us in prayer this evening." The sentiment would have felt genuine if not for the expression of annoyance on the priest's face. "I got the impression you and your, um, interesting friend, are not Catholic. So I'm curious why you attended our service this evening."

"Didn't see any sign banning Protestants from the building. I'm curious about something too. Why did you lie to me, claiming to be Mabel Trumbo's caretaker, Ridley Wickets?"

"I'm sorry if you mistook me for Ridley Wickets. I *was* Ms. Trumbo's caretaker, of sorts. But I never actually said I was Ridley Wickets."

I couldn't recall our conversation verbatim, but suspected he was being honest about never having actually verbalized the falsehood. "You never told me otherwise, either, when it was clear I thought you were Mr. Wickets. That's what's referred to as a lie by omission."

"Yes, I know. I'm sorry. My name's Chase Cumberland, but you can call me Chase. Ridley was Mabel's actual caretaker for the last eight or nine years, not that he was able to handle much of the work because of his age."

Before I could question Chase further, he looked up and saw another parishioner walking up the aisle to greet him.

"I can't really talk to you about it right now," he said softly. "Would it be okay if I stopped by the Heart Shack tomorrow morning so I can better explain my duplicity?"

"Yes, I suppose that'd be all right. Better yet, why don't you plan on joining my husband and me for supper tomorrow night? Can you be there around six, Chase?" I'd added his name just to see how it tasted on the tip of my tongue. It tasted bitter. Sort of like a heaping dose of chicory, or chicanery, in the priest's case. But I did have to admit, the handsome fellow looked more like a "Chase" than a "Ridley" to me. Chase was a strong name—the name of a handsome, strapping gentleman. Ridley sounded more like the name of an accountant, a shoe salesman, or perhaps a typewriter repairman, if there even was such a thing these days.

"That'd work just fine. I'm looking forward to dining with you and Mr. Ripple tomorrow evening. I shall arrive promptly at six."

There was a lot going through my mind as I walked outside to find Itsy. She was leaning against the railing of the porch at the entrance of the church, spewing a nasty stream of tobacco-laced saliva into the fragrant honeysuckle bush beside her. The departing congregation was giving her a wide berth, as if they'd just witnessed her being dunked in a baptismal vat of ricin.

I was glad the priest was available to join us for dinner the following evening. I was a bit surprised he'd even accepted my invitation. I knew his commitment to serving the Lord involved a lot of interaction with his flock. It occurred to me then what Chase Cumberland had meant when he'd told me his "boss" didn't miss a single thing. God, the all-seeing creator, was the very powerful boss he'd referred to. I had to wonder what his boss thought about the religious leader's deceptiveness.

That's no way for a priest to behave if he wants to be assured of a favored spot in heaven, I thought.

It probably goes without saying, but that was the one and only time Itsy and I ever paid a visit to the Sacred Heart Church on Falmouth Street. On that evening, it would have more aptly been named "Foul Mouth Street".

It wasn't until I was slipping into my pajamas about a half-an-hour later that it suddenly occurred to me why Itsy had never before attended a service at the catholic church. Unlike me, Mabel must have been wise enough not to invite her.

CHAPTER 22

When I pulled the truck over to the curb in front of Itsy's house, I thanked her again for accompanying me to the church service, and asked, "Got any notion what the Combs kids, and possibly Father Cumberland, might be looking for in Mabel's house? Do you know of anything she owned that might be worth the effort of scouring every nook and cranny?"

"Damned right, I do!"

Naturally, my interest was piqued. But then Itsy clammed up for such a long spell, I didn't think she was going to explain her emphatic response. I got the impression she had to give it considerable thought before replying. Fortunately, she finally decided to tell me the fascinating story. I turned the ignition off and listened in rapt attention, as Itsy must've done when Mabel had told her the story of her youth.

"Mabel didn't have the easiest childhood in the world. Her daddy, Oliver Wright, was twenty-five when he met her sixteen-year-old mother, Ingrid Anderson, in Eugene, Oregon in 1938. They married three months later and Mabel's older sister, Rosalyn, was born the following year."

"Is Rosalyn still alive?" I asked.

"No. As I've said before, Rosalyn was attacked and killed by a shark while on a family vacation in 1996. But I haven't gotten to that part yet. Anyway, in early 1942, with Ingrid pregnant with Mabel, Oliver was drafted into the army to serve in the war. A draft-dodger, Oliver took the family and fled the country, hiding out in a remote area of the Australian outback. In early 1943, unable to feed his family of four, he headed out to do a little prospecting at the Ballarat Mine in Victoria where a major gold strike had occurred in 1908."

"Did he find gold?"

"Yes. He hit a major gold vein that had somehow remained undiscovered. It was the mother lode, as her daddy put it. Oliver Wright became a wealthy man overnight. But he was a bit of a scoundrel, too, and he left a chunk of it in the Central Australian brothels. On August 14, 1945, the Japanese surrendered to the Allies, ending World War II, and Oliver took what was left of the gold nuggets he'd discovered home to Ingrid and their daughters. He also took home a bacterial infection called syphilis."

"Goodness gracious! Did it kill him?"

Itsy sighed. "If you'd quit interrupting me, Rapella, I'll tell you."

"Oh, okay. I'm sorry. Go on."

"No, the syphilis didn't kill Oliver, but he was generous enough to share the disease with his wife."

"Oh, no! Did she—?"

Itsy shot me a look that shut me up mid-sentence. "Their third daughter, Bella, was born in 1947 and Ingrid passed away from complications of syphilis the following year when Mabel was six."

"Did Ingrid pass the disease on to Bella?"

"No, thank God. Somehow Bella was unaffected by it."

"No thanks to Oliver. That slimy no-good bast—"

"So," Itsy drew the two letter word out for a dramatically long time to shut me up. "As Oliver got sicker and weaker from the disease, he depended on Mabel to take care of the cooking and the household chores, as well as watching over her younger sister."

"What about Mabel's older sister, Rosalyn?"

"I'm getting there, I'm getting there. Have patience, girl." Itsy shook a finger at me good-naturedly before continuing with the story. "Rosalyn was Oliver's go-to daughter until she ran away from home at thirteen. She got knocked up at fifteen, and she and her husband moved here to the states and bought—"

"Mabel's house, right?"

"No, of course not. They couldn't afford something that grand. They were both still kids themselves and had a bun baking in the oven besides. They scratched you-know-what with the chickens and were able to scrounge up enough to rent a small home on the wrong side of the tracks in Yakima."

"Oh, that's where Adelaide lives."

"Yeah, that's right. So, anyway, Rosalyn's daughter, Norma Jean was born in their tiny house in 1955 with the help of a midwife. The three got by with Rosalyn working two jobs and doing some tailoring jobs on the side. She knew her way around a Singer sewing machine, you see. When she figured out her lazy husband was nothing but a drunk and a bum, she dropped him like a bad habit and had to work even more hours altering clothes and doing odd jobs wherever she could find them. Rosalyn began to put a couple of dollars away each month and saved up until she could afford to take Norma Jean on a vacation to the coast. Unfortunately, that trip Rosalyn had dreamed about for several years, and pinched pennies to save for, ended in tragedy when she was nearly bitten in two by a great white off the coast of Newport, Oregon."

"Holy moly! Did Norma Jean witness the attack?" This time Itsy didn't admonish me for interrupting. She could see how involved in the story I'd become. She appeared to be just as invested in the telling of it.

"She not only witnessed it, she was standing next to her mother at the time and was knocked over by the shark.

Norma Jean was rescued by a young man who'd seen the shark attack her mother. Rosalyn bled out before they even got her back to shore. Norma Jean was twelve at the time and a hot mess from that moment on, which was a tragedy in itself."

"Oh, good Lord. What a story!" I wanted to hear more. "What happened to Norma Jean?"

"I'll get to that in a minute. First I need to go back to Mabel's daddy."

"Oh, of course." I tried to mask my impatience.

"When Rosalyn left, Mabel had to take over as head housekeeper and a mother figure to little Bella. A few years later, Bella, at age six, was sent to an orphanage in West Virginia, of all places, because Oliver didn't want an extra mouth to feed. Especially when the devastating effects of the syphilis was beginning to take a toll on him. Like Ingrid, he probably would have died of the disease too had he not been shot in 1957 for cheating at poker. Mabel, fifteen by then, packed up her most precious belongings and, reluctantly, her daddy's stash of gold. According to Mabel, it was around a hundred pounds' worth, which in today's market is probably worth over two million. She then left Australia for America in hopes of tracking down her two sisters, and never looked back."

"So what happened to Mabel next?" I had sat back in the truck seat and made myself comfortable as Itsy rambled on.

"Mabel ended up in a boarding house in Eugene, Oregon. At nineteen, she married Jackson Trumbo, a commercial fisherman about twelve years older than her and moved to this area with her new husband. About a year later, Jack died when the fishing boat he was on capsized and sank during a horrific storm at sea."

"Oh, my goodness. What a tragic story!"

"Yeah, it was. They had a full load of fresh Dungeness crab in the hull when the vessel went down. Do you know how much those things cost?"

"Um, yes. But I was actually referring to the loss of Mabel's husband and the rest of the crew."

"Well, yeah. There was that, too," Itsy replied. "But Mabel got a nice settlement out of it and bought the old Victorian, which at one time was a beauty to behold. As they say, 'all's well that ends well'."

"If you say so. But, gracious sakes, what a life story! I'm amazed at how precisely you've committed Mabel's life story to memory."

"In her later years, Mabel's memory slowly deteriorated. Along with everything else, she recited her life story on many, many occasions. Rather than embarrass her, I always acted as if it was the first time I'd heard it."

"And you said you didn't care all that much for your neighbor. You're as bad a liar as the priest!" I smiled as I spoke, and Itsy chuckled.

"Mabel was a really good person. We just disagreed on a lot of things."

"I understand, Itsy. So, tell me. Did Mabel locate Rosalyn and Bella?"

"Mabel never did discover what happened to Bella, and she only knew Rosalyn had relocated to the Oregon coast. That's why she and her husband moved to Oregon. But before Mabel could track Rosalyn down, she happened upon Rosalyn's obituary on a microfilm of the *Yakima Herald-Republic* that was on file at her local library. Mabel found Rosalyn's twelve-year old daughter in a state hospital in Yakima and formally adopted her, after finding out the girl's father wanted nothing to do with her. Mabel brought Norma Jean home and treated her as if she were her own offspring. Raised her right there in her own house until Norma Jean eventually got hitched to a loser named Roland Combs. Sydney and Adelaide were born soon after. Incidentally, Norma Jean and Roland's marriage crashed and burned after she caught him cheating on her with a much younger cocktail waitress. Tasman was seven at the time, and the twins were twelve."

"How sad is that?" I asked rhetorically. It was beginning to seem as if there was nothing but bad luck dripping from every branch of Mabel's family tree, particularly when it came to marriage. I realized once again how fortunate I was to have found the love of my life so early in life. I never once regretted my decision to marry him in the half-century that followed.

"Norma Jean did her best to raise her three kids properly and balance her struggles with her own personal demons for the next several years, before—poof!" Itsy stopped speaking abruptly, slapped her hands together as if wrapping up her story. "And the rest is history."

I felt as if I'd been reading a thrilling novel, and when I reached the climax of the story, the rest of the pages had been ripped out of the book. "What? It might be history to you, but it's not to me. What's 'poof' mean? I want to know what you meant by 'several years, before—poof!' Where's Norma Jean now? Why wasn't she here helping Mabel? Why didn't she inherit the estate? Why are the Combs' kids in Mabel's will instead of their mother, Norma Jean?"

"You sure have a lot of questions, Rapella. I ain't got all night, you know."

I just stared at Itsy, who was fidgeting in the passenger seat as if she was running late for an important engagement. I knew she didn't have a hot date. Sadly for her, *I* was her hot date that evening. Was she having nicotine withdrawal, or had she just grown tired of reciting her neighbor's life story? Whatever had made her nip the spellbinding story in the bud, she wasn't getting away with it! "Well, it's your fault, Itsy! You got me all keyed up about the tragic tale of Mabel's family, and then just left me hanging like a cattle rustler from a dead man's noose. I want to know what happened to Norma Jean. So spill it!"

"All right. All right." Itsy finally consented. "She died. Killed herself in Mabel's house, in fact. Shot herself in the chest in the drawing room. The bullet went right through her and embedded itself in the fireplace mantle. You'll see the bullet wedged in the mantelpiece if you look under the lace doily that's draped over it."

"But why would she do such a thing?" My voice

quivered in despair at the very thought of Sydney losing her mother to suicide.

"Norma Jean was suffering from hallucinations, bouts of severe depression, and a couple of other mental disorders. The twins were fifteen, and Tasman only eleven, when Norma Jean put a bullet through her heart right in front of Mabel and her children. As I said, 'Poof!'"

"Oh. My. God." I exclaimed, as if each word were a sentence in itself. "That's horrific!"

"I told you Norma Jean was a hot mess from the moment her momma died."

"Now I feel really bad for all three of the Combs kids. No matter how hard they try, it's something they'll never be able to 'unsee'."

"Yeah, I know. Mabel took it really hard, too."

"No doubt!" Then something hit me out of the blue. "Wait a minute, Itsy. Are you saying Mabel might've had some of that gold left when she died?"

"I honestly don't know. She never said, and I didn't ask. I would assume she did because she thought it belonged to the devil, and blamed her mother's death on it. She believed that money truly is the root of all evil, and wanted nothing to do with it. I know she never spent any of it in all the time I lived next door to her," Itsy said. Then, as if to change the subject, she added, "It's all water under the bridge now, I reckon. The three kids moved in with Mabel after their mother's death, and lived in her house until they were grown and out on their own. However, I think it was in Mabel's final years, after having had kind of a falling out with them, even Sydney to a certain extent, she decided to donate the bulk of her estate to the cardiac center. Along with the house, which she'd already included in her will, she wanted to bequeath the rest of her estate to the center so there'd be funds to go toward its maintenance and upkeep for years to come. Unfortunately, it was too late to change her will. Mabel would turn over in her grave if she knew those three Combs kids were going to get their grubby hands on any of her money, especially that no-account boy who ain't got two brain cells left to keep each other company. She did have a soft spot in her heart for Sydney toward the end of her life, though. And for good reason. Sydney donated a lot of her time and effort to look after her."

"Yes. Sydney's a very caring individual. But I'm curious about something you just said. Why was it too late for Mabel to change her will?"

"You have to be of sound mind and body to alter a last will and testament, you know. By then, the Alzheimer's was already beginning to manifest itself in a significant enough way to render her unqualified to alter her will."

"That's too bad. Alzheimer's is an awful, awful disease." Then something terrifying suddenly occurred to me. "Oh, my! So, you're saying there could still be two million dollars' worth of gold somewhere in her house?"

"It's possible. At least the Combs kids seem to think so. They just don't know where it is if it *is* still on the premises. I can't say I disagree with Mabel's view about the gold being akin to an evil curse. But, if I'd been her, I'd have gotten over it and wallowed in the lap of luxury until the day the Good Lord called my spoiled ass home."

I couldn't help laughing at Itsy's final comment. But the idea of having a treasure hidden somewhere inside the Heart Shack troubled me. I felt as if Rip and I were sitting on a ticking time bomb. I had no way of knowing who, and how many, knew of its existence and what those individuals might resort to in order to gain possession of it. The story answered one question, however. I now realized when I'd overheard Sydney say something to Adelaide that sounded like "wind the wold" during the bitter argument I witnessed between them at the hospital, she'd actually said "find the gold".

The realization made me wonder if I'd misjudged Sydney. Perhaps she was just as determined to find the fortune as her siblings. But, then, could I honestly blame her? I wasn't certain how I'd have acted had I been in her shoes, so it was hard to judge her behavior. It was unfair to judge it, as well.

I knew the trio could still be inside the house, hoping to find the treasure perhaps hidden within its walls.

I said goodnight to Itsy and thanked her for sharing Mabel's life story with me. It'd certainly shed new light on my feelings for Mabel's great-nieces and nephew. I had a great deal of empathy for them and what they'd been through with the tragic loss of their mother. But much of that empathy got washed down the creek when I thought about their single-minded lust for the gold.

The first thing I did after entering the house was walk into the drawing room and lift up the doily draped over the mantelpiece. When I eyed the hole from the bullet that had ended Norma Jean's life, I felt a sudden change in the atmosphere. It was as if the temperature in the room had suddenly decreased by fifteen degrees.

I set down on the couch with my head in my hands, tears flowing, and my heart aching, for a woman I'd never met. Mabel had experienced a lot more heartache in her lifetime than any one person ever should, and I vowed to find out the truth behind her death. If it was at someone else's hands, I was going to do all I could to make sure the owner of those hands paid for their horrendous crime. *Even if those hands belonged to Sydney,* I told myself.

I didn't have the heart to wake up Rip to tell him what I'd just learned from our next-door neighbor. I lay awake all night thinking about what that story might mean to the future of the temporary lodging facility and, more importantly, to the future of the couple currently occupying its master suite.

"You told me the two ladies didn't get along," Rip said after I reiterated Itsy's story the following morning as we lingered over breakfast. "How do you know she didn't make up that whole convoluted yarn?"

"Well, I can't be positive, of course. Itsy *is* kind of an eccentric character, but she sure seemed sincere when she told the story, and she made it clear the two were closer than she cared to admit. I think the tale's legit. We could be sitting on a small fortune here, and I don't like it one bit!"

"Don't worry, honey. I'll be here to protect you. I'm probably the only patient packing when he walks into the rehab facility for a therapy session. No one's safe anywhere these days."

"When terrorists start attacking cardio rehab facilities, it's time for us to dig an underground bunker and move into it." While I spoke, I topped off Rip's glass of orange juice.

"Not a half-bad idea."

"Itsy also made a good point that hadn't occurred to me yet."

"And what was that?"

"Mabel's last will and testament hasn't been altered in a number of years. She wasn't deemed of sound mind and body since she was diagnosed with Alzheimer's. Her gift of this house to the cardiac center stemmed back to the heart attack she suffered ten or eleven years ago. Remember Sydney mentioned that to us when I was concerned that whatever happened to cause Mabel's death might happen to you, too?" I asked.

"Yeah. I recall her saying Mabel had something called mycranial fracture."

"Yes, that's right. Although it's actually called myocardial infarction. Mycranial fracture sounds more like a complication from falling down a flight of stairs."

"Yeah, I guess you're right." Rip took a bite off his piece of toast and washed it down with juice. "So what's your point?"

"Adelaide and Tasman Combs have accused Sydney of coercing Aunt Mabel to change her will *after* her recent bypass surgery. But she made the decision to donate this house to the heart center around a decade ago."

"Surely Sydney's aware of that, too. Why hasn't she brought that to her siblings' attention?"

"I dunno. Maybe she has and they're just in denial. They probably refuse to believe a woman, who raised them like her own after their mother died, wanted anyone but them to have all her money when she passed. But according to Itsy, there was a falling out, and Adelaide and Tasman were the last two people Mabel would have wanted to benefit from her death."

"Well, dear, I guess you'll just have to accept that it is what it is." Rip had been stirring his bowl of hot cereal for over five minutes as if thinking the unappealing globby crap would eventually morph into a big pile of biscuits and sausage gravy if he played with it long enough. Oatmeal to Rip was like a unicycle to a goldfish. The two just did not go together.

He had at least acknowledged the fact he'd have to make some lifestyle changes and was making a half-assed effort to adjust. But I wasn't certain a half-assed effort was going to be enough to keep him alive, and that's what kept me up at night.

I turned my attention back to Rip as he said, "Speaking of Tasman, he was here for about an hour last night while you and Itsy were at church."

"Doing what?"

"I don't know. But I did hear him talking on the phone. I overheard him say something like, 'I'm worried they'll find out.'"

"Who was he talking to?"

"How in the hell would I know?" Rip barked gruffly. Somebody needed a nap already, and he hadn't even finished his breakfast yet. I listened as Mr. Grumpy Pants continued. "I'm not even sure I didn't misunderstand what he said. It's not like I could go ask him to repeat the conversation for me. He didn't know I was anywhere around when he made that remark."

"Hmm. That's interesting." I was naturally curious who Tasman had been conversing with and what he was afraid someone would find out, but I knew I'd gotten all the information I was liable to get out of Rip. With his hearing impairment, and his aversion to wearing his $5,000 hearing aids, it was possible the boy had said nothing of the sort. Tasman could have said something like, "I'm worried my pot supply is about out." Or, for that matter, even something as ludicrous as, "I'm worried the snowman will thaw out."

When the doorbell rang, I got up to welcome the cleaning crew, who were slated to finish up the job by noon. It was Thursday, Sydney's customary drop-by day, and she'd informed me she'd be by to pay them around eleven and check in on Rip at the same time. I suspected she might have another round of treasure-hunting in mind, as well. I wouldn't have been surprised to see Adelaide and Tasman show up, too. As far as I was aware, the gold had still not been unearthed—for the second time in its existence.

That thought made me wonder if Mabel hadn't buried the gold somewhere on the premises, a practice quite common back in the days of old. My pappy kept a Mason jar buried behind the chicken coop when I was growing up. But rather than two million bucks worth of gold, his jar had contained a handful of small change. He had a tendency to dig the jar up and clean it out before the coins could add up to more than a couple of dollars. It was definitely not from my pappy that I'd inherited my financially conservative nature.

When I responded to the ringing doorbell, I was surprised to find Itsy Warman on the front porch rather than the cleaners. I greeted her with a smile. As unpredictable as the lady was, I knew if I'd had a sister instead of all brothers, I'd have wanted her to be just like Itsy. She was fun to have around and would have kept me on my toes.

"Howdy, neighbor! What brings you over this morning?"

"I'm in a bind and was wondering if you'd be willing to take me into the city this morning. My car's in the shop getting a new alternator put in, and I need to drop something off at the bookie."

"Bookie?" Just when I thought nothing about Itsy could surprise me, I find out she's a gambler. I reiterated the word to make sure I hadn't misunderstood what she'd said. "Did you say bookie?"

"Yeah. It has to be today. It absolutely cannot wait another day."

I nodded my head slowly. I tried not to sound critical when I replied. "I'm surprised you'd have anything to do with something like that."

"Why's that? They say it's an activity that's helps keep an aging mind sharp."

"If you say so." I shrugged. I'd have thought gambling would keep an older person broke, rather than sharp. "You never cease to amaze me, Itsy. Anyway, I'm available, but the truck's not. Rip's going to need it to drive to the rehab center."

"Ain't the rehab center only two blocks up the street?" Itsy asked. She acted offended and probably thought I was looking for an excuse to get out of helping her. I felt bad, because she'd been willing to go to church with me the night before. But it's not like attending a Catholic mass was comparable to dealing with a bookie, which I wasn't even convinced was safe. I was embarrassed to ask Itsy if she was on top of her debt, or was in so deep she couldn't pay off her obligation. I've heard bookies could be downright brutal to clients who tried to renege on a losing wager. Itsy's insistence made me wonder if she'd been threatened with bodily harm if she didn't settle a debt today.

So, afraid for Itsy's well-being, I decided to help her out as much as I could. "Yeah, the rehab facility's nearby, but Rip's really limited about how much energy he can expend right now. In fact, today's the first day Rip's been allowed to drive. He'll be taking our only vehicle, but that doesn't mean we can't call Goober to come pick us up."

"Goober? Who's that?" Itsy asked. "Other than the mechanic on the *Andy Griffith Show*?"

"Good grief, girl. You've never heard of Goober? You are dreadfully out of touch, my friend. Have you not had any contact with the outside world in the last decade, or so?"

"Why would I want to immerse myself in the depressing reality of life any more than I have to? I'm happier not knowing what's going on in the world."

"You make a good point, Itsy. But burying our heads in

the sand won't get us to downtown Seattle anytime soon. Goober is like a modern day taxi cab, I hear. You call them and they send a car to pick you up and take you wherever you need to go."

"Hmm. Never heard of it. But then, I've never ridden in a taxi cab before, either."

"Wow! You *have* led a sheltered life, Itsy. Well, I'm almost sure the taxi company is called Goober. You just need to call the company and have them swing by and get us."

"I don't know how to call Goober, Rapella. I have this flip-top Jitterbug phone I got ten years ago. Can't you call them?"

"I don't know their number. Don't you have a phone book?"

"Gee whiz, Rapella. Even I know you won't find Goober in the phone book. Didn't you say you had a pod?"

"Huh?"

"A pod," Itsy repeated with a touch of indignation in her voice. "Or is it called an iPod? You know, that thing you use to Boggle things to find out more about them."

"It's Google I use to research different subjects. And you're talking about an iPad. I believe an iPod is one of those trailer things you can store stuff inside in lieu of renting a storage unit."

"Oh. Now that you mention it, I think I've seen one of those. The Nowacks down the street rented one of those iPods when they moved a couple of months ago," Itsy said. "Then the iPod company towed it to the Nowacks' new house when they were ready to unload their stuff and move in."

"Very convenient. Now wait here while I go Google Goober and make sure Rip feels comfortable not having me nearby for a while."

I was beginning to see Itsy's and my affiliation turning into the same kind of relationship that had probably existed between her and Mabel Trumbo. Itsy probably welcomed me as a replacement for her late neighbor, who'd most likely been the closest friend she'd had in the world whether she'd admit it or not. I was content knowing I filled some kind of void in Itsy's life, even if it was only destined to be for the next couple of months.

I asked Itsy to wait in the foyer so she wouldn't follow me into the kitchen. I didn't think our next-door neighbor needed to see a chubby, bald guy with a fresh zipper down his chest who was wearing nothing but a well-worn pair of boxer shorts and trying to choke down a bowl of what was now stone-cold hot cereal.

"Be careful," he said, after I informed him I was going on an errand with the neighbor. "Itsy doesn't sound like she'd be the safest driver on the planet."

I hadn't bothered telling him her car was in the shop and we planned to contact a transportation service called Goober for a ride. Like Itsy, he made no effort to keep up with current events, and I didn't have time to explain those new-fangled taxi cabs to him.

"I shouldn't be gone long." I kissed him on the top of the head and grabbed my purse off the counter. "I'm just tagging along on her quick little trip downtown. I'm sure I'll be back well before Sydney arrives at eleven."

I also didn't think Rip needed to know we were going to pay a visit to a bookie. He'd want us to wait until he could accompany us, and waiting was not an option. I didn't want Rip doing more than he should that early in the recovery process. It's not like he was in any condition to kick some bookie's behind should we be threatened. Besides, this would just be a speedy, uneventful trip into the city.

I didn't know it at the time, but it wouldn't be as quick a trip as I'd thought it'd be, and it certainly wouldn't be uneventful. Had I known what was in store, I would have faked a migraine, and stayed home to work on some mindless task all day. But I didn't. So off I went, like a heedless lemming racing toward the sea.

CHAPTER 23

"Regina? This is your mother," I said into the phone after I'd failed to find the transportation company on my iPad. When I'd Googled "Goober", I only found articles about the beloved TV character, peanuts, and a Nestle's candy product. As a last resort, I'd placed a call to my daughter.

"I know who it is, Mom. When you call, your name and photo pop up on my screen. Even if they didn't, I'd know it was you because you and Dad have your own personal ringtones."

"Oh?" It was flattering to hear our daughter had assigned us each our own tune so she'd know when we were calling. She must have wanted to make sure she'd never miss an opportunity to speak with us. "That's so sweet of you. And what are they, sweetheart?"

"Well, Dad's is Toby Keith's 'Who's Your Daddy'? And yours is 'Crazy Mama'."

"'Crazy Mama?'" I asked. I tried not to sound as offended as I felt.

"It's not what you're thinking, Mom. You know how much I love the Rolling Stones, and the title does have the word Mama in it, so—"

"Oh, never mind, Reggie." Itsy was waiting for me in the

foyer, and I didn't have time to dissect her reasoning behind the song choice. The fact she never wanted to miss a call from me was gratifying enough for now. "The reason I called is that I'm going with a friend to see her bookie and I can't seem to find Goober on my phone."

"Who? What? Her bookie? Did you say Goober?" Regina asked. She sounded agitated, as if I'd caught her at a bad time. "Your friend's bookie is named Goober?"

"No, of course not."

"Goober as in The Andy Griffith Show?"

"Now you're starting to sound like Itsy."

"Itsy?" Regina asked, clearly confused. I was even more convinced I'd caught her at an inopportune time; in the middle of a manicure, a real estate closing, or perhaps an argument with her cable TV provider.

Goodness sakes. She might have even just been in an accident, I thought. "You weren't injured were you, dear?"

"What? Was I injured?" Now Regina sounded more worried than flustered. "Mom, you haven't been cooking with sherry again, have you?"

"No, dear. The last time I tried that, it didn't turn out so well. Let me start over. I'm a little flustered at the moment."

"Yeah, no shit. I think that went without saying." My daughter's sarcastic response only goes to show why calling her was a last resort. Impatiently, Regina asked, "What's going on, Mom?"

"My friend, Itsy Warman, and I are trying to nail down a lift to town with that new Goober company that provides taxi service."

"Good Lord, Mother. It's not called Goober."

"Well, no wonder I couldn't find it on the Internet. What *is* it called?"

"Does Dad know about this?" Regina replied, instead of answering my question.

"Of course he does, sweetheart."

"Let me talk to him."

I glanced in the kitchen to make sure Rip wasn't

eavesdropping on my call. He wasn't. He was pouring his uneaten oatmeal down the garbage disposal and probably couldn't have heard my voice over the ruckus Goofus was making, anyway. I'd have bet the farm that ten minutes after I departed with Itsy, Rip would be eating cold pizza for breakfast that one of the Combs' kids had left in the fridge the previous night.

"Your father's at his rehab appointment."

"All right, Mom. Why don't you just let me arrange for the pickup for you two? I already have the app on my phone, and I don't have time to explain to you how to download it on yours and sign up for the service. I'll just need your current location and a destination address."

"Our address at the Heart Shack is 666 South Hart Street."

"Yikes, Mom. The number 666 is synonymous with the devil, you know."

"Maybe that's why this place seems to be haunted." I hadn't even considered the significance of the house's address before, but then, I'd never been particularly superstitious. "Downtown Seattle is our destination."

"Can you be a little more specific?" Regina asked, with a sarcastic tinge to her tone again. "Downtown Seattle's a little vague, considering the size of the city."

"I don't know the address, dear. Can't Itsy just tell the driver when he arrives?"

"I'll see what I can do," she replied. I detected a sigh on the other end of the line. I was beginning to wonder if she actually did answer her phone every time she heard "Crazy Mama" playing. She seemed to not have her phone with her quite frequently when I called. A few moments later, Regina said, "Don't worry about paying the driver. They'll just charge it to my account."

"Thanks, sweetie. I'll have Itsy reimburse you."

"Don't worry about it. It's really reasonably priced. Just have a good time and be careful. I can't believe daddy's letting you two make a visit to a bookie without him."

"He's not concerned, dear, so you shouldn't be either."

How could he be concerned about something he knows nothing about? I could have added.

"Well, all right. You two need to get outside where the driver can see you because he or she should be there in no time at all. I'll email you a screenshot showing the driver's name, license plate number, and vehicle make and model. Make sure they match before you get in. Okay?"

"Of course, dear. Thanks again."

"That blue car is slowing down. He looks like he's looking for someone. It must be our ride. Let's wave him down, Itsy." We'd barely made it to the curb when we spotted the car.

"Wow!" Itsy exclaimed. "That *was* fast. We ain't been standing here but a few seconds."

"Regina told me they'd be here in no time at all."

We both began waving our arms as if we were stranded on a deserted island and trying to flag down a plane flying overhead. The blue Chevy Cruze, which had a bashed-in headlight and mangled front fender, pulled over and stopped. The driver unrolled the passenger window and curtly asked, "Whaddya want?"

The disheveled driver had a ruddy face and bloodshot eyes that appeared to be aimed in two different directions. I was glad we could help him out with a fare. He was so slovenly, it was obvious he needed the money to buy some new clothes and help to get his life back on track. He needed to bone up on his social skills and manners, too. But I reckon no amount of money can buy respectability and politeness.

"We're your next ride, sir. My daughter said you'd be here soon, but that was crazy fast."

"What?" He looked dazed and confused. I thought Regina told me he'd know we wanted to go downtown, but then realized it was probably my fault for not knowing the exact address.

As the man stared at us with his mouth agape, Itsy and I climbed into the back of the Chevy and fiddled with our seatbelts. After we were buckled in, the driver continued to stare at us through the car's rearview mirror. He took a long draw from a flask he'd extracted from the console, which I assumed was water to help keep him hydrated on the warm day. I turned to Itsy, and said, "Give the gentleman the address."

Itsy tapped the driver on the shoulder. He was still silently staring at us through the mirror with his misaligned eyeballs. Itsy said, "We need to go to the bookie."

"What?" The man asked again. I knew by his incredulous tone he had no clue where Itsy's bookie was located. "Why should I take you there?"

"I don't think the purpose of our trip should be of any concern to you. We're paying you to take us where *we* need to go, not where *you* want to take us. We have plenty of money to pay you, if that's your problem," Itsy said icily.

I shook my head at her. "You big dummy. He needs an actual address. How's he supposed to know where the bookie is?" I glanced in the mirror to give the driver an apologetic smile.

"I don't know the exact address. I just know how to get there," she replied. She then tapped the driver on the shoulder again. "Can't you just drive down to the Pike Place Market and turn right?"

"Did you say you had plenty of money to—" the driver started to say, but I cut in.

"Yes, yes. Don't worry. You'll be taken care of, along with a handsome tip." I answered for Itsy because I hadn't had a chance to tell her Regina was planning to have our fare charged to her account. Reggie hadn't told me the company's tipping policy. But I knew you could draw more flies with honey, and I had a couple of dollar bills I was willing to part with if the man could get us safely to our destination.

The driver turned to face us with a gap-toothed grin. He not only lacked adequate clothing, but was also in dire need of some dental work. In comparison, he made Tasman Combs look like a viable candidate for a *Pepsodent* commercial.

"Whatever you say, ladies." He turned back around, reached down, and pushed a button on his door. I was relieved to hear the doors lock securely. I certainly didn't want to take a tumble onto the street should my seatbelt fail and my door accidently swing open.

I sat back in my seat as the car pulled away from the curb. While our driver was maneuvering wildly in and out of traffic, I kept my displeasure to myself and prayed for a quick arrival at Itsy's bookie's place. I couldn't help gasping after he yelled, "It's the pedal on the right!" out his open window to an old woman who looked as if she should have had her license pulled a decade ago. She was in danger of being passed on the passenger side by a young mother pushing a stroller down the sidewalk. I understood the driver's frustration at being unable to pass her due to oncoming traffic, as the elderly lady drove fifteen miles an hour in a forty-five miles-an-hour zone. But there was no call for using his left hand to flash an obscene gesture.

"We're not in that big of hurry, sir. I'm sure the woman is doing the best she can under the circumstances." I couldn't contain my disapproval any longer and didn't want the thirty-something driver to think we were in such a rush we'd condone him running the poor old lady off the road. Itsy's bookie would just have to cool his jets until we got there.

As if he hadn't heard me, the driver laid on his horn, scaring not only the older woman in the station wagon ahead of us, but also the two passengers in his back seat. I inhaled so sharply, I swallowed the entire peppermint lozenge I'd just put in my mouth to freshen my breath. As I tried to dislodge the lozenge by hacking harshly, I saw the elderly woman look into her mirror to see our driver waving his fist at her.

Suddenly, the mint shot out of my mouth, hitting our driver in the right temple just as the woman pulled off the road, ever so slowly and cautiously, into a tattoo parlor's parking lot. I'd have done the exact same thing, wanting no further interaction with the incensed driver making intimidating gestures.

With the slower vehicle out of his way, our driver sped up. I knew we had to have been exceeding the speed limit by at least twenty miles per hour. So far, I wasn't very impressed with the new taxi service, even though my daughter swore by it and thought it was the best thing since sliced bread.

Just then my phone pinged. I looked down to see I'd received a text from Regina. It said, DID YOUR RIDE ARRIVE ALL RIGHT?

I texted back to let her know it had and we were headed toward downtown Seattle. As I was typing my message, Itsy whispered, "I think he went the wrong direction."

"He probably knows a quicker way to get there," I whispered in response. I then sent another text to Regina.

NOT ONLY DID OUR RIDE ARRIVE QUICKLY, THE DRIVER APPEARS TO BE TAKING A SHORT CUT TO THE BOOKIE'S. ISN'T THAT NICE?

YES, Regina texted back. THEY SAID THEY DIDN'T HAVE A CAR NEARBY BUT WOULD HAVE ONE THERE WITHIN FIFTEEN MINUTES, SO I'M GLAD YOU DIDN'T HAVE TOO LONG OF A WAIT.

NOT EVEN A FULL MINUTE, I replied. BUT THE DRIVER SURE IS A BAD-TEMPERED YOUNG MAN.

REALLY? THAT QUICKLY? Regina's next text read.

YES. WE WERE IMPRESSED WITH HIS PROMTNESS.

YOU ARE IN THE VEHICLE LISTED ON THE SCREEN SHOT I E-MAILED YOU, AREN'T YOU?

I went to the mail app on my phone and opened up her message. On the screen shot photo it showed that a Carlos Medina would be picking us up in a white Toyota Rav-4, and there was a photo of a handsome Hispanic man, twice the age of the man in the front seat who was driving the blue Chevy Cruze. I hadn't had enough time to look at Regina's message earlier. However, now that I did, I didn't think our skinny white driver looked anything like Carlos, and he most certainly wasn't driving a white SUV. We had just assumed he was our ride because he'd been slowing down as if he were searching for someone as we spotted him coming down South Hart Street.

"Uh-oh," I said under my breath. I showed the information on the screen to Itsy. Her eyes opened wide in fear. I turned my palms up and shrugged in a "what do we do now" gesture. Before I could even ask the driver for his credentials, Itsy let out a loud groan and bent over, clutching her chest.

"What's wrong?" I asked her in alarm.

"Pull over, driver!" She hollered between dramatic moans. "I think I'm having a heart attack."

"Say what?" The driver asked in a panicky tone.

"We need to pull over so I can call for emergency medical assistance. My friend's having a heart attack!" I answered, a bit hysterically, now that my companion was writhing in agony.

"Are you sure?" He turned around in his seat to see what was happening in the back seat of his car. He looked at Itsy as if an alien being with two heads had just popped out of her belly button.

I thought the company he drove for should have covered that potentiality in their training manual, because it was clear our driver had no idea how to respond to an emergency in his vehicle. I guess it was just as clear I wasn't thinking straight at the time or it would have occurred to me that the man didn't work for the taxi-service company to begin with.

Itsy groaned again. It was so loud and terrifying, one would've suspected that both her kidneys were trying to pass two-pound stones at the same time. I yelled at the now frantic driver, who'd just missed clipping a parked ice cream truck by inches. "Of course, I'm sure. My husband just recently had a similar cardiac issue, so I know exactly what's going on with my friend."

The driver pulled over in the first gap between parked cars he came to. He pointed to the sidewalk and screamed, "Get out!" His order for us to vacate his car was even more infuriating than Goofus's constant demands for me to leave the kitchen. But with my friend in dire straits, there was no time to give him a piece of my mind. I helped Itsy out of the car. Her feet had barely cleared the back seat when the vehicle pulled away. When the driver gunned the engine, the back door slammed shut of its own accord.

Within seconds, the Chevy was a block away. I screamed pointlessly at the departing vehicle, unleashing my fury at its driver. "You have some nerve, you stinking creep! I hope you have a heart attack in the back of some ass-wipe's car some day and he drives off and leaves you on the side—"

"He can't hear you, Rapella!" Itsy said, interrupting my incensed tirade.

"I know, but it felt good to say it anyway. Now, lay your head on my thigh and don't try to talk. I'll have help here as soon as I can." I pulled my phone out of my pocket and began to dial 9-1-1.

Itsy, who'd stopped moaning the second the Chevy pulled away, slapped the phone out of my hand and asked, "What in the Sam Hill are you doing?"

"Calling for help. We need to get you to the hospital as soon as possible." I stopped when I noticed she was laughing. "Oh. You're not really having a heart attack, are you?"

"Of course not, you moron," she replied. "I did the first thing I could think of to get us out of his car. Having to jump from a moving vehicle can mess up a person's whole day, you know. Besides, I tried the door, and he had the child locks activated."

"How did you know he'd pull over and let us out?"

"Did you really think he was going to drive us to a

hospital or call the police to come assist us? Whatever his intentions were, they weren't to help us. I was correct in thinking he'd want us gone immediately if he thought some old lady he was hoping to rob was about to kick the bucket in the back seat of his car."

"You're right, Itsy," I said. I was shaking from the thought of what might have happened to us if not for Itsy's faked medical crisis. I owed her big time. Her quick thinking reminded me of my friend, Lexie Starr, who could always come up with a workable ruse at a moment's notice. "Oh, my goodness. He might have been planning to rape us."

"No. He wasn't planning to rape us. Trust me on this one, Rapella. It was the money we told him we had plenty of that the creep was interested in, not our smoking hot bodies."

"Oh, well. I suppose you're right." I felt a sense of dejection at her comment and I probably came across as disappointed that the man would turn his nose up at us that way.

"Seriously, Rapella?" Itsy stared at me as if I'd just told her I was going to pee on the fire hydrant next to us so I could mark my territory. "You're actually upset the man didn't think we were worthy of raping?"

"Don't be ridiculous." I shook my head in disgust. "I'd better text my daughter back before she begins to worry."

ALL'S GOOD, my message read.

"What's so freaking good about it?" Itsy asked, reading the text over my shoulder. "We're sitting here on a curb with no clue where we're at, and no idea how to get where we're going. You should have asked your daughter to hook us up with another ride. This time we'd promise to check out the driver's credentials before crawling into the back seat of his car."

"Never! For one thing, I don't want my daughter to think I'm a nut job. Her ringtone already indicates she thinks I'm crazy. Nor do I ever want to get a ride with that company again."

"But that weirdo doesn't even work for the company, Rapella. We're the idiots who flagged the dude down and hopped into his back seat without verifying he was the driver assigned to pick us up. Worse yet, we told him we had plenty of money and insisted he drive us somewhere."

Itsy was smarter than I'd given her credit for. She'd impressed me as a gal who'd be perfectly at home in the backwoods of the Ozark Hills, smoking a corn cob pipe and running a moonshine still. Yet here she was, showing a lot more sense than I was.

"Yeah, I guess you're right. As much as I hate to, I'll have to give her a call. Let's walk down to the bridge so I can get an address off a building."

Itsy stood up and looked in the direction I was pointing. She exclaimed, "Hey! That's the Desimone Bridge!"

"So?"

"I know where we're at now. That bridge is by Pike Place Market. The bookie is only a couple of blocks from there, on East Pike Street. It's not but a ten-minute walk from here. Let's get that taken care of, and then we'll worry about how to get home."

I tagged along beside Itsy as we walked to her bookie's place. I hadn't wanted to appear meddlesome and ask her what she needed to see her bookie about. I wasn't sure I even wanted to know. Oh, who am I kidding? You and I both know I was itching to ask about it. Somehow, I managed to remain silent.

In lieu of me asking nosy questions, we talked about how lucky we were that Regina texted me when she did. If she hadn't, we might have found ourselves in deep doo-doo. We could easily have become victims, or worse, statistics!

Suddenly, Itsy stopped. "Well, here we are."

I looked up to see a metal sign over the doorway of a small hole-in-the-wall type store. The sign read, "Book-E", and below the name of the store was their facetious slogan. "Used Books at like-new Prices."

"Used book store?" I asked in astonishment. I'm not sure what this says about me, but I felt an overwhelming sense of disappointment. "Book-E? I thought you said we were going to see your bookie. As in gambling, like on horses or something."

"Gambling?" Itsy replied. "Do I seem like the betting type to you? Good grief. I can't believe you'd think I was anything but a normal, run of the mill, retired senior citizen. I ain't got the resources to gamble even if I wanted to. You didn't see any money trees growing in my yard, did you?"

"Well, I can't honestly say I'd ever consider you normal or run of the mill, Itsy. But I'm sorry for the misunderstanding. I suppose the 'E' stands for the fact it's located on 'East' Pike Street. So what's so important that you had to come here today?"

Itsy pulled a hardback out of her oversized satchel. The book had to do with the identification of common North American bird species. She explained her desire to borrow it. "I was curious about this orange-beaked critter that frequents one of my backyard feeders. This place lets you borrow books free, but if you're late in returning them, you're assessed a fine. It operates just like a library, except you can buy the books if you feel like wasting perfectly good money. Their clever slogan is not far off the mark. So I prefer to borrow them and save my dough for more important things. This was due three days ago and they only allow a four-day grace period."

I was so flabbergasted, you could have knocked me over with one of those orange-beaked critter's feathers. I couldn't believe we'd put our necks on the line only to prevent my abnormal, and hardly run-of-the-mill, neighbor from having to pay some measly penalty for a used book that was a day or two overdue. "How much would the fine have been?"

"It's a quarter to begin with. But it accrues another dime with each week that it's late. That can add up fairly quickly. Don't you see?" Itsy asked in earnest.

"The only thing I see is possibly the only person in the world who's a bigger cheapskate than I am. No telling what my daughter's going to be charged after the real driver pulled up in front of your house only to find we'd bailed on our end of the rider-driver arrangement. And all to save a measly quarter! You could've waited until fall and only owed a couple of dollars on the stupid book. Or probably bought the blasted thing for a buck. To think I was just admiring you for the common sense you exhibited when you faked the heart attack. And we still have to figure out how to get home from here. I can't call Rip to come get us because I took our only phone."

"You can use my phone to call him," Itsy said after we'd left the book store. She didn't even have the courtesy to look embarrassed for putting us both through such a traumatic event over something so trivial.

I was practically screaming when I replied. "I have our only phone, Itsy! Our *only* phone! I don't have a clue what the landline number is for Mabel's house phone because I've never had a need to ask about it. If I used your phone to call Rip, our *only* phone, which is in my back pocket, would ring and what good is that gonna do us?"

"Okay, okay. I get it! You don't have to make a production out of it. After all, I know Mabel's landline number," Itsy said. Her tone was a mixture of annoyance and guilt. I guess I should have realized she'd know Mabel's number. She probably dialed it on her Jitterbug a dozen times a day while Mabel was alive.

I didn't want to call Regina to arrange another ride for us. I was even more opposed to the idea of asking Rip to come rescue us, especially when it was the first day he'd been released to drive. I wasn't looking forward to the lecture I'd get from him either.

I was weighing my options when Itsy spoke up. "Well, I guess if you'd rather, we can always take the mass transit bus. It picks up passengers every half-hour at the bus stop a block down the street and will drop us off at the hospital, which, as you know, is only a couple of blocks from home."

"Are you freaking kidding me?" I screeched. It was all I could do to resist the urge to shove Itsy off the curb into the path of an approaching three-wheeled meter maid buggy. I gave myself a few seconds to collect myself, and said, "Fine! Let's go!"

I stomped down the sidewalk ahead of Itsy. I was so ticked off at her I couldn't see straight. I'd have asked why we didn't just take the stupid bus to Book-E in the first place but I already knew the answer. Itsy had hoped to avoid the cost of the transit fare. She followed me down the street to the bus stop, wisely keeping her pie-hole shut.

It didn't help my anger decrease any when I read the sign next to the bench that read, "King County Metro Transit, ORCA bus stop. Adult fares $2.50 to $3.25, depending on zone. Seniors $1.00, all zones."

I could feel steam coming out of my ears. My exasperating next-door neighbor had inconvenienced me when I had more important things I could've been doing, so she could save a grand total of two bucks on round-trip bus fare. I was beginning to wonder how exasperating Mabel Trumbo must've been if Itsy Warman found *her* to be annoying. Could anyone be more aggravating than Itsy herself?

CHAPTER 24

◆

I could tell Itsy felt bad about the incident when she insisted on paying for my bus fare. The fare was nominal, but I noticed when it was her turn to pay, she opened up a small coin purse and began to count out a fistful of small change. I began to wonder if her penny-pinching behavior wasn't more a matter of being strapped for cash than merely being a tightwad.

Rip and I were on a fixed budget, like many retirees, but we never worried about where our next meal was coming from. We always had an emergency fund to fall back on should the need arise. I felt a sense of shame for assuming Itsy was in the same financial condition as we were. She lived alone, and having never been married, she didn't have a husband's social security or retirement pension to help subsidize her expenses.

I stepped in front of Itsy and handed the attendant two dollar bills. "Let me get it, Itsy. I promised I'd get you to town and back and feel obliged to stand by my word."

"But—"

"No, Itsy. I've got this. Let's get on the bus and find a seat."

I followed Itsy to the third row from the rear. We relaxed in relative silence as the shuttle bus made its rounds.

I was going to call Regina when we got home and insist on paying her back however much she was charged for the taxi service—hopefully without having to reveal that we never got in the white SUV she'd arranged to have pick us up.

When we pulled over at one of the bus stops, Itsy nudged me and pointed to a couple of women walking out of an office that had "Joe B. Vise—Attorney at Law" etched on the glass door. I instantly recognized Sydney and Adelaide Combs. Both were wearing identical scowls and looked as if they'd been involved in a dispute. We watched as they picked up their pace in order to catch the bus before it pulled away from the curb.

"Duck down!" I told Itsy. "I don't want them to see us."

"I wonder what they were doing at that lawyer's office," Itsy whispered as we crouched behind the seat in front of us.

"I don't know. But I'm sure it has something to do with Mabel's estate. The girls didn't look too happy, did they?"

"Nope. They were definitely pissed off about something." Itsy smiled. She was clearly pleased the twins were upset about their meeting with the attorney. "Probably found out they couldn't get what they wanted, even if they contested their aunt's will."

We weren't surprised when the girls got off at the stop closest to the Heart Shack. I was certain they were about to commence on another fortune-hunting flurry. I didn't want them to know we'd witnessed where they'd been that morning, so I asked Itsy if she'd mind walking the few extra blocks if we waited until the next stop to get off the bus.

"Not at all, Rapella. I owe you that much."

You owe me a lot more than that, I thought, but kept my opinion to myself.

Rip was sitting at the kitchen table when I walked in the door. He was concerned because he'd expected me to be back an hour or so earlier. He looked tired, as if he'd overdone it at his rehab session. He asked, "Did you two run into some kind of trouble, honey?"

"No trouble. It was just a slight hiccup that made our trip take a little longer than expected. Don't you think you should be upstairs, relaxing in the recliner?"

"Yes, but I wanted to get Goofus back in his cage first."

"Why isn't Goofus in his cage?"

"You must have left the cage open after you fed him this morning. He's been flying around the house since you left. All three of the Combs kids were running around, trying to capture him for a while. Then they just threw their hands up and went back to their rummaging. Shortly afterward, the twins left for an appointment they said they couldn't miss, and Tasman continued going from one bedroom to the next upstairs, sorting through closets and drawers. When he started to search our room I told him there was nothing in there he needed."

"What'd he say to that?"

"Nothing. Just glared at me, muttered under his breath, and headed to the next room up the hallway. I guess the knot-head thinks his aunt was incompetent enough to stash two million dollars' worth of gold into a chest of drawers in a guest bedroom. I even heard him up in the attic for a while. I knew it was him because I heard his phone playing some kind of crap music when a call came through for him."

"I think you meant rap music, not crap."

"Is there a difference? Anyway, I'd heard the same song last night when he told the caller he was worried about someone finding out about something."

"Itsy and I saw the twins come out of an attorney's office before they boarded the same bus we were on. Where are they now?" I asked.

"Who knows? When they came in, they headed straight to the basement. I don't know if they're still down there. They've been going through the place with a fine-toothed comb. I've been waiting for them to ask me if I'd consent to a cavity search. Did you say you two boarded a bus? Why'd you—"

"Cavity search? That's so funny." I responded quickly because I didn't want to go into the details of our trip to town. Before Rip could revert the conversation back to the bus ride, I told him he was free to go upstairs and rest now that I'd returned. I'd try to catch Goofus and take a sandwich up to him for lunch after I got the bird back in his cage. "I could swear I shut the door on Goofus's cage after I refilled his water bottle this morning. Are you sure you didn't see one of the kids open it?"

"Nope. Why would they do something that would delay their search for the gold or whatever they're all determined to find? You've been under a lot of pressure, dear. Don't feel bad if you forgot to shut the door on the bird cage."

His attempt to pacify me irritated me instead. Yes, it was true I'd been under a great deal of stress the last few weeks, but I would never forget to close Goofus's cage door. The last thing I'd want is for that obnoxious bird to get loose. Now I had to figure out a way to capture him without being clawed or pecked to death.

"Yeah, whatever, Rip. I'll be up with your lunch in a bit."

"Okay, thanks," Rip said wearily. "Oh, and can you ask Sydney about hiring an electrician to check the wiring here? She mentioned there was a fund for the repairs and maintenance of the place. The lights have been flickering on and off all over the house. The phone is messed up, too. It rang several times, but I couldn't hear who was on the other end of the line when I answered it. Plus, I think the contractor missed a hole in the roof. I've heard loud wailing several times that sounds like it's coming from the attic. Wind blowing through a gap, I'd guess. If I felt up to it, I'd check it out myself."

"I know, dear. Until you're feeling stronger, it's probably best to let a professional handle something like that." Although I'd never say so out loud, I didn't want my husband, who wasn't the handiest guy in the world, messing with faulty electrical wiring. I didn't want him to survive the heart incident only to be fried by a red wire that should have been black. "You know, I'm beginning to believe this place really is haunted. Mabel, Norma Jean, or someone doesn't seem to want us here."

Rip laughed, as if he thought I was kidding. I wasn't. There were too many odd things going on in the house. In the previous week, I'd heard the piano playing several times at night. I didn't bother trying to get Rip to go down and check it out. Through no fault of his own, he was slower than frozen molasses right now. Even at his best, prior to his operation, he was no faster than room-temperature molasses.

I went downstairs myself once to try and detect who was tickling the ivories in the wee hours of the morning, and thought I'd seen a ghost disappearing around the corner as I inched my way into the drawing room. It had frightened me so much, I hadn't even considered going down the next couple of times I'd heard the music.

Itsy had given me an idea when she'd made a comment on the bus ride home about concealing myself and waiting to see who came into the room to play the piano. Apparently she thought I was more courageous than I was. I'd been locking our bedroom door every night, and although Rip slept with a loaded pistol on the nightstand beside the bed, I'd considered asking him to install a deadbolt on our door.

But Itsy's suggestion reminded me of the motion-sensing game camera I'd purchased at a garage sale in Buffalo, Wyoming, earlier in the year. It had served to help us identify a suspect then, so maybe it could help identify a piano-playing prowler now.

After throwing a blanket over Goofus as he pranced back and forth across a shower curtain rod in one of the guest suite's bathrooms forty minutes later, I wadded him up inside the material, careful not to hurt him. I might occasionally wish him dead, but I never wanted to see him injured.

The task wasn't graceful, and it wasn't pretty. It wasn't without bloodshed either. After I bandaged the hand Goofus tried to annihilate with his beak, I prepared a ham salad sandwich and added a small Tupperware container full of apple slices to the plate before taking it upstairs. As expected, Rip was out cold. I sat the plate down on the table and then went back downstairs.

I needed to go outside and get the spare container of cat litter out of one of the under-carriage compartments in the Chartreuse Caboose. Dolly had been staying in the house with us and had become best buds with Gallant, who tiptoed around her as if she were a full-sized mountain lion instead of an overfed tabby. He'd stepped out of line with her once, and in return he'd been unmercifully bitch-slapped by our undaunted cat. Initially I'd been afraid Gallant would hurt Dolly. Now it was Gallant I worried about. He was too much of a softie; laid-back, obedient and loving. He'd let Dolly have her way with him if she so chose.

While I was in the trailer, I took the game camera out of the storage compartment under the queen-sized bed. Before I turned in for the night, I'd try to conceal the camouflaged device as well as I could in the drawing room.

In the meantime, I needed to decide what I would prepare for supper. I was expecting Father Cumberland to arrive around six, and I wanted to have everything ready by then. I could hardly wait to hear why he'd thought it necessary to be so ambiguous with me the afternoon he'd come into the Heart Shack uninvited.

I'd soon discover the answer was a zillion and eight light-years away from what I was expecting.

CHAPTER 25

I decided to serve a fruit salad with garlic bread and vegetable lasagna for supper, just in case our dinner guest was a vegetarian or vegan. It was a healthier option for us, as well. The lasagna recipe I used called for a variety of different veggies, all of which I had, except for frozen chopped zucchini. I didn't feel like making a trip to Safeway, even though the store was less than a mile from the house.

I needed to figure out something I could substitute for the zucchini. During the bus ride, Itsy had told me Mabel had maintained a large garden in her back yard until her heart issues began to incapacitate her. Itsy had indicated that Mabel grew ten times more than she could consume on her own, so there was a chance she'd frozen some of the garden produce and stored it in the chest freezer in the garage. Despite the fact the frozen veggies might be a decade old, once blended with the rest of the ingredients, they probably wouldn't taste too awful.

As I walked out the front door, I saw that all three of the Combs kids' vehicles were gone. I was glad to have the search party out of our hair and the house to ourselves. It would make our dinner conversation with the priest much easier.

I went into the garage, which had moss growing on its roof from built-up dirt and debris. Its interior was dank, dark, and smelled of mildew and old gasoline. Sorting through the various packages inside the chest freezer, I found meat that looked as if it'd been purchased the year the house was built.

In a Safeway bag on top were four bags of frozen vegetables: two of broccoli florets, one package of Brussels sprouts, and a bag of cubed zucchini. Bingo! The last bag was exactly what I had hoped to find. It looked new and would be ideal for the lasagna dish.

I noticed the receipt from the purchase was still in the bag. It'd been wadded up, and there was a black smudge on the back of it. I always scrutinize any purchase receipt to make sure I hadn't been screwed over by an inattentive or opportunistic sales clerk. Out of pure habit, I glanced at the receipt. It was dated one week prior to Mabel's passing, which seemed odd to me. Along with the packages still in the bag, there were other items listed on the receipt: two more bags of Brussels sprouts, two cans of spinach, and several pounds of fresh broccoli.

The list of products sounded like a healthy mix of vegetables for an elderly person, or nearly any person, for that matter. But, they were the absolute wrong foods for someone who'd just had a double-bypass and was taking a blood-thinning medication. Everything on the list was extremely high in Vitamin K, which Sydney had warned us worked against the medication by thickening the blood and making clotting a risk. The physician on the news, Dr. Gupta, had said the same thing.

Mabel had died from a pulmonary embolism, according to the post-exhumation autopsy. Had she eaten the produce that was now missing from the bag? If so, I could understand the medical board's decision to question the cardiac center's staff. Why hadn't they informed Mabel of the dangers of foods high in the risky vitamin? Granted, she was beginning to show moderate signs of Alzheimer's, but she had Sydney taking care of her after her operation.

There was also Patricia Lankston, the day nurse, who took care of Mabel when Sydney couldn't be present. Hopefully, even Tasman had enough brain cells left to know he couldn't feed those vegetables to his aunt on the two Sundays he covered for Sydney.

Had Patricia Lankston been brought up to speed on the specifics regarding Mabel's diet and medications? Could she have made an honest mistake? Was Tasman aware of the dangers of those items? These were the questions racing through my head as I dug through the chest freezer's contents. I found nothing else of interest, other than a bag filled with approximately five hundred dollars worth of paper money.

I removed the bag so I could turn the cold-hard cash over to Sydney. I suppose I'd have found this discovery odd had I not currently had a roll of twenty-dollar bills hidden in the hollow leg of our trailer's kitchen table. People from our generation found it hard to completely trust banks after hearing horror stories from our parents about the stock market crash of 1929.

Suddenly, an unfathomable thought hit me like a tire iron to the noggin. I grabbed the bag of zucchini, tucked the receipt into my bra for safekeeping, and rushed back into the house. I went upstairs to the master suite, checked to make sure Rip was resting, and then quietly opened the closet door.

When I'd placed our toiletries in the drawers of the restroom vanity a couple of weeks earlier, I'd gathered the items that belonged to Mabel and placed them inside a plastic grocery bag. I'd then placed the bag inside an unused pillow case and thrown it into the bottom of a laundry hamper in the closet. I needed to make sure those personal items were given to Sydney, as well. I retrieved the bag and carried it into the bathroom and closed the door so Rip wouldn't be bothered by any noise I made.

I dumped the bag on the counter and sorted through the items until I located the three medication bottles I'd remembered removing from the top drawer of the vanity.

The medications consisted of a statin for lowering cholesterol levels, a blood pressure medication, and a popular anti-coagulant. All three bottles had Mabel Trumbo's name on the labels. It could've been Rip's medicine drawer, as he was currently taking the exact same medications. Not surprising, since they were both patients of the same cardiac surgeon, Dr. Manual Murillo.

I wasn't particularly interested in the first two medications, but I studied the pharmacy label on the anti-coagulant bottle and dumped its contents onto the counter. It took some calculating to figure out that Mabel had not taken all of the medication she should have. It looked as if she'd missed two days' worth during the two weeks between her release from the hospital and the day of her death. But that wasn't a significant enough finding to conclude an improper dose of medication had been a factor in her death. An untaken pill or two could have easily been an oversight, but doubtfully a fatal one.

I felt an enormous sense of relief and returned all of Mabel's toiletries and medications to the plastic bag.

It occurred to me as I dropped the pillow case containing the bag into the hamper, if anyone had been looking for the medication bottles so they could remove them from the premises and dispose of any evidence they might provide, they probably never would've thought to search in a hamper that appeared to contain nothing more than a few pieces of laundry. I doubted any of them, even that halfwit boy, were interested in keeping their elderly aunt's dirty underwear as a family keepsake. If Tasman *had* entertained that thought, he had even more serious issues than I'd given him credit for.

While I was standing in the closet, I heard the sound of footsteps on the ceiling above me. I assumed one of the kids was up there searching through the attic. Those three were persistent, I'll grant them that. Then again, two million smackaroos was a powerful incentive.

I checked Rip once more, covering his bare feet with the blanket haphazardly spread across his slumbering body.

For once, Dolly was not attached to Rip like a furry parasite, but was curled up in the middle of our bed. I smiled and hurried back downstairs to resume the task of preparing supper.

As I gathered the ingredients for the lasagna, I closed the pantry door and leaned over to scratch the snoozing dog's head. When something jumped out of my cleavage and came to rest on his muzzle, Gallant's eyes popped open in alarm. I straightened up instantly and grabbed my chest because, to be honest, the suddenly-appearing grocery receipt startled me, too. I laughed at both of our reactions and tossed the receipt in the junk drawer next to the refrigerator.

Chase Cumberland was due to arrive in two hours. I couldn't see how he could've had anything to do with Mabel Trumbo's death. Nor could I think of any reason her death might benefit him, but that didn't eliminate my curiosity about why he had led me astray as to his true identity. According to Sydney, he may have done some searching in the house, as well.

It promised to be an interesting evening. Rip and the priest had not yet met, and it was important that Mr. Cumberland be judged fairly. I'd have to remind Rip to keep an open mind, remembering his own words about people who were skilled at putting up a front.

As I was placing the final layer of noodles across the top of my lasagna, another disturbing thought crossed my mind. I'd assumed the footsteps I'd heard coming from the attic had belonged to one of the Combs kids. But I recalled noticing their vehicles were gone when I'd gone out to the trailer and then the garage. Which meant the trio was already gone prior to the footsteps I'd heard in the attic. As I ruminated over the significance of that, I raced over to the window to peer toward the street. The curb was void of vehicles.

So who is in the attic? I wondered, not sure I wanted to know. But I had to be proactive about it, since Rip was not yet strong enough to do much. I couldn't just pretend I hadn't heard the footsteps. I realized I was going to have to go upstairs and see if I could crawl into the attic through the opening in the guest bathroom, whether I wanted to or not.

In the meantime, I'd try to summon up the courage to act on my plan. It was going to take a heap more than I currently had at my disposal.

CHAPTER 26

"What do you mean when you say you were helping Mabel out around this place because you were being blackmailed?" I asked Chase Cumberland as I placed the pan of lasagna on a hot pad on the table.

"That's all there was to it," the preacher said.

"But, why in the—" I began.

Rip, afraid I might offend the religious leader by being too direct, cut me off. "She must've had *some* kind of leverage on you to be able to force you into performing free labor."

"Yes. She did," Father Cumberland replied. He seemed unable to make eye contact with either of his dinner companions. After I sat down, he reached his arms out to join hands with us and said, "Let us bless our meal before I explain."

After saying a prayer of appreciation for the meal we were about to partake in, he continued, "I'm not proud to admit what I've done, but I hope you two won't feel compelled to see me crucified for what I'm about to share with you. No one else knows about the arrangement between Mabel and me prior to her passing."

"You needn't worry about that, Father," Rip said. "We have no personal vendetta against you. It's really none of our business to begin with if you'd rather not share."

I gently kicked Rip in the shin. I didn't want the priest to take the easy way out. He had deceived me, and I thought I deserved an explanation. Chase seemed to agree with me. When Rip grimaced and grunted from the blow to his lower leg, our dinner guest smiled.

"That's all right. I owe Rapella an explanation."

Chase had taken the words right out of my mouth. I returned his smile. "Thank you, Mr. Cumberland. I was confused by your reluctance to correct me when I misidentified you as Mr. Wickets. It will put my mind to rest to know why you weren't upfront with me, but I certainly wouldn't want you to be crucified, as you put it, over something for which you're not responsible."

Because the man was a devout Catholic and the leader of an impressive-sized flock, I wanted to give him the benefit of the doubt. I'd been assuming he was not accountable for whatever it was that Mabel thought she had on him. Therefore, I was taken aback when he responded.

"That's just it, Ms. Ripple. I *am* responsible for the predicament I found myself in. I've no one but myself to blame. I have committed a sin for which I've asked forgiveness from the Lord and repented. But that doesn't mean I've forgiven myself."

Rip, whose curiosity was pathetically lacking, began to ask him if he was certain he wanted to proceed with his story. I bit my tongue despite the fact I wanted to tell him to zip it and let the man talk.

"I think getting this off my chest might be therapeutic for me, Mr. Ripple. And, like I said, I need to explain to your beautiful wife why I misled her."

After a remark like that one, I was ready to forgive him without even hearing his explanation. Anyone who called me "beautiful" was golden in my book. That thought reminded me of a promise I'd made to Sydney. "Before you begin, Mr. Cumberland, I have a question to ask you. Did you leave a threatening note, along with my new gold ring, in a music box upstairs the night you lubricated the door hinges?"

"Heavens no! I'd never do anything of the sort!" Chase looked stunned, as if I'd poked him in the eye with my salad fork.

I had tried not to sound as if I was accusing the priest of malice as I'd spoken, but it didn't prevent Rip from returning my kick to the shin. I winced before carrying on with my inquiries. "Ouch! So, tell me, Father. Did you spend any time in the storeroom that night?"

"Please, call me Chase. And, no, I didn't. I'm sorry, Rapella," he said. "I had time to take care of the hinges on this main floor and on all of the doors upstairs, but it's a time-consuming job. It was almost daybreak when I finished. Why in the world would you think I'd leave you a nasty note?" The priest now appeared as if his feelings had been hurt and I felt terrible for having ever doubted him. It looked as though my customary apology tour was going to commence earlier than it usually did after I'd stuck my nose into a murder investigation.

"I apologize for being so blunt, but someone tried to frighten me into leaving here not long after you left. Then Sydney told me someone had scoured through her aunt's personal files that evening, as well. I promised her I'd ask you about it, so I felt obligated to do so. Do you recall if there was anyone else in the house that night who might've been responsible for either, or both, incidences?"

"I could hear someone working on something downstairs," the priest responded thoughtfully. "That's another reason I didn't go down to finish the hinge-lubricating job. I assumed it was one of Mabel's nieces, or her nephew, and I didn't want to disturb them in case they were involved in something important."

"Of course," I said. "Again, I'm sorry if I offended you. I truly never believed you'd do something so vile, but I was obligated to ask."

"I understand," Chase replied.

Rip, who looked as if he'd rather be doing squat thrusts on the kitchen floor than be involved in my conversation with the priest, said, "Why don't you go ahead with what you wanted to share, son? It's getting late, and there's a pan of lasagna calling my name."

"There's no meat in it, honey." I thought it only fair to warn him. "It's a vegetable lasagna."

"Oh," Rip muttered. "Well, then, take your time, son."

"Okay," Chase replied with a knowing smile. "Anyway, just over twelve years ago when I was ordained, I took a vow of chastity, as most Roman Catholic clerics of the Latin-rite are expected to do. I'm ashamed to say I broke that sacred vow. Sydney and I—"

"Sydney?" Rip and I asked in unison, both of us were nearly shell-shocked. If Sydney wasn't such an unusual name, I'd have thought he was referring to someone other than Mabel's great-niece.

"Yes," Chase hung his head as he continued. "We didn't actually engage in, er, well, you know, intercourse. I can't honestly say I didn't want to in the heat of the moment, but I came to my senses in time to back away from the temptation."

"So you didn't really commit a sin, after all. Right?" I asked. I found his shyness about the subject adorable.

"In the eyes of the church, it is sinful to engage in any sexual activity, or have any sexual thoughts or feelings, whether they result in copulation or not."

Rip studied the sorrow in the priest's eyes and laid his hand on the man's wrist. "Son, you need to stop beating yourself up over something that happened several years ago. You asked for forgiveness and repented. I'm sure our Lord has forgiven you and is proud of the way you've served him every day since then."

"How did Sydney feel about it?" I asked. I needed all of the juicy details to satisfy my inquisitive mind.

"I don't really know, but I hope she understood."

"So what's Mabel's got to do with this?" I asked. I felt bad that the kind man was harboring such guilt over something I thought was quite trivial. But I still had unanswered questions, and he seemed to be willing to answer them.

"Well, you see, I met Sydney when she accompanied Mabel to an Easter sunrise service about three years ago. I was so drawn to her that I asked her out for supper that evening. I should've given it more thought and canceled the date. When we met for supper a second time, I accompanied her home afterward. We began to make out, but I stopped short of engaging in intercourse. I explained to Sydney why I couldn't go through with it and it seemed at the time as if she understood my plight."

"Of course, she did, Chase. So what's Mabel got to do with this?" I asked again.

"It soon became apparent that Sydney had said something about the incident to Mabel. I haven't spoken with Sydney since. I knew it was wrong to avoid her like I did, but I was too embarrassed and ashamed to discuss the matter with her."

When Chase stopped talking, I could sense there was more to the story, so I prompted him to continue. "Go on, Father."

"Mabel approached me the week before the fundraiser that included raffling off the Steinway. She nonchalantly mentioned she knew what had happened between Sydney and me, and inferred if she didn't win the raffle she might be persuaded to share the information with the rest of the choir. Just the mention of an incident like that could cause great upheaval within the congregation, and especially with the elders. Can you imagine how quickly the news would have spread if she'd told a dozen or more women in the church choir about it?"

"That grapevine would've had smoke rolling off of it," Rip said. It irritated me when men assumed every woman loved to gossip. Naturally, a few of them do, but not all of us. There are men who are prone to tittle-tattle, too. But I didn't want the conversation to veer away from the subject at hand, so I didn't respond.

"What'd you do?" I asked, ignoring the look of aggravation Rip cast my way. For the life of me, I couldn't figure out how he wasn't dying to know how the priest reacted to Mabel's thinly-veiled threat. Did my husband not have one inquisitive bone in his body?

"The piano's in the drawing room, isn't it?" Chase replied with a distinct tone of bitterness in his voice. I nodded and waited for him to give a more thorough explanation.

"As the head of the church, I was selected to pull the winning ticket out of the hat. Mabel bought one ticket, which I palmed when I reached into the hat full of folded-up tickets. Lo and behold, Mabel's ticket was the winner of the valuable grand piano. And that bothers me more than anything. A lot of folks bought multiple tickets in hopes of being the lucky winner. I stole every one of their chances to win. I kept that straw basket, still full of the tickets purchased by the others. One of them was the rightful owner of that Steinway piano that's in the drawing room. I keep it on a table at the end of my bed, so every morning when I wake up, I'm reminded of the sin I committed."

"I understand how you feel, son." Rip said, "but it's time to let it go. Mabel Trumbo is with the Lord now, and all of those who didn't take home the piano that day have moved on. You need to move on, too."

"I suppose you're right. Wallowing in self-loathing isn't doing me any good. Or anyone else, for that matter. Maybe I'll start by finally getting rid of that basket of tickets."

"Very good. I hope you do."

"I agree," I said. "But why don't you put the basket of tickets in your basement and hang on to it for a little bit longer. I have a feeling you might need it in the near future."

Chase Cumberland gazed at me in puzzlement, but nodded his head anyway. I wasn't satisfied yet, though. I wanted all the juicy details, even if the lasagna became colder than a well-digger's behind before we dug into the rapidly cooling pasta dish. "So, how did that lead to you being her handyman?"

"Fear, I suppose. To keep her quiet, I was desperate to keep her happy any way I could. The work was simple enough, and I really didn't mind helping out. I have to admit I thought the jig was up when I walked into her kitchen one day and was surrounded by a swarm of women from the church choir. To my relief, Mabel never brought it up. In fact, she was fawning all over me like I was the golden boy, or something."

You were, Father. She was showing you off to make her friends' envious. I wanted to tell Chase, but thought better of it. Instead I focused on his story as he continued.

"At some point, as her memory began to fail, I couldn't even be sure she remembered the incident, but I was committed to taking care of the little repair issues by then. And I wasn't going to take a foolish risk on the off chance she remembered the incident clearly. Her official caretaker, Ridley Wickets, was seventy when he first came to work for Mabel, and at his age there were a lot of things he found difficult to handle. By the time I came along, he was more of a fixture in the house than an employee. At his height, even changing light bulbs was a challenge." Chase laughed, and as he did, a light bulb came on over my own head—the imaginary kind powered by an "aha!" moment that never needs changing.

"So the little fellow who reminded me of a leprechaun truly *is* the real Ridley Wickets, as he professed to be the day I ran into him in the drawing room, isn't he?"

"Yes, ma'am."

"And you realized he was who I was talking about when I mentioned him the day we first met, didn't you?"

"Once again, I apologize for not telling you about Ridley then."

"That's okay. I understand your reasoning now."

"Well, truthfully, I had another reason for keeping mum about him. You see, Ridley came over to America in 2008 on a temporary work visa for a brief stint with the Seattle Symphony, one of the nation's most renowned symphonies. When the short-lived stint ended, he desperately wanted to remain in the U.S., for some reason I was never privy to. Ridley answered an ad for a handyman that Mabel had put in the classifieds in 2009, after the last of the Combs kids moved out, and he's been living here in the house ever since. He was in constant fear of being discovered and returned to Ireland, where he'd likely be banned from returning to the United States for a number of years. Mabel kept Ridley hidden, so to speak, and was content to let him fly under the radar in her home for as long as he wanted. Mabel had to clue me in about him because of my frequent visits to address various issues around the house."

"Of course," I said. "You were apt to cross paths with him at some point, and Mabel knew it'd be best to forewarn you about her houseguest."

"Exactly. When you asked about him, Rapella, I didn't want to rat him out and possibly get him evicted from the only place he had to call home or, worse yet, get him deported from the country. Mabel hired the lawn work done all those years, because Ridley was even afraid to go outside, which explains why his skin is the color of typing paper."

Chase's comments made me wonder three things. First of all, had the old caretaker been playing Mabel like a fiddle all those years? Secondly, with his extremely pale skin, was Ridley the ghostly apparition I thought I'd seen one night when I went downstairs after hearing music? If he played in the Seattle Symphony, he was clearly our nighttime pianist. And, lastly, how much did Itsy know about Mr. Wickets? She seemed to be familiar with him when she talked about him not attending church and behaving like a vampire. I now understood her remark about it being dangerous for him to be seen in the daylight. I was almost afraid to ask Mr. Cumberland my next question.

"Where is Ridley now?"

"Somewhere in this house would be my guess. I'd bet Ridley could go undetected for months. He had years of practice at being invisible. And, being so tiny, he moves more quietly than your fat cat."

"Hush, son," Rip said in a serious manner, with an index finger against his lips. "Dolly could be lurking somewhere in the vicinity. Like her daddy, she's very sensitive about her weight."

We all laughed at Rip's comment. Even to the priest, who had just met Rip, it was obvious that neither Rip nor Dolly gave a flying fig about their waistlines.

As the men wolfed down their second helpings of lasagna, I thought about the footsteps I'd heard minutes earlier. The petite and elderly caretaker, who'd be around eighty now, might be more agile than I thought when it came to climbing up into the attic through the access panel. He definitely could disappear from sight in a flash. Perhaps Ridley was the one who wanted us out of the house, and not Mabel or Norma Jean haunting us from beyond. I figured Chase Cumberland, in his handling of repairs in the building, would know about its ins and outs. "Do you know if there is access to the attic other than one in that farthest bathroom upstairs?"

"Yes," Chase said. "There is access in the maintenance room behind the furnace that heats the top floor. A ladder is propped up against the wall that leads to an opening in the ceiling. That's the ladder I used to take down the draperies for you. Why do you ask?"

"I heard footsteps coming from the attic and wondered if Ridley could be living up there."

"He could be. There's a small room with a cot in it on the far west end of the attic. I noticed it when I was up there checking out a furnace duct not long ago."

"Okay. Good to know," I said. "Now finish up your supper, men, before the peach cobbler I made for dessert gets too cold."

Rip's head popped up like a prairie dog looking out of the hole above his burrow. "Did you say peach cobbler?"

"Yes, dear. I thought you deserved a reward tonight for all the hard work you've been putting into your therapy sessions and exercises at home. I didn't think one piece of cobbler was going to kill you."

"That's what I've been trying to tell you," he retorted.

"I said *one* piece."

"You'd better listen to her, man. You have an angel in Rapella, and she deserves to have you around for many years to come," Chase said as he picked up a handful of dishes and carried them to the sink.

"Thanks, but I'll get these." I took the stack of dirty plates from him and motioned for him to go back to the table.

"Whose side are you on, son?" Rip asked in jest.

After a hearty laugh, Chase turned serious. "So, Rapella, am I forgiven?"

"Of course you are. As Rip said, you're not only forgiven by me, but I'm certain by God, as well. Now sit down, pull your ears back, and dig in," I replied as I placed a bowl of cobbler in front of both men.

Other than small talk, there wasn't much chit-chat as we ate our dessert. I realized a person who felt as if he was being blackmailed might have a motive to eliminate his blackmailer. But I couldn't picture this kind man harming a flea, when a mere flirtation had left him in a state of anguish for so long.

After supper, we moved to the drawing room. The first thing Chase did was stop and admire the new vertical blinds the heart clinic had sprung for. He nodded his head, and said, "Perfect! The blinds make all the difference in the world. You've done a good job with the place, Rapella."

"Thank you. I feel comfortable here now." I'd done some redecorating and thought the house felt more inviting. "By the way, Father, you don't have to spend one second worrying about your story going any further than us. As they say, 'what happens in the Heart Shack, stays in the Heart Shack.'"

"Thank you. That means a lot to me." Chase's relief was evident. He grinned, and added, "Don't you think that 'Heart Shack' is—"

"A silly name for the place?" I said, finishing the question for him. After his amused nod, I said, "I did, but it's starting to grow on me. Do you mind if I run something by you that also goes no further than the three of us?"

After he agreed, I told him about the vegetables I'd found in the chest freezer and the slight discrepancy in Mabel's prescribed medications. "Do you think there's a chance Sydney could've had a hand in her aunt's death?"

"I can't honestly say," he replied. "I didn't really know her that well. She didn't impress me as having an evil side, however. What's your gut feeling?"

"That she'd never hurt another living soul," I said honestly. "But with all of the signs pointing toward her, I don't think the possibility can be overlooked. I have just one more thing I'm curious about. Did Mabel really pay you twenty-three dollars?"

The priest laughed. "No. I'm sorry. I really hated to lie to you, but felt I had no choice. I thought by making my made-up story more elaborate, it'd be more believable. As if it would absolve me, I guess, I picked twenty-three because it's my favorite psalm. You know the one? The—"

"Lord is my shepherd. I shall not want..." Rip and I joined in and all three of us recited the entire psalm together.

"Amen!" Rip said when we finished. Then, in an obvious attempt to veer the subject away from Mabel Trumbo's death, he asked, "So, how about those Mariners, Father?"

Rip and Chase both took a seat in the drawing room. While the two men debated the chances of the Seattle baseball team going the distance that season, I returned to the kitchen and began to clean up the dishes. Goofus, who'd been silent all through supper, squawked at me. "Scwam Sam. You're a bad boy. Can't eat that, Skid."

I froze at the bird's last words. I observed how the bird could instantly pick up on a phrase and repeat it, even though he tended to speak with a speech impediment. Syd could be a nickname in the Combs' family, just as Addie and Taz had proven to be. I couldn't help but wonder if Goofus had heard Mabel say, "Can't eat that, Syd?" With the way the bird pronounced certain words, Skid could very well stand for Syd.

After our dinner guest had departed, I talked it over with Rip. Like me, he didn't want to believe Sydney would have done anything to harm her aunt. Not for fame or fortune or even life itself. But we couldn't deny the fact the evidence was piling up against the seemingly angelic nurse.

The evening had answered a lot of questions, but it'd also brought up a few new ones. For starters, was Ridley Wickets still residing in the Heart Shack? The following morning, I planned to visit the little room in the attic and see if I could locate an out-of-sight sprite.

CHAPTER 27

A s it turned out, I didn't have to crawl up into the attic the next morning on a hunt for Ridley Wickets. I happened upon him after I awoke with an upset tummy. I went downstairs at the crack of dawn to get a couple of saltines to settle my stomach.

Wearing the same plaid shirt I'd seen him in before, a sound-asleep Ridley sat cross-legged on the floor with Gallant's big head lying in his lap. They both were startled awake when I stepped into the room and switched on the light.

Alarmed, Ridley jumped to his feet, causing Gallant's chin to fall to the ceramic floor. After collecting himself, he said, "Good morning, me lady. What brings ya down so early?"

"What brings you down at all? Have you been living in this house since my husband and I moved in?"

He had the grace to look down. "Yes, me lady. Much apologies to ya. I have no place else but to go."

"Why didn't you just tell us you were staying here? We wouldn't have booted you out. It's clear Mabel was content to let you stay here as long as you wanted to, and who are we to upset the apple cart? Are you camped out in the attic?"

"Yes, me lady."

"Not any more. You have no business going up and down that ladder in the maintenance room. As long as the cardiac center doesn't force you out, you are more than welcome to utilize one of the guest rooms. It was you behind all of the odd noises, the howling sounds in the attic, the flickering lights, the phone calls, and the other strange happenings. Wasn't it?"

Ridley nodded without making eye contact.

"You're our mysterious nighttime pianist too."

"Yes, me lady. Much apologies. I was afeared you'd find me."

"Why were you afraid? Rip and I aren't terrible people, Ridley. Like you, we're getting a little long in the teeth. In fact, in my case, I don't even have any real ones left. And the other one of us has a sticky ticker, at least until he's completely recovered. It's just not safe to frighten people our age."

"Much apologies," the Irish man repeated.

Even though Chase had told us why the old caretaker was afraid of being discovered, I was still rather pissed about Ridley's trickery. But I could understand why Mabel wanted him to have access to the Steinway piano. Not that wanting the talented musician to have a quality instrument to practice his skills on excused the way she went about acquiring the piano.

"You're a very gifted pianist, by the way. But you nearly scared the bejesus out of me numerous times, and had me thinking I needed to see a shrink. Why not just inform us that Mabel had granted you free occupancy, at least until the cardiac center took over ownership of the place?"

"Was afeared you'd kick me to the curb if you's be to know I was about, now that it's the hearty home, and all." I found Ridley's use of "afeared" in lieu of "afraid" endearing, but I was still a bit irritated with him. Ridley stared at the red socks on his feet. They did nothing to make him look less elf-like.

"I would've never done that, Mr. Wickets. So there was

no call to give me the fright of my life by putting the threatening message and my gold ring in the music box."

"Whatcha be talking about?" Ridley asked, staring straight into my eyes for the first time. He appeared genuinely befuddled.

"I'm talking about the note you put in the music box that said I didn't belong here. Were you trying to scare me away?"

"I be hoping the noisies and flicking lights would make you goes away so I wouldn't not have to go, but I know not about a note or box." Ridley's poor grammar and double negatives were at times hard to follow, and his voice was soft and barely audible. Despite all that, I recognized sincerity when I heard it, and I believed him.

"If you didn't do it, who did?" I asked.

Ridley shrugged. "The boy be me guess. He be in my stuff one day."

"Ah, I see." And I did. Rip had said he'd heard Tasman's phone playing rap music in the attic when he was up there sorting through things. He'd been going through Ridley's private property, but may not have realized who it belonged to.

"Does Tasman know about you? Or the twins?" I asked.

"Me no think so, except maybe the nurse girl. I see them but they not never meet me. Can't trust them kind."

I couldn't disagree with that. I didn't trust them either. I told Ridley he was free to move into one of the available bedrooms right away, and I'd assist him if needed. I also let him know he could play the piano any time he had a hankering to. "I believe music breathes life into a home. Even though I don't condone her actions, I can see why Mabel wanted you to have the church's magnificent piano."

"Yes, me lady. She do that for me. I do things for her too. Even after I old." Ridley Wickets and Mabel Trumbo must have been close, I realized. It seemed as if the arrangement had been a beneficial one for both of them. It kept both of them from living alone, and gave them someone else in the house to interact with. At his current age, he probably didn't have the funds or the wherewithal to relocate. He was obviously not receiving a Social Security check on the same day every month, like most folks his age, having expatriated from his native country nine years earlier.

I invited Ridley to join me for a cup of coffee. I then called the phone number Father Cumberland had given me and asked him if he'd mind helping move Ridley's stuff down from the attic. Chase was delighted to hear I'd offered the elderly caretaker a bedroom on the second floor and said he'd be happy to assist.

After he'd drained his cup of coffee, I invited Ridley to join us for supper. I doubted he'd had a warm meal in ages, but didn't want to embarrass him by asking. I had to assume the reclusive gentleman was behind the disappearance of random food items, including the bag of Oreos I'd accused Rip of eating while I was downtown with Itsy. Ridley accepted my dinner invitation and excused himself in his usual delightful manner. "I be gone."

Another piece of the Heart Shack puzzle had fallen into place. Now I wouldn't need to conceal the game camera in the drawing room. I'd set it on the kitchen counter the night before with plans of relocating it in hopes of catching the piano-playing intruder. After our discussion with the priest, I'd forgotten to remove the camera from the kitchen. I realized now that there was no intruder whose image I needed to capture. The Heart Shack was really more Ridley's home than it was ours.

I could understand Ridley's concerns and wasn't sure I wouldn't have done the same thing. I'd see what I could do to make sure the elderly pianist was welcome to stay in the house as long as the place was inhabitable.

The following morning, after I fed the two pets and took Gallant out for a short walk, I took a carton of eggs out of the refrigerator. Ridley would be joining us for breakfast, so Rip was getting a respite from oatmeal and whole wheat toast.

Before starting breakfast, I decided to take the game camera back to the trailer. As I walked into the Chartreuse Caboose, I noticed on the camera's display there'd been four images captured. The camera was aimed at the door leading to the back yard overnight, and its motion-sensing element had somehow been accidentally activated. I hadn't walked over to that corner of the room, so I assumed the photos must've been of Gallant as he'd meandered about the kitchen at some point during the night.

I took the memory card out of the slot and stuffed it into my front pocket, hoping to download the images to my iPad while Rip was at his rehab appointment. If I was lucky, I might have captured a cute photo of the St. Bernard who'd wormed his way into my heart.

I'd captured something in the images, all right, but it wasn't Gallant who'd been meandering through the kitchen in the middle of the night.

I was rendered speechless that afternoon when I looked at the images on the memory card. Clear as a bell was the image of our next-door neighbor, Itsy Warman, letting herself into the house through the back door. The time-stamped image was taken at 02:16 a.m. earlier that morning. The second image was of her standing in front of the junk drawer, which was directly below the one that held the silverware. The drawer contained miscellaneous items such as a roll of scotch tape, rubber bands, a dog-eared recipe book, and some loose change. And, like any junk drawer worth its salt, there were off-the-wall items in it, too, like a Butterfinger bar that was so old it had literally turned to dust, a golf ball signed by Arnold Palmer, a button that said 'I Like Ike' on it, and a dried up tube of depilatory cream.

In the third photo, Itsy stood with her back to the camera. The final shot, taken at 02:31 a.m., was of her opening the back door to depart. The images stymied me. What in the world was she doing sneaking into Mabel's house in the wee hours of the morning? It appeared she'd spent a total of about fifteen minutes in the house.

As you can imagine, I was anxious to find out what Itsy had been up to. I marched directly to her house and rang the doorbell.

"Good morning, neighbor," she greeted me cheerfully.

Without returning the greeting, I held my iPad up to her face so she could see the incriminating image on the screen. She visibly blanched as she recognized herself in the photo.

"Oh, yeah," she said. "I was going to walk over and tell you about that today. You see, I'd been thinking about baking a cake for you and Rip to thank you for going downtown with me. But a couple of weeks before Mabel passed, she'd borrowed my Bundt pan. I couldn't sleep last night and was sitting out on my front porch when I remembered I'd never gotten it back. Well, you'd mentioned on the bus ride home from the Book-E store that the cardiac center would be taking possession of the house soon. So, using a key to the back door that Mabel gave me years ago, I let myself in to retrieve the pan. I couldn't find it, though."

She finished explaining with an expression on her face that I deciphered as, "I wonder if she bought that load of bull crap?"

"And you thought Mabel had stashed your Bundt pan in a drawer that wasn't more than four inches in height?" I asked, as I scrolled to the next image in my photo file.

"Well, no, of course not." Itsy stopped talking for several long moments, as if trying to come up with a reasonable excuse for her actions. Finally, without addressing the question about why she was looking in the junk drawer, she continued. "I realized the pan was probably in the pantry and I didn't want to startle the dog by making too much noise. I knew if Gallant began to bark and raise a fuss, you'd hear it upstairs and be frightened."

"No more than I was when I heard Ridley Wickets, whom I didn't even know was in the house, playing the piano in the middle of the night. Why didn't you tell me you knew it was him playing it, and that he was the man I asked you about that reminded me of an elf?"

"Mabel made me promise I'd never tell anyone about Ridley. And since you're as 'anyone' as the next guy, I aimed to stay true to my word. But I knew you were frightened by Ridley's nighttime piano-playing, so I hoped you'd find out about him on your own rather than me ratting him out. That's why I suggested you conduct a stakeout in the parlor."

"Okay. I get it," I said. "I appreciate your concern for me. And keeping your word was an honorable thing to do, but I also noticed you helped yourself to the change in the drawer. Itsy, if you're in a financial bind, you could've just asked me and I would have loaned you some money. You didn't have to steal Mabel's coins, for goodness sakes!"

Itsy had initially appeared humiliated by my remarks, but after a few moments of silence, she reacted defensively. "Well, it ain't like Mabel's gonna need those few coins to purchase a soda pop or a postage stamp. They don't have vending machines in heaven, you know."

Not knowing how to respond to a remark like that, I just stared at Itsy. The silence must have made her uncomfortable because she tried to clarify her comment, by adding, "I'm sure God hands stuff like that out for free up there, kind of like we do candy bars on Halloween down here."

Her justification for stealing the change made me laugh. I would add that I was laughing with her, not at her, if not for the fact she wasn't laughing at all. I realized then that her amusing response had been intended to cover up her shame and embarrassment. I felt bad for humiliating her. I should have thought before speaking. There was no reason to bring up the fact she might be short on cash. Stealing a couple dollars' worth of small change wasn't that big of deal. It was no wonder she wanted to retrieve her cake pan while she still could. She probably didn't have the money to replace it.

"I guess you're right, Itsy. I was just curious why you came into the house last night. I'll see if I can find your Bundt pan in the pantry. If I do, I'll bring it by later on."

"Thanks, I'd really appreciate it. I got my car back and

will pick up a cake mix when I go to the Safeway over on East Pine later today. I'll bring the cake over this evening. I guarantee you my cake will be a lot moister than any cake Mabel ever baked. She could make a mayonnaise cake turn out drier than a popcorn fart. So, do you prefer white or chocolate?"

"I appreciate the offer, but it's not necessary. I'm trying to avoid having anything with too much fat, sugar or salt in the house. Rip's having enough trouble getting acclimated to healthier eating habits without having his will power tested by having a cake within arm's reach." I smiled to show I truly did appreciate the kind thought.

"Well, all right. If you're sure."

"I am. But thank you anyway, Itsy. I'll see you later. Okay?" I wasn't sure why I was even surprised that Itsy would let herself into the house to retrieve her cake pan in the early morning hours. There was an obvious connection between the two ladies, even if they'd had a habit of bickering over everything from who had the prettier lawn to who made the moistest cake.

CHAPTER 28

◆

I called Sydney later that afternoon and asked her if she could swing by the house the next time she had the chance. I wanted to see what could be done about assuring Ridley Wickets would not be put out on the curb like yesterday's trash once the cardiac center took legal possession of the Heart Shack. I'd be careful not to reveal too much information about the caretaker, so as not to cause him any problems with immigration officials.

I also was going to feel her out about the frozen vegetables in the chest freezer. I knew instinctively someone had intentionally fed Mabel the vegetables high in Vitamin K. Were they hoping she'd form a clot that would break loose and travel to her lung—exactly as it did—or had it been an accidental oversight?

I pulled open the same junk drawer Itsy had stolen the coins from and checked to make sure the receipt for the vegetables was still in the drawer. Knowing Itsy had issues with Mabel, the thought had crossed my mind that she might've had a motive to eliminate Mabel that I wasn't aware of. However, seeing the receipt was still in the drawer convinced me Itsy was innocent of any foul play. She wouldn't have left such compelling evidence in plain sight had she been guilty of utilizing Brussels sprouts as a murder weapon to kill her neighbor.

The idea made me stop and consider how many zillions of ways there are to commit a homicide. I doubt anyone has ever thrown a bag of frozen veggies into their grocery cart and thought, "I sure hope someone doesn't break into my house and murder me with my own spinach."

The idea of shopping for a murder weapon in the frozen foods aisle reminded me of something Itsy had mentioned earlier. She'd said she was planning to make a trip to the Safeway on East Pine Street. The few times I'd made a grocery run, I'd gone to the Safeway on Fourth Street. It seemed Itsy preferred the Pine Street location, even though it was a longer commute. My guess is the Safeway on Pine Street offered a double-coupon day, to which I could relate. I'd been known to drive to a different town, fifteen miles away, to take advantage of double-coupon opportunities.

I looked at the receipt I now held in my hand and saw printed on the top of the receipt: Safeway #1958. My iPad was lying on the kitchen table so I Googled the store number. I was surprised to discover Safeway store #1958 was located in Tokeland, Washington—the home town of none other than Tasman Combs! I remembered the town's name vividly, because the first time I'd heard it, I'd thought it was ironic for Mabel's pot-smoking great-nephew to live in a town with such an appropriate name.

Sydney had told me Tasman took her place watching Aunt Mabel on Sundays because the day nurse was off that day and Sydney worked a long shift. Mabel passed away on a Monday. If Tasman purchased the vegetables and fed them to her on Sunday, he could also have convinced her she'd already taken her anti-coagulant medication. With her memory impairment, it wouldn't have taken a great deal of persuasion. If Mabel recalled she wasn't supposed to eat a lot of green leafy vegetables, she might've said to her nephew, "I can't eat that, kid." It was very similar to the phrase I'd heard Goofus repeat several times—"I can't eat that, skid."

The pieces seemed to be falling into place. The day I'd

witnessed the spat between the twins in the cardiac ward of the hospital, Sydney had mentioned that Tasman had been fired from the fast food restaurant after being caught smoking marijuana. I'd photographed what was undoubtedly his roach clip on the marble table in the foyer, which meant he'd been in and out of the house at least once without my knowledge. He'd left behind his sunglasses on another occasion, but I couldn't be certain I was away from the house at the time.

Tasman's devious plan could possibly have been without either of his sisters' knowledge. On the flip side, all three could've been in on it. I'm sure they'd all heard the tale of Mabel's childhood and knew there was likely two million dollars' worth of gold somewhere on her property.

Even so, because of the store receipt, I was leaning toward Tasman. I hadn't trusted the boy since the moment I'd laid eyes on him. Tasman was a sleazy character with only his own best interests at heart. With his Aunt Mabel gone, he'd be in line for a healthy inheritance, and money is a great motive when it came to murder. But, as far as I knew, the gold nuggets had yet to be found.

I ran upstairs to show the receipt to Rip and explain why I thought Tasman Combs was responsible for the murder of his Aunt Mabel. Rip would know what I should do, who I should call, and where I should take the receipt so Tasman could be apprehended and brought to justice.

The relief I felt was palpable. Not only was I glad the killer would not walk away a free man with hundreds of thousands of dollars falling into in his undeserving hands, I was also convinced with near certainty Sydney had nothing to do with her aunt's death.

Meanwhile, my shoulder was almost out of alignment from patting myself on the back. Once again, I'd be the individual primarily responsible for solving a homicide. Even though the hospital board was pursuing their investigation, the police department didn't seem compelled to look any deeper into Mabel's death. The results of the autopsy left the homicide detectives uncertain as to whether the death was accidental, or the result of foul play, and they seemed content to sweep the case under the rug as long as none of the family members stirred up too much of a fuss. *No big rip,* I thought. *I'll just have to stir it up myself.*

I now had a piece of evidence I hoped would encourage the police department to open a full-blown homicide investigation. I just *knew* I'd discovered Mabel Trumbo's killer.

But, for the umpteenth time in my sleuthing career, I was mistaken!

CHAPTER 29

At the police department, I turned over the Safeway receipt and explained the extenuating factors that pointed an accusatory finger at Tasman Combs. The detective I met with was appreciative of the evidence and information I'd provided. He told me he was a rookie, and I knew solving the murder case of a prominent citizen like Mabel Trumbo would be a big fat fluffy feather in the detective's cap.

When I received a call to come to the police station the following day, I naturally thought I was about to be awarded with my second commendation plaque in as many months. Together, Rip and I had been given one when we solved the death of a Buffalo, Wyoming, RV park owner in April.

Imagine my surprise when the clearly disappointed detective informed me that four fingerprints were found on the receipt, and none of them belonged to Tasman Combs. One print belonged to me and one belonged to a clerk at the Tokeland Safeway store, but no match was found when the other two prints were run through IAFIS, the national fingerprint database. Tasman was in the system from a prior DUI arrest, but whoever the prints belonged to was not, the detective informed me.

"Does that mean he didn't kill Mabel Trumbo?" I asked Detective Akers.

"No, but it does mean we don't have enough evidence to charge the young man in question with murder."

"But he lives in Tokeland, where the items were purchased." I'd thought I'd explained the Vitamin K aspect thoroughly to the detective.

"Do you have undeniable proof it was Tasman Combs who made the purchase?" The detective asked. "I spoke with Dr. Thies, the medical examiner who performed the autopsy, and he agrees with your premise. Whatever Ms. Trumbo ate the previous evening was likely responsible for the clot in her lung that killed her. But for right now, we're at a dead end unless we can determine who made the black smudge on the back of the receipt."

"What?"

"There was a fifth print that was rendered useless because of the smudge. The trace evidence from the substance that caused it was sent to the lab and came back as containing formaldehyde, cyanide, arsenic, and polonium."

"Oh, my! Are you saying Mabel Trumbo was killed with a cocktail of poisonous chemicals?" I was dumbfounded. "Why were none of those toxins discovered in the autopsy?"

"Because none of those chemicals were ingested by the victim," the detective explained. "Believe it or not, those same chemicals are found in smokeless tobacco. The smudge on the receipt was residue from chewing tobacco, and was most likely left behind by the killer. Do you have any proof that Tasman Combs chews tobacco?"

I felt shock radiate to my spine, like I'd been struck upside the head by a Louisville Slugger. My mouth dropped open so wide, my dentures nearly fell out. I could barely answer the detective as I realized an idea that'd been festering in the back of my mind could actually be correct. "No, I don't think Tasman uses smokeless tobacco, but I know someone close to the victim who does. Can you run a name through a computer database that will show what her maiden name was?"

"Sure," he replied, hesitating before he asked his question. "What's the name?"

"Itsy Warman."

The detective came back a few minutes later. It seemed as if I'd been holding my breath the entire time. "There was no Itsy Warman, but there's an Isabella Wright Warman who lives on South Hart Street, next door to—"

"Next door to Mabel Trumbo's house. Oh my goodness," I mumbled, as the truth hit me. "Isabella Wright Warman, also known as Itsy Warman, is Mabel's sister."

It's no dang wonder Itsy knew Mabel's life story so precisely, I thought. How could I not have seen it immediately? Itsy was Mabel's younger sister, Bella, the six-year-old sent to an orphanage here in the states a few years after their mother died. Being siblings explained why Itsy felt such a close bond with Mabel, and yet she could be annoyed by her at the same time. I often felt the same way about a couple of my brothers. Although they irritated the crap out of me sometimes, I still loved them with all my heart. Blood was thicker than water and, apparently, stronger than intense exasperation.

"What motive could Itsy have had to kill Mabel?" Detective Akers asked. I could tell by the tone in his voice that the detective's interest was renewed. Earlier in the conversation, he'd sounded as if he'd be happy to sweep the entire case back under the same rug I'd forced him to retrieve it from.

"Well, I can think of two million reasons right off hand."

"Huh?"

I told the detective the story about Mabel's childhood and explained my theory for a motive. "I believe you'll find that money is the motive behind Mabel's murder. It's quite likely Mabel hid roughly two million dollars' worth of gold nuggets on her property. Gold that once belonged to their father. Itsy had just as much right to half of it as Mabel did. After all, she was only a year old when their mother died.

Itsy might've seen the money as her justifiable reward for having been sent away to live with strangers in a foreign land when she was only six. And now it would serve as salvation from her lack of funds. She no doubt loved her sister, but Mabel's determination not to share their family fortune might've resulted in the love/hate relationship they shared. With Mabel, who was already showing signs of Alzheimer's, dead and out of the picture, Itsy could try to locate where Mabel had hidden the gold."

"Go on." The detective encouraged me to continue. I sensed he was taking notes as I rambled on.

"To complete her scheme, once Itsy found the gold, she probably planned to sell it on the black market and use the cash to live out her life in stress-free comfort. Well, as stress-free as one can be with the threat of being caught, arrested, and tried for murdering her own sister, hanging over her head."

After the detective told me he was sending a couple of officers out to apprehend Itsy and bring her in for questioning, I went home, feeling deeply troubled. Although I was relieved it now appeared as if the truth had come out, I was saddened to find out a woman I'd have enjoyed having as my own sister was actually a killer. To me, taking another person's life, especially one's own sibling, was an inconceivable and unforgivable sin.

It was just another example that proved the love of money truly was the root of all evil.

CHAPTER 30

I almost fainted when I answered the front door of the Heart Shack a few hours later to see Isabella "Itsy" Warman standing on my doorstep. With her hands planted firmly on her hips, she looked mad enough to bite a rusty nail in half. "Why in Sam Hill did you go and turn me into the cops? If you'd just asked, I would've told you Mabel was my sister."

Rendered speechless, I just stood there and stared at the irate woman. Finally, Itsy said, "There's a reason I didn't want anyone to know who I was, Rapella. But I certainly would never have killed the only family member I had left in this world—other than those Combs brats, of course."

I just stood there staring at Itsy, seemingly unable to utter a single word.

Itsy's eyes filled with tears of grief. "I never even told Mabel I was the sister she'd tried to locate for years. When she'd talk about finding her 'long-lost sister', I'd try to convince her it wasn't worth her time and trouble because I didn't want my identity to be discovered."

"But why not?" I was truly perplexed at why the woman wouldn't want her sister to know who she was all those years.

"Don't you see? She'd think I only tracked her down to

get my half of our father's gold. I was afraid it'd drive a wedge between us that could never be removed. That was the last thing I wanted, and the money wasn't *that* important to me. So I changed my name to Itsy and took the surname of my last foster family so Mabel wouldn't put two and two together. Even though she didn't know we were sisters, I did, and I wanted to remain close to her. After all, she'd raised me by herself until I was six and sent away by our father. So when the house next to her became available in 1962, I bought it. I spent the next thirty years working for a landscaping company in order to make the payments and put food on my table. I draw a small pension and social security, of course. It's not a lot, but it's enough to scrape by."

"Now I see why you have such a green thumb. Why don't you come inside so we can chat over a cup of coffee? It seems we have a lot to talk about," I said. Itsy looked lost and forlorn, standing on the porch with tears now streaming unchecked down her cheeks. I had a feeling it was the first time she'd allowed herself to grieve the loss of her sister.

"Don't you have any tequila or whiskey, or something a little stronger than coffee?"

"You betcha, I do. After today's events, I could use a strong drink myself."

We spent the next hour discussing what had brought Isabella to where she was today as we sipped a mixture of tequila and orange juice. I knew, without a moment's hesitation, Itsy was being totally honest with me.

"Why didn't you ever marry?" I asked, despite knowing it was known of my business.

"Why, you ask? I'll tell you why," Itsy was intense as she answered my nosy inquiry. "I never had any desire to marry after seeing the way my father treated my mother. Her death was ultimately at his hands, you know."

"I understand completely." I decided not to ask Itsy any more prying questions, but as it turned out, I didn't need to. Itsy's emotions were flowing out of her now, like rain water out of a downspout.

"Mabel was difficult to get along with at times, but then I reckon I could be, too. I knew she thought the gold was evil, a reminder of the depravity that killed our mother. I couldn't disagree. She suffered through a lot more strife with that miserable father of ours than I did. I didn't want my sister to ever have a single doubt about my intentions and I truly never gave the hidden treasure a second thought until Mabel died of what I believed to be mysterious causes."

"So what did you do then?" I asked.

"What *could* I do? Tell the cops I had a gut feeling one of those kids was behind her death? Without proof of any wrongdoing, I was basically up a creek without a paddle. The Combs kids had no clue that, like Mabel, I was also their great-aunt, and that's the way I wanted to keep it. I wanted nothing to do with them because I really didn't like the way they treated my sister."

"How'd they treat her?"

"As soon as she showed the first sign of having memory issues, they wanted to put Mabel in a home where her dementia could be monitored and controlled."

I wasn't certain that would've have been such a bad thing to do, and told Itsy so. She replied, "The truth was, her memory issues hadn't yet reached the point where she was a danger to herself or anyone else."

"Was that the falling out you mentioned when you told me about her childhood?"

"Yes."

"I have to ask, Itsy. How did your chewing tobacco end up on the sales receipt I gave to the police?"

"I was the one who discovered my sister's body. I'd gone over to visit as I did nearly every morning, and when she didn't answer the doorbell or my raps on her door, I went back to my place to get my key to her house so I could let myself in. I found Mabel slumped over the kitchen table, cold and lifeless."

"Oh, no! I'm so sorry, Itsy." Although I didn't mention it, I was greatly relieved to discover Itsy's sister hadn't died in the exact spot I laid my head every night.

"Thanks. So anyway, I called the police. While I waited for the emergency workers to arrive, I noticed a sack of thawed-out vegetables on the kitchen counter. Since Mabel's freezer was stuffed to the gills, I ran the bag out and tossed it into the old chest freezer in the garage. Although Mabel didn't use it anymore, she'd never unplugged it. I think I was in shock, reacting as if she wasn't really dead and might want to cook the frozen veggies in the future. I wasn't thinking straight at the time, or I'd have left the sack on the counter. If I had, the emergency personnel might have made the connection to Mabel's death. I told the investigators that same thing when I was interrogated today." When she'd finished, Itsy gave me a venomous look, as if suddenly reminded of the fact I was the turncoat who'd precipitated the humiliating injustice she'd been subjected with.

"I'm sorry I doubted you. But what was I supposed to think? I was seeking justice for your sister. I did the same thing you'd have done had you been in my shoes."

"Yeah, I suppose you're right."

Now I knew how the tobacco got on the receipt and that the bag wasn't deposited in the freezer until after Mabel's death. But the missing items from the bag were most certainly the murder weapon, and I'd thought for sure the receipt for them was the smoking gun. To see if Itsy was in agreement, I asked, "So, do you still believe, as I do, that despite what the detective said, it was Tasman who killed Mabel?"

"Yes, but what good does that do us?"

"We need to go to that detective's office and demand he listen to all the reasons why we think Tasman's responsible for your sister's fatal pulmonary embolism. The receipt makes it probable that Tasman purchased the vegetables with the intention of killing Mabel with them. The detective I met with agreed the evidence was damning when I presented it to him this morning, but he told me it wasn't enough to charge Tasman with murder."

"Is that when you decided it must've been me who killed

Mabel, and then told the cop to come cuff me and stuff me in the back of his patrol car in front of all of the gawking neighbors?"

"Oh, come on, Itsy! Give me a break!" I was naturally defensive when I explained my actions. "Detective Akers told me there was chewing tobacco residue on the grocery receipt. As much as I hated to do it, I had to tell him that you were a tobacco chewer."

Itsy actually laughed at my discomfort, and said, "Oh, all right. Go on with your evidence against Tasman."

"Well, Mabel died the morning after he spent the day in her home 'taking care' of her. Tasman took care of her, all right. Maybe with both of us demanding action, we can persuade them to interrogate him and delve further into the case."

"I agree."

"Good. So will you help me nail the little bastard?" I asked.

"You better believe I will, Rapella."

I reached across the table and clasped her hands in mine as a gesture of solidarity and our newfound friendship. "Let's see to it that little creep spends the rest of his life behind bars."

"There's nothing I'd like better."

CHAPTER 31

The next morning was an off day on Rip's rehab schedule, so I drove the truck to the police station to meet with Detective Akers. Itsy sat in the passenger seat. I turned to her and asked, "Would you prefer I call you Bella?"

"I've been Itsy a lot longer than I was ever Bella, and that name probably suits me better, anyway."

"Because you're itsy-bitsy?"

"I thought we'd gone over that before." Itsy had a stern tone to her voice, but the twinkle in her eyes belied her attempt to sound perturbed.

Once we were seated in the detective's office, I asked Mr. Akers to bring out the grocery receipt I'd given him the previous day. I then went over all the reasons I was convinced Tasman Combs had deliberately caused his aunt's death: my first exchange with him in the foyer, his persistent search for the gold, the threatening note he'd left for me to find, his "I'm worried they'll find out" comment to some unknown listener on his phone, his expensive drug habit that had to be hard to afford after being fired for smoking weed on the job, and the fact Mabel didn't trust him.

Itsy chimed in once in a while with examples of why

she'd never trusted Tasman to be alone with her sister, and why she'd always thought he'd knock Mabel off, given the opportunity. The detective nodded numerous times, but never voiced an opinion on the evidence and reasoning we presented.

Finally, he said, "My biggest concern is that from what you two have told me about him, Tasman doesn't sound like he has the sense God gave a left-handed monkey wrench, much less the wherewithal to know he could kill his aunt with broccoli and Brussels sprouts."

"Do *you* have the sense God gave a left-handed monkey wrench, detective?" I asked. "I feel as though I do."

Detective Akers stared at me silently, obviously taken aback by my question. His expression was one of a man who'd just been asked if he was smart enough to breathe on his own, or if instead he'd require constant reminders. As expected, he didn't respond and I continued.

"My point is that I would've had no idea I could kill someone in Mabel's position with veggies high in Vitamin K. Would you have? But, everyone knows how to use the Internet to research information, particularly people in Tasman's age group. If I was determined to build an atom bomb, thanks to the World Wide Web, I could learn how to do it."

"Okay, I see your point, Mrs. Ripple. I suppose it wouldn't hurt for us to have a little chat with him. If he *is* guilty, and thinks we have solid proof of his culpability, he may feel compelled to confess. But don't get your hopes up, ladies. I've seen many murder cases go sideways when we least expected it."

"Will you let us know if you're able to break him and get him to confess?" I asked.

Detective Akers turned away to pick up the phone, but not before I saw him roll his eyes. He glanced at Itsy, who returned his look with a pleading expression on her face. "Well, I guess since you're Ms. Trumbo's next of kin, I can give you a call after we talk to him."

"Thank you," Itsy replied. "But call Rapella's cell phone, please. She's the one spearheading this investigation."

The look the detective gave me after Itsy's remark was difficult to decipher, but it was probably for the best I didn't know what was going through his mind at the time. I smiled apologetically at the officer, grabbed Itsy's arm, and steered her toward the door. "Okay, let's get out of the kind gentleman's hair so he can get to work on the case."

The next six hours dragged on like an Oscar winner's acceptance speech. While Rip watched TV and did his assigned exercises, Itsy and I sat on the front porch in a couple of comfortable rattan chairs I'd found in the basement.

We sipped on glasses of sun tea, and on occasion Itsy would stuff some tobacco in her mouth. I'd found an empty coffee can in the pantry for her to use as a spittoon. I'd also found her Bundt cake pan. It looked like something she'd picked up at a garage sale for a quarter. However, when I returned it to her, you'd have thought I'd uncovered a long lost diamond ring someone dear to her heart had given her. But then, who am I to throw stones when I resided in my own little "glass house"? I'd have wanted the cake pan back, too, because it'd cost ten to twenty hard-earned bucks to replace with a brand new one.

As we chatted about her and Mabel's childhoods, we glanced at my phone on the wrought-iron table every minute or two, trying to will it to ring. Itsy told me about her struggles growing up, being shuffled from one foster home to another and never feeling loved, or even wanted, at any of them. The Warmans, who'd been her final foster family, had been the most welcoming of all, even though she'd counted the days until she could pack her bags and take off on her own. Her story moved me, even though I sensed no self-pity in her telling of it.

Itsy and I glanced at the phone again, thinking the detective wasn't going to keep us in the loop after all. Finally, just when we were about to give up, the screen on the phone lit up and it began to ring.

"Hello." I enabled the speaker on the phone so Itsy could

hear both sides of the conversation, and answered breathlessly.

"This is Detective Akers. I'm afraid we've had to clear Tasman Combs of any wrongdoing."

"What?" I then repeated my question, hoping I'd misunderstood what he'd said. "You had to do what?"

"During the interrogation, he said his sister, Sydney, showed up at Mabel's house around five the night before the woman's death and told him he was free to go. She'd said she'd gotten off early and would see that Mabel got fed and settled before she went home. Apparently, Mabel Trumbo was actually their great-aunt, but that's beside the point."

"Yes, I know. Saying great-aunt every time is cumbersome."

"Exactly," the detective said. "So, anyway, as he was preparing to leave, Sydney removed several bags of frozen vegetables from a Safeway bag she'd brought in with her. Tasman questioned her about them because earlier she'd told him to make sure Aunt Mabel didn't consume any green or leafy vegetables. Sydney had actually made a list for Tasman of foods to avoid, which is now in our evidence locker."

The detective cleared his voice and went on with his explanation. "Sydney told him it was true Mabel shouldn't eat foods high in Vitamin K under normal circumstances, but the solonga level in her system was too low, and the veggies would help return it to its recommended level. He didn't question her decision. After all, Sydney was a cardiac nurse and knew just about everything there was to know about heart health."

"Solonga level?" I asked. "Seriously? We weren't warned about monitoring Rip's solonga level after his bypass surgery."

"I'd never even heard of it," Detective Akers said. "Anyway, it looks like Tasman's in the clear."

"But—"

"Tasman also said Mabel had been confused all day and

acting strangely, as if she'd been drugged or something. From what you two told me, Tasman should recognize that look as well as anyone. In fact, although he didn't come right out and say it, he inferred he'd smoked a little weed just before Sydney arrived and he wanted to escape before Sydney noticed it and climbed all over his...well, you-know-what."

"Was Tasman able to prove his whereabouts afterward? Could he prove he went home to Tokeland after he left Mabel's house?" I was grasping for straws, but I could feel the case beginning to slide sideways, as Detective Akers had said they frequently do.

"No, better than that. He was able to prove he went to the biker bar on First Avenue by the Alexis Hotel. The bartender vouched for him, saying he arrived around five-thirty and was there all evening. He even had Tasman on a security camera video, drunk as a skunk and trying to pick up a chick who was even more trashed than he was. According to the bartender, he left with that gal just before closing time and stayed overnight at her apartment."

"Could Tasman prove that?"

"Yes. We recognized the woman on the video and she verified he spent the night with her. She said the details of that evening were a little hazy, but she was positive Tasman was there all night and didn't leave until she had to get up the next morning to get ready to go to work at, believe it or not, the police station."

"Really?" I asked.

"Yes, she's our dispatcher here. But, that's neither here nor there, and you didn't hear it from me. Understood?"

"Absolutely. Our lips are sealed."

"So, that's that."

"Yes, if you can believe a word the little pothead said." I knew I sounded defensive, but I'd been so sure we'd had the little jerk dead to rights.

I hated to ask, but I wanted to put the case to rest. Was it possible Sydney was responsible for her Aunt Mabel's death? After all, by her own admission, she was the person who purchased all of the woman's groceries. She knew exactly what a high level of Vitamin K could do to a person on blood thinner medicine following bypass surgery. I couldn't imagine why she'd purchase the frozen vegetables in Tokeland, unless she was there visiting Tasman. And the more I thought about it, the more convinced I was that there was no such thing as a solonga level. So-long-a? Seriously? I was sure it'd been a pitiful attempt at humor on some insensitive fool's part. Was Sydney the insensitive fool in question?

Despite the outcome, I had to know the truth. Itsy deserved closure as well. I bit the bullet, and asked the detective, "So, I assume you're going to look into any possible alibi Sydney Combs might've had?"

"Absolutely! Detective Riley's on the way to the hospital now to pick her up for questioning."

"Okay, thanks." Itsy and I were both disheartened by the turn of events. "Will you let us know what happens after Sydney's questioned?"

It took a long time for Detective Akers to respond, and when he finally did, his voice sounded reluctant. "I suppose so."

It was a long evening, and I was understandably upset by the outcome of Itsy's and my visit to the police station. I couldn't deal with my sense of guilt at being behind Sydney's apprehension. I kept wondering if she'd been humiliated at being led away from her work at the hospital by a homicide detective. I was praying she hadn't been "cuffed and stuffed" like Itsy had.

"It's not your fault," Rip said in an attempt to console me. "Besides, dear, if Nurse Combs did the crime, she should have to do the time. Mabel deserves justice as much as anyone."

"I know. I just wish it hadn't been Sydney behind her aunt's death. I was so certain it was her brother who'd killed Mabel."

"We don't know for certain yet that Sydney was involved. Keep the faith, darling."

* * *

The phone rang the next morning while Itsy and I were conversing over coffee in the drawing room. The caller ID on my phone indicated it was the Seattle police department calling. Afraid of what the detective might tell me, I had to force myself to answer it.

"Mrs. Ripple? This is Detective Akers."

"Good morning, detective," I replied. An eternal optimist, I added, "I suppose you're calling to tell me Sydney's been charged with first degree murder."

"No," he replied. "Actually, I was going to inform you that she's been cleared, as well."

I breathed an audible sigh of relief. The detective asked me if I was all right before he finished his explanation as to why Sydney was also off the hook. "Dr. Murillo, a cardiac surgeon at the heart center, confirmed Sydney assisted him throughout a long surgery that began at four o'clock in the afternoon and wasn't completed until after midnight. Apparently, a patient had been brought in for emergency surgery to repair an aortic aneurysm."

"That is music to my ears." When I realized how dispassionate my remark sounded, I clarified it. "I meant that Sydney's innocent, not that the patient needed emergency surgery, mind you. Go on."

"So anyway, we know Tasman was at the bar when the vegetables were ingested, which the coroner, Dr. Thies, estimated took place in the six-hour window between four and ten the evening prior to her death. Dr. Thies has now determined the victim's death was an accident. Most likely she was hungry and decided to fix the vegetables for herself. With her memory issues, she probably didn't think twice about what she was eating."

"Can the coroner's determination be proven without a shadow of a doubt?" I asked. I was hoping it could be, but something told me there was more to the story than met the eye.

"Probably not, Mrs. Ripple. But even if someone else intentionally fed her those vegetables, we know it wasn't Tasman, or his sister, Sydney. Because, let's face it,

Sydney couldn't have been at two places at the same time."

Itsy and I looked at each other with identical stunned expressions. Something had dawned on both of us at the exact same moment. I took a deep breath and said, "Maybe it only appeared as if she was in two places at the same time, detective."

"Huh? What do you mean by that?"

"Sydney has an identical twin! The two are nearly indistinguishable from each other."

"Really? We weren't aware of that." The detective was clearly astonished. "Tasman never mentioned a second sister, much less that she was Sydney's twin. You may be on to something. What's her name and where can we find her?"

I gave the detective her name and told him she lived in Yakima. I recalled hearing Sydney say Adelaide worked at the First Cut Hair Salon, which was most likely in her home town. It was a weekday, so there was a good chance they could find her there.

I thanked the detective and ended the call, overwhelmed with relief that it hadn't been Sydney who'd killed her aunt. My prayers had been answered.

Although it wasn't Tasman as we'd originally thought, we were hopeful we'd found Mabel Trumbo's killer. We were afraid to be overly confident, having been convinced we'd found the killer before only to be disappointed.

I sat back in the rattan chair with what was, no doubt, a smug, self-satisfied expression plastered on my face. I had the satisfaction of knowing my warning to Adelaide the first time I'd met her seemed as if it might have turned out to be prophetic in nature. Karma may truly had come back and bit the evil twin in the butt.

CHAPTER 32

The following day, Adelaide Combs was arrested on first-degree murder charges. Detective Akers was kind enough to tell us that, during an intense interrogation, she'd admitted to having planned the murder in order to capitalize on her inheritance, not knowing at the time the house had been bequeathed to the heart center. She'd also hoped to find the gold nuggets her Aunt Mabel was alleged to have stashed away somewhere on her property, but, to her dismay, her victim had hidden the booty too well. As a pathetic attempt to justify her actions, Adelaide had claimed to be "putting the old broad out of her misery" because, after all, Mabel Trumbo "couldn't remember shit, you know". Hearing that only served to give me more satisfaction in knowing the despicable young woman was going to get what she had coming to her.

In the days that followed, we found out a lot of details about the murder via the sizzling grapevine, Detective Akers, and the local news coverage. It seems Adelaide had purchased the frozen vegetables in Tokeland the week before Mabel's death when she'd picked Tasman up on her way to visit their biological father, Roland Combs, in South Bend. After researching the connection between Vitamin K and blood clotting, along with how much of the sleep aid medication Adelaide had been prescribed years earlier it would take to cause confusion and sedation, she'd devised her murder plot.

A few days before Mabel's death, Adelaide had stopped by Mabel's house on the pretense of being concerned about her health. While there, she'd sneakily removed all of the anti-coagulant pills from the prescription bottle on the kitchen counter and replaced them with off-brand Vitamin K tablets that were nearly identical in appearance. The swap ensured Mabel's blood would thicken up faster during the several days prior to the Sunday Tasman was due to watch over Mabel.

In Mabel's weekly pill organizer, Adelaide had also slipped a couple of her sleeping pills into the Sunday morning compartment and two more in the noon slot. They were small and easily overlooked in the cocktail of medications Mabel took.

On the fateful Sunday evening, Adelaide had dressed in a set of scrubs, purchased earlier in the week in Yakima, and confirmed by a sales clerk at the uniform store. She then went to Mabel's house and pretended to be her identical twin, Sydney. Adelaide breezed into the house and cheerfully greeted her aunt. "Hi, Aunt Mabel. It's me, Sydney."

Aunt Mabel, who was off in another world due to all of the sleeping pills she'd ingested that day, easily fell for the ruse. Adelaide, still pretending to be Sydney, told Tasman he was free to go. She'd stay and see to it that Aunt Mabel was fed and put down before she went home. Little did Tasman know that she meant the term "put down" literally. He hadn't questioned his sister's identity, as it was difficult for even him to tell them apart, unless they were standing side by side. The fact Adelaide wore the scrubs she'd recently obtained and called him Taz, a nickname Sydney often used, made him even less suspicious that he was being duped. Having a buzz on didn't help matters, either, he'd admitted.

After Tasman left and headed to a nearby bar, Adelaide

had convinced her Aunt Mabel, who was loopy at the time, to gobble down large amounts of Brussels sprouts, broccoli, and canned spinach because her solonga level was critically low. Solonga was indeed a made-up term Adelaide created for her own amusement. Adelaide then gave her aunt her evening medications, which had included no anti-coagulant pills, but plenty of Vitamin K tablets. She put her aunt to bed, locked the front door and left to let "nature" take its course.

Adelaide had no way of knowing at the time if her scheme would work. But it did. Aunt Mabel suffered a fatal pulmonary embolism early the next morning. As Adelaide had hoped, a blood clot formed, then broke loose and traveled through Mabel's blood stream to her lung.

Adelaide's plan had been well thought out and executed precisely. It would've worked perfectly, too, if not for one thing—a stupid, old, nosy-ass woman named Rapella Ripple, who helped karma come back and kick Adelaide Combs in her skinny-jeans-clad rear end. And I could not have been happier about it!

To my relief, Ridley Wicket's citizenship was never questioned and at Sydney's request, he'd been granted free use of one of the suites for the remainder of his life by the director of the heart center. Ridley never explained his reluctance to return to his native country, and Rip and I never asked. Rip didn't think it was any of our business, and I wasn't sure I really wanted to know.

The aging caretaker told us he'd witnessed one of the twins—he couldn't distinguish between the two either—messing around with Mabel's weekly pill organizer four or five days before Mabel's death. After a couple of weeks of troubling contemplation, his scruples kicked in, prompting him to phone in an anonymous tip to the local police station. Ridley knew he stood the chance of being discovered and booted out of the country, but by then his conscience wouldn't let him harbor the secret any longer.

I was surprised when Ridley told us it hurt his arthritic

fingers to play the piano these days, and he was going to have to give it up. Or, to be more exact, Ridley said, "Me old fingers hurt. Me no play no more."

Although saddened to hear that the ravages of time were going to still the beautiful music his hands created, I was happy when he suggested the Steinway be donated to charity.

Because I had a better idea.

I called Chase Cumberland, who was in complete agreement with my suggestion of holding a second raffle for the piano. By doing this, he could right a wrong and, to a certain extent, redeem himself. This time around he planned to pull a ticket out of the same straw basket of tickets that'd been purchased by various folks the first time the raffle was held.

Now, although long overdue, every individual who'd purchased a ticket in the past would get a fair chance to win the pristine instrument and take the prize home with them. That included a few participants who had since passed. However, should a deceased individual win the raffle, Chase said he'd see to it the piano went to the winner's family.

I assured Chase there was no reason anyone needed to know anything other than Mabel had requested a second winner from the initial raffle be awarded the piano. It'd be one of those little white lies that harmed no one and let water that'd been long under the bridge stay that way. The second raffle would simply be Mabel's way of giving back to the church that had been such an important part of her life. Enough said!

Sydney stopped by shortly after the arrest of her twin sister. She was naturally upset, but appreciative of my efforts to save her from being dragged through the mud. Along with a host of other emotions, she was excited to find out Itsy was her great-aunt. She said, "I often thought the two ladies were so like-minded they could've been sisters. Those two fought like siblings at times, but were also quick to jump to each other's defense and could be counted on to support one another when the chips were down. I wish Adelaide and I could've had the same tight bond those two had."

"I do too, honey," I said sincerely.

Sydney then shared an amusing anecdote. "I remember once when Aunt Mabel and Aunt Itsy didn't speak to each other for two months after an argument over whether it was correct to have the loose end of the toilet tissue roll coming over the top, or coming from behind on a toilet paper holder. Crazy, huh?"

"Yeah, crazy!" I'd agreed, even though Rip and I had occasionally disagreed about toilet paper etiquette ourselves. No one will ever convince me that toilet tissue shouldn't drape over the top of the roll. I may be open-minded about almost every other subject, but when it comes to how a roll of toilet paper should be hung, I am dead-set on my opinion.

On a warm afternoon, about a month later, Itsy walked into the kitchen through the back door of the Heart Shack as I was putting the final touches on a low-fat, sugar-free strawberry cake. I'd made it to celebrate Rip's release from rehab. It'd become routine for Itsy to pop in whenever the mood struck her, which was just fine with me because I always enjoyed her company. I would miss my eccentric new friend when Rip and I moved on.

After discussing her sister's "drier than a popcorn fart" cakes, I asked Itsy, "Why have you never even attempted to locate your daddy's gold? Sydney said Mabel's will clearly states that other than her house, everything in her estate was to be awarded to her closest next-of-kin, which would be you. I'd help you, you know, and Sydney said she would, too. The gold's likely hidden on this property somewhere and if you don't find it soon, it'll be too late. Someone will eventually discover the nuggets and then the money will probably end up in the hands of the heart center."

"I realize that, Rapella. But I have to think that's what Mabel would have wanted to happen."

"I disagree, my friend," I said. "Mabel's in heaven now and your identity is no longer a secret. I believe she knows now that you're her little sister, Bella, and I think she'd want you to make the decision on what ultimately happens to the gold."

"You think?"

"I do, Itsy. I also believe the last thing Mabel would want is for you to struggle financially when the gold could help you live more comfortably, or wallow in the lap of luxury, as you put it."

"You might be right, Rapella. Even though I've never had the opportunity to try it before, I think I could learn to wallow quite admirably."

"Oh, Itsy," I replied with a laugh. "I've no doubt that given the chance, you could wallow with the best of them."

After sharing a good chuckle, we called Rip into the kitchen and sang a hideously off-key rendition of "For He's a Jolly Good Fellow". After laughing at Goofus's "Tanks you!" when the song ended, the three of us dug into the strawberry cake. My husband of fifty years was back to his old self, justice had been served for Mabel's death, and life was good once again!

EPILOGUE

A few days later, Rip and I were sitting on the front porch of the old Victorian home, enjoying our tradition of one after-supper highball. The Heart Shack had celebrated its grand opening, and the first family of a recovering heart patient had moved into the suite across the hall from Ridley's in the new temporary housing facility. They appeared delighted with their accommodations. I had noticed, however, that they avoided the always unfriendly, and occasionally downright hostile, cockatoo in the kitchen as much as possible. I couldn't say I blamed them. I'd been feeding the sassy bird for two months and he'd yet to warm up to me. He was lucky I hadn't put him out of my misery with one of Mabel's cast-iron skillets, as I'd been tempted to do on many occasions.

Rip and I were planning to head to northwestern Missouri in a week's time. We'd received an invitation from Lexie Starr and Stone Van Patten requesting our presence at a wedding which would unite Lexie's daughter and Stone's nephew in holy matrimony. We'd been present for the marriage proposal, so there was no way we were going to miss out on the actual wedding.

As we chatted about inconsequential topics, Rip said, "I

was walking around in the back yard this morning and noticed there were a couple of volunteer tomato plants coming up in that area that used to be a vegetable garden. Too bad we won't be around when the tomatoes are ready to pick."

"Dang it! I love vine-ripened tomatoes. We'll have to go to that farmer's market in Rockdale while we're there for the wedding. Too bad there weren't still canned tomatoes from all of the canning Itsy told me Mabel did before she got too ill to tend to a garden."

"I wonder what she did with all of those canned veggies. I also wonder why, since the veggies are preserved in jars, it's not called jarring instead of canning," Rip said before he took a long draw on his one allotted alcoholic drink for the day. He'd been as delighted as a kid in a candy shop when Dr. Murillo had told him continuing our long tradition should not adversely affect him.

I smiled as Rip continued. "My mother used to store her Mason jars in our root cellar along with potatoes, onions, and other root vegetables from the garden."

"When I was young, our neighbors had a root cellar, too," I said. "You reckon there's one in the back yard we don't know about? Mabel had to store all of those jars somewhere. That whole back corner is a tangled mess, you know. Apparently, someone thought that'd be a good place to stack up all of the brush, tree trimmings and limbs that fell during wind storms over the years."

"It's worth a look around," Rip replied. "Speaking of which, the new guy they hired to manage the Heart Shack called to tell me the lawn maintenance people are coming tomorrow."

We discussed the new manager, who seemed as nice as he could be, and then talked about Tasman adopting Gallant. The next time I'd seen the kid, he admitted to me he'd picked up my ring off the marble table in the foyer where I'd left it to protect it from the harsh chemicals I was using to clean the house. He had written the threatening note and left it and the ring in the mahogany box, turned the music on, and then hid in a closet in another guest bedroom while I had ten years of my life scared out of me. He told me the prank had been Adelaide's idea. I believed him because I thought it was probably too elaborate a hoax for him to have come up with on his own, which is pretty sad. As Detective Akers had said, Tasman truly didn't appear to have the sense God gave a left-handed wrench.

Tasman apologized for frightening me and I accepted his apology. I then threatened him with *his* life if he mistreated Gallant in any way or harmed one hair on the sweet dog's body. Tasman promised to give Gallant a good home and treat him with tender loving care. I had a feeling if I ever saw the St. Bernard again, he'd be higher than a kite from inhaling second-hand marijuana smoke.

I was happy when Sydney opted to give the obnoxious cockatoo a home after the cardiac center informed her the pets needed to be found new homes due to liability reasons. "I told Sydney her decision to adopt Goofus was bass-ackwards. She should have chosen the lovable dog and said vamoose to that mouthy Goofus. She told me she'd much rather have had Gallant, but was afraid her yorkies would make mincemeat of the lovable mutt."

Rip laughed. "Does Sydney know the average lifespan of a cockatoo? It's like half a century, I've heard. They're similar to parrots when it comes to how long they live."

"Goofus was fortunate to have made it a week after I took over responsibility of caring for him. For awhile I thought the silly bird was trying to tell me who was responsible for killing his master. Now I realize he was probably just carrying on to hear himself talk."

"Kind of like you do?" Rip asked.

"Watch it, Buster Brown, or you'll be eating kelp on a bed of steamed couscous for supper tonight."

"I found the root cellar!" Rip exclaimed from the rear of the property. I was admiring the volunteer tomato plants while he poked around in the jungle of brush the landscaping crew was going to clean up later on that afternoon. "It's hidden beneath all this debris. I cleared the stuff off the door, but there's a padlock on the latch."

"I wonder if that small key with the old skeleton keys goes to that lock." I'd placed the key ring in the back of my underwear drawer after new locks had been installed on the house. Why? Because I'd had a gut feeling that one day I might find a lock to fit that extra key, and I always take my hunches seriously.

"It very well might fit this lock," Rip said. "Can you go get it?"

The lock was rusty and had obviously not been opened in a long time, but Rip fiddled with it until it finally clicked open. "How about that? I'm glad Sydney didn't pitch this little key when she couldn't figure out what it went to. Not that I couldn't have used bolt cutters or busted the lock open with a sledge hammer."

"You've come a long way in your recovery process, but I don't think you're quite ready to be swinging a sledge hammer yet." I patted Rip on the back and followed him down the chiseled-out steps with my hand on his shoulder.

Down inside the hand-dug cellar were dozens of cases of canned vegetables. Behind the cases, was a large wooden crate. Just out of curiosity, which you know has an unshakable hold over me, I cautiously opened the lid to see if the crate contained more jars, hoping it didn't contain something like a coiled-up copperhead instead.

It contained neither canning jars nor a venomous snake. But what it did contain was approximately one hundred pounds of gold nuggets.

I'd been a little disappointed when Itsy made no concerted effort to locate the gold after our discussion about searching for it. I think I'd wanted Itsy to have it more than she did. So I'm happy to report that after the gold was redeemed for two million, one hundred and seventy thousand dollars, the money was finally Itsy's to do with what she wanted.

In a letter we received from Itsy a few weeks after we'd

arrived in Missouri, she explained that she'd given two-hundred-thousand dollars to Sydney. I knew the generous gesture was not required of Itsy, but rather done out of the kindness of her big heart. To be fair, she'd given the same amount to Tasman, in hopes he didn't use it to kill himself with a drug overdose. She'd donated Adelaide's share to the heart center to go toward the future maintenance and upkeep of the Heart Shack, as she knew Mabel would have wanted. And, believe it or not, Itsy had included two one-dollar bills in the envelope to pay me back for the bus fare I'd paid when we went to the Book-E store to return her borrowed book.

As for the rest of the money, I can't say for certain but I assume Itsy will be using it to "wallow in the lap of luxury until the day the Good Lord comes to take her spoiled ass home". Whatever the case, I have to believe Mabel is looking down from heaven at her beloved little sister, Bella, with a huge smile on her face.

Turn the page for an
excerpt from

RIPPED
APART

A Ripple Effect Mystery

Book Five

Jeanne Glidewell

"**Y**our daughter doesn't have the sense God gave a day-old boll weevil!"

"*My* daughter?" I asked my husband, Clyde "Rip" Ripple. "I could've sworn you were present when Regina was conceived."

"Why would she and Milo ignore a mandatory evacuation order?" Rip was too tense to appreciate my attempt at levity. "It's not like Mayor Wax would issue one for no reason."

"When I spoke to Reggie on Friday, I literally begged her to flee the coastal area." My eyes grew misty as I spoke.

"Well, at that stage of the game, it was probably best they stay put rather than risk getting caught up in the storm while traveling in their vehicle," Rip replied.

I swallowed hard at the thought Regina may have reconsidered my pleading advice and, in order to appease me, convinced Milo to evacuate too late, placing them at even greater risk.

Our fifty-one-year-old daughter, Regina, and her husband, Milo Moore, lived on Key Allegro Island in Rockport, Texas. In the wee hours of Saturday, August 26, 2017, Hurricane Harvey had made landfall as a category four storm in our quaint little hometown of approximately ten thousand people, causing massive, catastrophic devastation, according to the latest weather report.

Reggie had informed me just hours before the storm hit that they planned to ride it out in their waterfront home. I saw no particular honor in their decision to "go down with the ship" if the hurricane was as destructive and life-threatening as anticipated, and I told her so. Three or four times, in fact! But, unfortunately, my words appeared to fall on deaf ears.

Just a few hours later, the hurricane came roaring into Rockport, with all its pistons pumping, and wreaked havoc on everything in its path. It'd been reported that all of the town's utilities had been put out of commission indefinitely. This included cell phone and Internet service, leaving us no way to contact our daughter to see if they'd survived the storm.

If they did, I'd be tempted to strangle them both for causing us such angst by behaving so recklessly. Rip had just recovered from a triple bypass. The last thing he needed was to be stressed out about their safety.

Just after noon on the twenty-seventh, Rip and I were in the parlor of the Alexandria Inn with our friends, Lexie Starr and Stone Van Patten, who owned and operated the renovated Victorian bed & breakfast facility. We'd been glued to the TV for hours, watching the Weather Channel and anxiously waiting for updates on the progress of the still-churning hurricane and the devastation it was leaving behind in its wake.

We gasped in unison as meteorologist, Jim Cantore, predicted Hurricane Harvey would inundate the Houston area with over fifty inches of rain. Fifty inches of rain!! I couldn't quite wrap my head around the idea of over four feet of rain falling in one storm! The magnitude of this forceful storm, that had strengthened for days in the Gulf of Mexico before making landfall in Rockport, was unprecedented and expected to become one of the costliest, if not *the* costliest, tropical cyclone on record.

Through it all, we had no way of knowing how Regina and Milo had fared, or if their beautiful home was still standing. Rip and I were in Missouri and felt helpless, knowing it was unlikely we'd be able to get to our daughter's side for days. The damage reports were not exactly encouraging, either. Local airports, and nearly every thoroughfare leading from Houston to south of Corpus Christi, were closed indefinitely. Thousands of power poles that'd been snapped in two, downed electrical lines, uprooted trees, debris, and various other hazards were making every road in the vicinity impassable.

I shook my head in despair. "Even if the kids survived the storm, I doubt their fancy-pants home did."

"Let's not borrow worry, Rapella." Rip tenderly stroked my back. "We need to hope for the best, even as we prepare for the worst."

Just then our cell phone rang.

"It's Regina!" I exclaimed. Flustered, I grabbed the phone, accidentally disconnecting the call.

"What the − ?" Rip looked at me as if I'd just hung up on the Pope. When the phone rang a second time, he snatched it from my hand. "Sweetheart? Are you kids all right?"

I nervously watched as Rip strained to hear Regina's response. As usual, he'd left his hearing aids in the safety of his toiletry bag, which was a constant source of irritation for me.

"Give me the blasted thing!" I snatched the phone back.

"Mom?" Regina sounded on the verge of hysteria. Her voice was cutting in and out. "I___ ___ one bar___ ___ ___first time___ ___get out all___."

"I can't understand you, honey. Are you and Milo okay?" I asked.

Her barely audible reply sounded like, "I'd prefer banana pudding on my radiator."

"Your what? Did you say radiator?" Between a terrible connection and her obvious distress, I was unable to make out much of what she said. I took comfort in knowing if she was able to speak, she was at least alive and conscious.

"All roads closed___ Milo ___ ___the roof___ ___ wind___ is dead___ ___ ___ripped apart___ ___ the pier___ dog___ ___ big mess___ ___ ___what to do."

That's all I could make out before the call dropped. I immediately tried to call her back, but to no avail.

Everyone gathered in the parlor stared at me in trepidation. I'm sure my expression was that of a person staring straight into the eyes of a rabid coyote, snarling and licking his chops at the same time.

"I, um, I think she was trying to tell me that Milo's dead." I was so choked up, I could barely speak. "And something to do with the dog making a mess."

"What?" Rip asked, clearly perplexed.

"Then again, maybe it was their dog that died."

"They don't *have* a dog!" Rip replied impatiently. "What exactly did Regina say?"

"I think she might've said Milo fell off the roof due to the wind." I was desperately trying to make sense of what few decipherable words I'd heard. "And something, or someone, was ripped apart."

"No doubt a lot of things were ripped apart, but even Milo's not foolish enough to stand on the roof in a hurricane. Did Regina specifically say he'd been killed?" After a career in law enforcement, Rip was more focused on facts than emotions.

"I'm not sure. There *was* a lot of static on the line."

"I reckon all we can do at this point is to wait for Regina to contact us again," Rip said after a heavy sigh. His voice was composed, but his expression was anything but.

Although I was extremely relieved to have heard Regina's voice, I remained distraught the rest of the evening over the possible fate of her husband. Sleep that night eluded me. I lay in bed, staring at the ceiling. An uneasy feeling churned in my stomach, letting me know that unforeseen changes were just over the horizon.

RIPPED APART

available in print and ebook

THE RIPPLE EFFECT COZY MYSTERIES

Also by Jeanne Glidewell

RAPELLA'S HEART-HEALTY MEAL

Garlic-Roasted Salmon & Brussels Sprouts*

Ingredients:

14 large cloves of garlic

1/4 cup extra-virgin olive oil

2 tablespoons finely chopped oregano, divided

1 teaspoon salt, divided

3/4 teaspoon pepper, divided

3/4 cups of white wine, preferably Chardonnay

6 cups of Brussels sprouts, trimmed and sliced

2 pounds fresh salmon filet, skinned and cut into 6 portions

Lemon wedges

Preparation:

Preheat oven to 450 degrees. Mince 2 garlic cloves and combine in a small bowl with oil, 1 tablespoon oregano, 1/2 teaspoon salt and 1/4 teaspoon pepper. Halve the remaining garlic and toss with Brussels sprouts and 3 tablespoons of the seasoned oil in a large roasting pan. Roast, stirring once, for 15 minutes.

Add wine to the remaining oil mixture. Remove the pan from oven, stir the vegetables and place salmon on top. Drizzle with the wine mixture. Sprinkle with the remaining 1 tablespoon of oregano and 1/2 teaspoon each of salt and pepper. Bake until the salmon is just cooked through, 5 to 10 minutes more. Serve with lemon wedges.

*As you have already learned from this story, you should

not consume large amounts of Brussels sprouts if you are taking an anticoagulant drug.

Oreo "Ripple" Coffee Cake

Ingredients:
> 20 reduced-fat Oreo cookies, coarsely chopped
> 1/3 cup of unbleached flour
> 3 tablespoons of light margarine, melted
> 1/3 cup of semisweet chocolate chips
> 16-ounce pound cake mix
> 3/4 cups of water
> 2 whole large eggs
> *Glaze:* 1 cup powdered sugar and 4 teaspoons of fat-free milk

Preparation:
  Preheat oven to 350 degrees. Prepare a 10" tube (Bundt) cake pan with cooking spray and flour, and set aside. In a small bowl, combine Oreos, flour, margarine, and chocolate chips. Mix well and set aside. In a larger mixing bowl, combine cake mix, water, and eggs. Pour half the batter into prepared pan. Sprinkle two cups of cookie mixture over the top of the batter. Top with remaining batter and cookie mixture, pressing cookie mixture gently into batter. Bake for 50 minutes. Cool in pan for 10 minutes. Remove from pan and invert cake to cool completely. Meanwhile, prepare the glaze by combining powdered sugar and milk in a small bowl. Mix until drizzling consistency. Drizzle over cake.

Jeanne Glidewell, lives with her husband, Bob, and chubby cat, Dolly, in Bonner Springs, Kansas, during the warmer months, and Rockport, Texas, the remainder of the year.

Besides writing and fishing, Jeanne enjoys wildlife photography and traveling both here and abroad. This year Jeanne and Bob traveled to Australia and New Zealand with friends, Sheila and Randy Davis, in February, and while Bob fished with friends in Canada, Jeanne and her friend, Janet Wright, enjoyed a Caribbean cruise in May. They look forward to returning to their newly rebuilt south Texas home in October 2018.

Jeanne and Bob owned and operated a large RV park in Cheyenne, Wyoming, for twelve years. It was that enjoyable period in her life that inspired her to write a mystery series involving a full-time RVing couple—The Ripple Effect series.

As a 2006 pancreas and kidney transplant recipient, Jeanne now volunteers as a mentor for the Gift of Life of KC program, helping future transplant recipients prepare mentally and emotionally for their upcoming transplants. Please consider the possibility of giving the gift of life by opting to be an organ donor.

Jeanne is the author of a romance/suspense novel, Soul Survivor, six novels and one novella in her NY Times best-selling Lexie Starr cozy mystery series, and four novels in her Ripple Effect cozy mystery series. She is currently writing Marriage and Mayhem, book seven in the Lexie Starr series, and hopes to have it released in the fall of 2018. The Ripple Effect book 5, Ripped Apart, will follow, hopefully in the early spring of 2019.

CPSIA information can be obtained
at www.ICGtesting.com
Printed in the USA
FFOW03n0056230418
46301106-47840FF